"Books, dogs, and food—and ... fun—connect almost all of Vale... ... mysteries, regardless of pseudonym."

—*The New York Times*

"Cold nose, warm heart—Bailey the Bloodhound is everything you want in a pet detective. Read with extreme caution: this deliciously fun series could become highly addictive."

—#1 *New York Times* bestselling author Laura Childs

"Kallie E. Benjamin has created a warm, relatable heroine and a welcoming small-town setting. Add in a friendly bloodhound, a spot-on supporting cast of characters, an intriguing mystery plus emergency pie(!), and you get a charming tale that cozy readers will savor. The Bailey the Bloodhound mysteries are just plain fun!"

—*New York Times* bestselling author Sofie Kelly

"A dog lover's delight! Bailey the Bloodhound is such a good boy. This loving, mischievous, smart fellow has no idea that he's a 100-pound dynamo. Set in an old-fashioned town with a homey diner and a gossipy salon, this book is delightful and even includes an entertaining romance! But it's the kind, warm characters who will keep readers coming back for more."

—*New York Times* bestselling author Krista Davis

"*Sniffing Out Murder* is a strong series starter that introduces a likable protagonist, charming setting and characters, sizzling romance, and a twisty mystery."

—Mia P. Manansala, Agatha Award–winning author

"A delightful start to a new cozy mystery series! *Sniffing Out Murder* is a hit for cozy fans with its quirky characters, clever mystery, and sweet romance budding in the air. But the star of this fun and murderous tale is Bailey the Bloodhound, a lovable pooch who is smart, loyal, and the perfect sidekick. A surefire hit for Kallie E. Benjamin!"

—*USA Today* bestselling author Abby Collette

"A complex whodunit, with a feisty heroine and her delightful bloodhound, Bailey. Pour a nice cup of tea and be prepared to read *Sniffing Out Murder* in one sitting."

—Terrie Farley Moran, award-winning author of the Murder, She Wrote novels

"You will love spunky Pris and her canine companion, Bailey the Bloodhound. Prepare for lots of doggy kisses and bloodhound heroics."

—*USA Today* bestselling author Victoria Thompson

"Kallie Benjamin's fictional middle-grade author Pris Cummings lets her protective bloodhound, Bailey, help sniff out who's behind the murder of a body the dog digs up in the town park. Pris, back in her hometown of Crosbyville, Indiana, to pursue her writing career, is a determined and loyal sleuth in this delightful new series even as romance blooms, suspense mounts, another body drops, and Pris

works to keep her dog and her beloved circle of humans safe. A must-read!"
—Maddie Day, bestselling author of the Country Store and Cozy Capers Book Group Mysteries

"A scentsational start to a fun new series, readers will enjoy this cozy murder mystery for its endearing cast of characters, humorous moments, and sweet touch of romance."
—Diane Kelly, author of the Southern Homebrew Mysteries

"Kallie E. Benjamin spins a charming tail, with a protagonist you want as your best friend, a hound to love you, and a town you want to live in. More, please!"
—Sherry Harris, author of the Sarah Winston Garage Sale Mysteries

"Framed by the importance of family and friends, this dog-centered cozy series starter, with its cast of well-drawn characters, will appeal to dog-lovers and fans of Laurien Berenson's Melanie Travis dog-themed mysteries."
—*Booklist*

"Writing as Kallie E. Benjamin, V. M. Burns introduces a charming cast of characters in this new cozy series. Fans of Burns's Mystery Bookshop series, featuring an author and poodles, will appreciate."
—*Library Journal*

"For fans of cozy mysteries with partners that woof!"
—Book Riot

HOUNDING A KILLER

KALLIE E. BENJAMIN

BERKLEY PRIME CRIME

NEW YORK

BERKLEY PRIME CRIME
Published by Berkley
An imprint of Penguin Random House LLC
1745 Broadway, New York, NY 10019
penguinrandomhouse.com

Book design by Elke Sigal

Library of Congress Cataloging-in-Publication Data

Names: Benjamin, Kallie E., 1964- author.
Title: Hounding a killer / Kallie E. Benjamin.
Description: First edition. | New York: Berkley Prime Crime, 2025.
Identifiers: LCCN 2024035039 (print) | LCCN 2024035040 (ebook) |
ISBN 9780593547373 (trade paperback) | ISBN 9780593547380 (ebook)
Subjects: LCGFT: Detective and mystery fiction. | Cozy mysteries. | Novels.
Classification: LCC PS3602.U767525 H68 2025 (print) | LCC PS3602.U767525
(ebook) | DDC 813/.6—dc23/eng/20240802
LC record available at https://lccn.loc.gov/2024035039
LC ebook record available at https://lccn.loc.gov/2024035040

First Edition: May 2025

Printed in the United States of America
1st Printing

The authorized representative in the EU for product safety and compliance is
Penguin Random House Ireland, Morrison Chambers, 32 Nassau Street,
Dublin D02 YH68, Ireland, https://eu-contact.penguin.ie.

In loving memory of my parents, Benjamin (11/2/1938–12/21/2023) and Elvira (10/12/1938– 1/24/2013) Burns, for your love, support, encouragement, and prayers.

CROSBYVILLE ANNUAL FALL FESTIVAL

Saturday

Time	Activity	Location
10:00–8:00	Games, Food, Rides	Old Dairy Barn
10:00–12:00	Show Jumping	Equestrian Center
12:00–1:00	Dressage	Equestrian Center
12:00–2:00	Search and Rescue	Outbuildings
2:00–8:00	Pony Rides, Hayrides	Stables

Sunday

Time	Activity	Location
10:00–8:00	Games, Food, Rides	Old Dairy Barn
10:00–12:00	Pet-Assisted Reading Demo	Outbuildings
12:00–1:00	Baking Contests	Cottage
4:00–6:00	Pony Rides, Hayrides	Equestrian Center
6:00–8:00	Music	Stables

Chapter 1

"Have you contacted the police?" Anna asked.

"The police can't help me. I need Bailey the Blood-hound to find Max before it's too late."

"What do you mean?" Anna asked.

"In three days, Max will inherit fifty million dollars, IF he appears for the reading of his late uncle Herbert's will. So, you see, it's critical that we find him."

Anna turned to her partner. "What do you think?"

Bailey the Bloodhound's gaze moved from Carey to Anna. After a moment, he stood up and barked.

"Looks like Bailey the Bloodhound, Pet Detective, is on the case," Anna said.

I read out loud the words I'd just written while I sat at a picnic table waiting for Gilbert and Marcie—my boyfriend and my best friend—to get back from the food tents at the Crosbyville Fall Festival. We knew from experience that the lines at this two-day annual festival would be crazy long. My aunt Agatha was one of the food vendors and suggested that arriving early on the first day would improve our odds of eating before we were ready to pass out, but I wasn't so certain. Still, it's good to have a plan, so while Gilbert and Marcie braved the food lines, my dog, Bailey, and I secured a seat, which we also knew would be scarce as the day progressed.

I loved writing outside and today the weather was perfect. Not too hot. Not too windy. And not raining. Crosbyville, Indiana, had had more than its fair share of rain this fall, which had threatened to cancel the festival. However, a change of venue and a streak of good weather saved the day and the festival.

"Should I add that Max is a dachshund?" I glanced down at Bailey, my three-year-old bloodhound, but he didn't bother lifting his head from his paws. His dark soulful eyes held mine for a few moments, and then he closed his always-droopy lids and returned to sleep.

"You're not helping. We need to get this book written. My editor says if I can get this third book finished by the end of the month, he can get it typeset and printed this year. Then it will be in bookstores in six months. And you know what that means, right?"

Bailey didn't budge.

"It means we'll get paid. Which means that I can buy

new tires before winter and you, my muse, can get those expensive liver treats you like."

That did it. The L-word got Bailey's eyes open. He stood up and glanced around as though looking for those elusive snacks.

I chuckled and scratched Bailey's floppy ears. "Calm down, boy. They aren't here now. We have to finish writing *The Case of the Dancing Dachshund,* the next book in The Adventures of Bailey the Bloodhound first."

"Who are you talking to?"

I froze and racked my brain to remember what I'd said, apparently out loud. I turned and glanced up into the deepest blue eyes I've ever seen. "Excuse me?"

"I heard you talking and wondered if you were on the phone, but I don't see earbuds. Before I interrupted you, I was . . . never mind. Are you free, love?" Handsome Blue Eyes flashed a pearly white smile. A thirtysomething-year-old man with a lovely accent stared down at me.

His question—"Are you free?"—reminded me of the classic line from a 1970s Britcom, *Are You Being Served?* A love of mysteries, classic movies, and old sitcoms was one of the things my best friend, Marcella Rutherford, and I had in common. "Um, yes. I'm free."

Blue Eyes smiled. "Great, my name's David. David Townsend. I'm looking for—"

"Oh, you're David Townsend." I stared for several moments and then pulled my gaze away from the pool of blue. I shook my head to clear my thoughts and then cleared my throat. "I'm sorry, it's just we've been expecting you. I mean, we've all heard you were coming and— Condolences."

He tilted his head to the side and stared. "Expecting me?"

"News travels fast in a small town. Even though your grandfather didn't interact with a lot of people in the community, we all knew that he was expecting his grandson to arrive. We've all been excited to meet you."

He straightened up and grinned. "How well do I measure up? I expect the old man may have built me up too much."

The twinkle in his eyes told me that David Townsend was fishing for a compliment. Still, the heat rising up my neck meant that I had fallen into his trap.

"Oh no. You're fine . . . I mean, you're not a disappointment."

"Good. I would hate to disappoint." David Townsend laughed. "Before this week, I hadn't seen the old man in years. I heard he was a recluse?"

"He was one of the richest men in the state . . . well, in the country, but rarely left his house and only interacted with a small number of people. This is my first time visiting his farm."

"Oh really? I assumed you knew him."

"Your grandfather kept to himself, but he loved my aunt's cooking. She owns the Blue Plate Special Café downtown. It was one of the few places that he visited regularly. He got to be good friends with my aunt Agatha. In fact, I always thought he had a bit of a crush on her."

"Thank you, love." David Townsend smiled. "Now, I'm supposed to be awarding the ribbons at the equestrian event, and I haven't visited the old place in donkey years. Could you perhaps . . . give me directions?" He waved an arm. "The estate's massive and I've gotten a bit turned around."

"Directions? Oh, you want me to . . . Sure." I glanced at my phone. "Bailey and I need to head that way, too. I promised one of my students I'd watch her in the show jumping, which starts at ten." I tucked away my notepad and pen and shoved them in my backpack. I got up from the table where I'd settled in to sneak in a little writing.

Bailey stretched as though he'd just been running a marathon instead of napping under the table. He sniffed David Townsend. He didn't seem impressed. He snorted and turned his back.

"Bailey?" David Townsend pointed.

"Yes." I slipped my backpack on, grabbed Bailey's leash, and headed off in the direction of the equestrian ring, which I'd seen on the festival map along with the itinerary.

David Townsend matched my pace, which allowed me to steal a glance out of the corner of my eye. He was tall and thin with dark hair, blue eyes, and a strong jaw. He was handsome and something in his bearing, the tilt of his head or the way he walked, told me that he was well aware of the fact that women found him attractive. But it made him even less attractive to me. He walked as though he owned the earth, which, given how rich his grandfather had been, probably wasn't far from the truth.

Townsend was wearing caramel brown linen slacks and a cream shirt. His shoes were the same color as his pants and looked as soft as butter. They were extremely nice. Too nice for tramping through the grass at a festival, but I supposed he could afford to replace them if they were ruined. Maybe he had an entire closet of Italian leather shoes. When one pair was ruined, he tossed them away and pulled out another. That wasn't my reality. Still, it must be nice.

It was a beautiful autumn day. The leaves were changing colors and while the sun was shining, there was a slight nip in the air that indicated it would be a cool night. We walked across the expansive lawn over the one hundred–acre estate that had belonged to Edward Townsend, toward the stable and equestrian center in companionable silence.

"I feel at a disadvantage. You know who I am. I've met Bailey, but . . . I don't know the name of Bailey's lovely owner."

I felt my face flush. "I'm sorry. My name's Priscilla Cummings, but everyone calls me Pris."

"Pleased to meet you, Pris." He extended his hand, and we shook. He held on to my hand a bit too long and gazed into my eyes with a lopsided grin. After a few beats, I pulled my hand away and felt the heat rush up my neck.

We continued our walk across the grass, which was thankfully dry, weaving through the crowds who were standing around the grounds of Townsend Farms eating roasted corn, funnel cakes, and other fair foods as they enjoyed the games, food, and activities of the fall festival.

"So, Pris. What's the town saying about me?" He leaned

close and flashed a smile. "I want all of the gossip, and please don't spare my feelings. I want to know what the people of Crosbyville are really saying about me."

"I have no idea what you mean. Gossip? What gossip?" I was a horrible liar and even to my own ears, I didn't sound truthful.

"I grew up in a small village in England before moving to Australia with my dad. I know how small towns are. *The estranged grandson of a wealthy old man returns to the family estate days before the old man kicks the bucket.* There's no way the town's busybodies aren't gossiping. Now, spill it, and don't spare my feelings."

Heat rushed up my neck and I glanced away to avoid making eye contact.

"That bad, huh?" David Townsend threw his head back and laughed. "Crikey. The prodigal has returned?"

Crikey? I haven't heard anyone use that word since I used to watch episodes of The Crocodile Hunter *on television. I guess Aussies really did use it.*

"No, of course, well, there were stories, but everyone's been . . . well, they've been curious, and grateful."

He stopped to look at me. "Curious I understand, but grateful? Why grateful?"

"The Crosbyville Fall Festival is important to the community."

He shrugged. "Why? What's the big deal about a festival?"

"The festival is an annual event that funds local nonprofits. Each year, the town council receives hundreds of applications from organizations that use the money they receive from the festival to provide services for the community. Twenty organizations were selected this year. All of them are worthwhile. This year, the pet-assisted therapy reading program and the Crosbyville Search and Rescue Association were recipients. Since Bailey and I work with both organizations, that means we aren't here to simply enjoy the festival and eat. We're working."

He glanced at Bailey as he loped beside me with his nose glued to the ground. "Brilliant."

"The festival has always been held at the county fairgrounds. At least, that's where it's been for as long as I can remember. But Mother Nature has a wicked sense of humor and wreaked havoc at the fairgrounds this year with an off-season storm. High winds downed trees and the St. Joseph River overflowed its banks, leaving the grounds too soggy for the volume of traffic that would attend the festival. For a while, it looked as though the festival would have to be canceled. Thankfully, Edward Townsend came to the rescue and offered his ample estate for the festivities, and at no cost. So, everyone's grateful."

"I used to enjoy going to fetes in England when I was a lad. Tombolas, white elephant stalls, cakes, and coconut shies."

"What's a tombola?" I asked.

"I think you Yanks would call it a raffle."

I decided I'd google *coconut shies* later rather than continue to highlight my ignorance. "It sounds like a lot of fun."

"We had those photo booths and my mates and I would

take goofy photos. Those were fun times." He smiled at the memory and then came back to the present. "I'm sure the old man would have wanted to continue the festival. It's good for the public image." He must have noticed the surprised expression I wasn't swift enough to hide, because he quickly added, "Of course, it's good for the town, too."

"Plus, even after your grandfather's sudden death, you're allowing us to still have the festival here. So, everyone's grateful."

"I'm glad for the gratitude, but my grandfather's death was hardly sudden. He was eighty-five, after all. Plus, he had a bad ticker." He thumped his chest a couple of times with his finger.

"Oh, I had no idea about his heart. He seemed to be in such good health when I saw him last week at my aunt's diner. He used to come to my aunt's restaurant every Sunday."

"Really? I thought the old man was a bit of a recluse, not getting out much."

"I wouldn't call him a recluse. It's true he didn't interact much with the people in town. In fact, the only person he talked to regularly outside of his staff was my aunt Agatha. But he loved horses more than people. He could talk about horses for hours. But he talked to Aunt Agatha. He loved her fried chicken. They used to sit and talk for hours. Like I said earlier, I think he had a crush on my aunt." I smiled. "I had no idea he had a bad heart. He never mentioned it."

"Vanity. The old man didn't want anyone to know." He put his fingers to his lips to indicate silence.

"Of course."

"Well, I can tell you that everyone in Crosbyville is very grateful."

"Good." David Townsend smiled. "A sinner like me can use all of the goodwill he can get."

We rounded a corner and continued toward the horse stables.

"Bailey!"

I turned as three young girls headed full steam ahead in our direction. Mary Elizabeth Hicks, Hannah Morgan, and Clarice Kelley ran toward me and then immediately dropped to the ground around Bailey and began an ear-scratching lovefest with Bailey in the center, drooling like a faucet.

"Whoa. Bailey is one popular dog," David Townsend said.

"Well, duh! He's famous." Clarice rolled her eyes.

David Townsend raised a brow and glanced in my direction.

Before I could explain, Hannah jumped in.

"He's Bailey the Bloodhound," Hannah said dramatically.

"Pet Detective." The three girls giggled.

"These lovely girls used to be my students, back when I was still an elementary school teacher. Now I write children's books featuring a bloodhound who is a detective." I flushed. I hadn't figured out how to talk about my writing without blushing. My first book, *The Case of the Missing Maltese*, had been a huge success, and my publisher was feeling confident that the second book in the series, *The Case of the Barking Beagle*, would be equally successful.

"Ah . . . I see. All this time, I had no idea that I was hanging around a celebrity." David Townsend winked at me.

Before I could respond, the show-jumping competitors were ordered to make their way to the arena. The competition was about to start.

David Townsend motioned to me that he was receiving a call and stepped several paces away.

"My goodness. I better go." Mary Elizabeth stood up and gave Bailey a big hug. "Wish me luck, Bailey."

Bailey gave her face a lick, which she seemed to take as a good sign.

Mary Elizabeth brushed the dirt from her khaki riding breeches. She was wearing dark riding boots and a white shirt. Her stepbrother rushed out of the stables leading a large brown horse.

"There you are. You better go. Prince has the jitters. If you hurry, you'll have a few minutes to take him around so he can get rid of some of his pent-up energy." He handed Mary Elizabeth a navy show coat he had draped over the saddle.

Andrew Hicks was only a few inches taller than me and probably weighed twenty pounds less. The rumors around Crosbyville claimed that Andrew Hicks had three loves—horses, liquor, and gambling. He was only in his mid-twenties, but he looked older. Aunt Agatha said alcohol, hard living, and disappointment had aged him beyond his natural years. I heard he'd once wanted to be a jockey. A riding accident ended that dream and left him with a love-hate relationship with liquor, a bad temper, and a limp. Now he lived out his equestrian dreams by training young riders at the Townsend stables, working as a groom, and betting on horses at the racetrack.

Mary Elizabeth had been in Crosbyville for only one year, but she had been one of my brightest students. If her parents had listened to the principal and had her tested, I feel confident that her IQ would have been in the genius category. Despite pressure from the principal and the school board, they decided against testing. They hadn't wanted Mary Elizabeth saddled with a label. She loved school and learning, and that was enough for them. I found her to be inquisitive, well read beyond an eleven-year-old level, and an all-around nice kid. She was well liked by her classmates and got along with everyone. What more could parents want? Beyond that, she was also a committed animal lover. The biggest problem I encountered involved attempts to sneak her two guinea pigs, Molly and Scout, into class.

She slipped on her show coat and buckled her helmet.

"Can we come watch?" Hannah asked.

Andrew nodded. He tipped his cap to me, then rushed Mary Elizabeth off to her competition, followed closely by Hannah and Clarice.

At nine, Hannah Morgan and Clarice Kelley were younger than Mary Elizabeth. All three girls were transplants from bigger cities to Crosbyville. Hannah Morgan—the only child of my boyfriend, the chief of police—relocated from Chicago after the death of her mother. Clarice Kelley relocated from Indianapolis, the state capital, to live with cousins after her parents died. A murder and recent incarceration meant Clarice was now staying with a different cousin. Mary Elizabeth had been out of the country with her parents, but had moved here when her stepbrother got a job working for Edward Townsend. The Crosbyville rumor mill speculated that she was a distant cousin of Edward Townsend.

When they were gone, David Townsend finished his call and rejoined me. "Sorry, love."

"No problem. We've reached our final destination, anyway." I waved my arm to indicate the equestrian center. "Will you be competing?"

"Gawd, no. What made you ask that?" David Townsend asked.

"Earlier today, I saw all of the trophies your grandfather had displayed in the equestrian center, and I just assumed." I tried to hide my confusion. "Your grandfather was so proud of your accomplishments. When he was at the diner last Sunday, he boasted that when you arrived from Australia, you'd show us Americans the art of horsemanship."

"Well, I suspect my grandfather's mind must have slipped a bit in his old age." David Townsend chuckled. "Actually, I have a bit of an injury that prevents me from riding at the moment."

"I see."

"Pris! We've been looking all over for you." My best friend, Marcella, and my boyfriend, Gilbert Morgan, rushed over to where we stood.

"Well, I best be off. Thanks, love." David Townsend turned and limped away.

"Was that David Townsend?" Marcie handed me a funnel cake.

"Um, yeah. He asked for directions to the stables." I bit into the huge funnel cake and wiped powdered sugar from my shirt. "Hmm. This is delicious, but what took you so long?" I said in between bites of the warm fried dough.

"There was a long line." Marcie shrugged. "Was David limping?" She asked in a way that sounded casual and unconcerned to everyone except for a friend who knew her like a book.

"He said he had an injury, but I didn't remember him limping earlier as we were walking here."

Marcie frowned. She bit into her funnel cake, which hid her expression from my scrutiny, but it was too late. I'd already seen her face and I knew something was bothering her.

Marcella Rutherford was tall, dark, and stunningly beautiful. The offspring of a Nigerian mother and a Taiwanese father, she had dark, smooth, flawless skin and was a talented art and music teacher. I, on the other hand, was five feet three, curvy, with a lighter complexion that was prone to acne, and curly hair that was prone to frizz at the slightest sign of humidity. Thankfully, I had discovered a fantastic hairstylist in town who helped me tame my curly mane—well, mostly.

Gilbert had two glasses of apple cider, but seeing that my hands were full with Bailey's leash and a funnel cake, he exchanged the leash for one of the ciders.

"Thank you," I mumbled.

Gilbert took a finger and wiped powdered sugar off my chin with a gentle gesture that was more of a caress.

I smiled and wondered for the millionth time how I'd been so lucky as to attract the attention of someone who was tall, dark, and ruggedly good-looking like Gilbert. He was ex-military, and he had an authoritative bearing that was evident even when he wasn't in uniform, but today he was fully geared up. Crosbyville's police force consisted of sixty-four sworn, full-time officers, and every available officer was needed to maintain peace and order, especially with a large event like the fall festival.

"That has to be the fanciest barn I've ever seen," Gilbert said.

I glanced back at the enormous structure. "Well, Edward Townsend was an extremely wealthy man who loved horses," I said.

"His sons competed in dressage, show jumping, and polo," Marcie said. "I think David's father, James, had dreams of being a jockey and racing horses."

"What happened?" I asked.

"Too tall." Marcie shrugged.

"You know quite a bit about the Townsend family," Gilbert said.

"I grew up here." A small flush rose up Marcie's neck.

"I don't know much about the younger Townsends," I said, "but Edward Townsend was a nice man. He used to love talking to Aunt Agatha. Now that he's gone, I wish I'd taken the time to sit and listen to him more."

Gilbert reached over to kiss me, but right before his lips

touched mine, a bloodcurdling scream ripped through the air.

Gilbert hesitated a split second, his hand on his holster. "Stay here." He ran toward the screams.

Marcie and I stared at each other for a few moments. Then a thought sent shivers down my spine.

"Hannah."

We rushed in the direction of the scream.

Chapter 2

A crowd gathered in front of the barn and blocked the stable door. I stood on my tiptoes and craned my neck to see.

Marcie was taller than me, and it didn't take long before she patted my arm. "Pris, over there." She pointed to the side.

That's when I saw Hannah and Clarice in the pasture outside of the barn. They were standing next to Mary Elizabeth, who was dismounting from a large brown horse.

Mary Elizabeth tossed the reins to Hannah, pushed her way through the crowd blocking the stable door, and entered.

Marcie and I hurried over to Hannah and Clarice, still frozen in place. "Are you two okay?"

Hannah nodded. "We were just waiting for the dressage

ribbon ceremony when we heard a lot of shouting and then someone screamed."

I hesitated between wanting to go after Mary Elizabeth and staying to make sure that Hannah and Clarice were both safe. Marcie must have noticed my indecision because she inclined her head toward the barn.

I rushed toward the crowd in the direction that Mary Elizabeth had taken. It took a lot more pushing and jostling, but I eventually made my way inside and toward the front of the crowd.

That's when I saw David Townsend with a bloody nose and Gilbert handcuffing Andrew Hicks while Mary Elizabeth lunged and pummeled Gilbert's back.

I rushed forward and threw my arms around her.

She resisted for a few moments, but her energy was spent, and she collapsed in tears.

I was always amazed at how quickly Gilbert was able to flip a switch and transform from father of Hannah and my boyfriend into Chief of Police Gilbert Morgan, law enforcement officer. He was now in full-blown policeman mode.

Chief Morgan looked stricken. His jaw was clamped shut and the vein on the side of his head was pounding. He tilted his head to the side to indicate that I should take Mary Elizabeth outside.

Unlike entering the barn, where I had to push my way through, leaving was an entirely different matter. Like Moses at the Red Sea, the crowd parted and Mary Elizabeth and I walked outside.

Clarice and Hannah rushed to Mary Elizabeth's side and comforted their friend. After a few moments, I felt Marcie's hand patting my shoulder. I gave Marcie a bewildered look when the crowd parted again, but this time, Chief Morgan's voice boomed like waves crashing against the rocks.

David Townsend, with a handkerchief to his nose, marched out of the barn.

"Okay, keep it moving. Show's over," Chief Morgan ordered.

The crowds reluctantly pushed backward out of the doorway, although most still milled around at the outskirts of the barn in case the action wasn't finished. The ones who waited were quickly rewarded when, moments later, an uncuffed Andrew Hicks burst through the door. He paused for a few moments before he spotted Mary Elizabeth.

"Mary Elizabeth." He crouched down and opened his arms wide.

On hearing her name, Mary Elizabeth turned, spotted her stepbrother, and then hurled herself into his arms.

"It's okay. Don't worry. It's okay," Andrew Hicks repeated over and over as he comforted his stepsister.

David Townsend grabbed Chief Morgan by the arm. "Aren't you going to do anything?"

Chief Morgan gave a frosty authoritative stare to the hand that gripped his arm, until it dropped.

"Brr." Marcie rubbed her arms.

"Look here, mate. You can't be planning to let him go free! Why is he no longer in handcuffs? He assaulted me.

The man is dangerous. He deserves to be locked up," Townsend said. "How can you just let him go free?"

"I'm releasing Mr. Hicks based on my investigation. I have eyewitness testimony from people who are willing to swear that the two of you had words. Things got heated and the two of you came to blows. It—"

"He hit me. Look at me." David Townsend pointed at his shirt, which was torn, and the bruise under his eye, which looked well on its way toward changing from dark red to purple. By tomorrow, he would definitely have a black eye. "The man is dangerous. He deserves to be locked up."

"All of the witnesses claim you threw the first blow. You failed to hit your mark. Mr. Hicks was merely defending himself," Gilbert said.

"Defending himself? You have got to be kidding me. What kind of hick town is this where prominent members of the community, who are responsible for paying a substantial amount of the tax dollars that fund your salary, are treated like second-class citizens? I want this ruffian arrested. I want justice. I want you to do your job and—"

That was a big mistake. Nothing irritated Chief Morgan more than to have people who felt entitled order him around.

"Mr. Townsend, I know my job. I don't need you or anyone else telling me how to do it." Chief Morgan glared.

"I was merely—"

"You were trying to throw your weight around, but that's not how things work around here. I have five witnesses who will swear that you threw the first punch." Chief Morgan paused. When David Townsend didn't respond, he continued. "Now, I can arrest both of you for disorderly conduct, which is a misdemeanor and a fine. However, I didn't think that would be the way that our newest community member and the host of the town's festival would want things to go down."

David Townsend stared from Chief Morgan to Andrew Hicks and then his gaze moved to the crowd that was eagerly watching. Townsend's brow unfurled and his lips curved upward in a fake smile that never reached his eyes. "Of course, I wouldn't want the festivities tainted by such an ugly display."

"Good. Then, we agree," Chief Morgan said.

Townsend grudgingly nodded. Then his gaze moved to Andrew Hicks and his brow furl returned. "Hicks. You're fired. I want you off my property."

"Fine, but I have a contract. You owe me one month's wages." Hicks was still holding Mary Elizabeth's arm and yelled over her shoulder.

"Contract? You have got to be joking. I'm not paying you one dime."

"Then, we'll let the court decide. Your grandfather signed a one-year contract."

"My grandfather's dead. That contract is void."

David Townsend and Andrew Hicks lobbed threats back and forth like tennis pros at Wimbledon.

"Chief Morgan, I think I've been more than patient here. I want this man removed from my property at once," David Townsend said.

Before Chief Morgan could respond, Natalie Evans sauntered over and placed her hand on David Townsend's arm. "David, what on earth is going on?"

Natalie Evans was five feet six with shoulder-length hair in a shade of blonde that nature never created. A prominent lawyer who commutes several days per week from Chicago to handle Edward Townsend's legal affairs, Evans was new to Crosbyville and fit in about as well as a shark in a goldfish tank. She wore a lavender Sergio Hudson safari suit and matching four-inch heels that would have been perfect for *The Real Housewives of Orange County* but stood out like an elephant at a bunny farm at an outdoor festival in Crosbyville, Indiana. Her makeup was heavily applied and looked great from a distance. Up close it was overwhelming. Especially the eyelashes that sat on her cheeks like spiders.

"Her eyelids have to be strong to wear those," Marcie whispered to me, reading my mind.

Chief Morgan explained the situation to her, and a look passed between Natalie and David that made me wonder if there was more than the normal client-attorney relationship going on between them, but the look disappeared quickly.

Natalie threw back her head and let out a cackle that didn't suit the carefully cultivated exterior facade she projected, which normally screamed champagne, caviar, and lunch at the country club. But her laugh, and something in her voice and mannerisms, shouted beer, brats, and peanuts from the cheap seats at Wrigley Field.

"I'm sure all of this was a simple mistake." She waved her hand and flashed a fake smile at the crowds. "Irregardless of whose fault it was, I think you can afford to be magnanimous, David. Forgive and forget."

"Did she just say 'irregardless'?" Marcie whispered again.

"She did, and my left eye is starting to twitch." I closed my eyes and tried to cleanse that misuse of the English language from my brain. Everyone has a pet peeve. One word or phrase that grates their nerves. For me, it's *irregardless*. If Natalie Evans wasn't aggravating enough, she'd triggered my inner English major and sent it into hyperdrive. Marcie patted my arm and drew me back to the conversation.

"We don't want to bother Chief Morgan with minor scuffles like this, do we?" She forced a smile, but her eyes shot daggers into David Townsend.

"No. I suppose you're right." Townsend extended a hand to Gilbert. "Sorry, Chief. No hard feelings, eh?"

Chief Morgan hesitated a half second before shaking. "No hard feelings on my part."

I was standing close enough to Townsend to see him swallow hard and then walk over to Andrew Hicks. He extended his hand, but Hicks glared. Townsend smacked him on the back and chuckled. "Cute kid." He tried to pinch Mary Elizabeth's cheeks, but she turned her head away.

"Great. Now that that's all settled, David, lend me your arm, and help me back to the house. This grass is ruining my shoes." Natalie laughed again.

David Townsend extended his arm. Natalie wrenched her heel out of the soft ground and took his arm.

The crowd was still muted, shaken from the outburst in the barn. Luckily, help arrived in the form of my aunt Agatha driving a food truck with her café's name painted on the side, *The Blue Plate Special Café*.

"Pie and ice cream. Baked fresh today. *Hand-churned* ice cream," Aunt Agatha said.

The smell of pies wafted through the crowd and broke the cloud of anger that had descended over the group and replaced it with sugar, spices, and warm pastries. Within minutes, a line of people gathered at the truck awaiting their pie and ice cream.

Natalie Evans and David Townsend continued up toward the house. Interestingly, David Townsend wasn't limping anymore. Natalie spoke with her hands, and her body language indicated that she wasn't pleased with her client's behavior.

I turned to talk to Marcie and caught a look that on anyone else, I might have labeled jealousy, but my brain couldn't accept that. I had to be wrong. "Marcie, is there something you want to tell me?"

Instantly, her mask was back in place. "Nothing to tell. It was a long time ago and obviously didn't mean anything." Marcie shrugged and walked off.

I glanced around and saw that Hannah, Clarice, and Mary Elizabeth were all occupied with pie and ice cream. No tears in sight. Gilbert was talking to another officer I recognized from the Crosbyville Police Department. The scene looked as peaceful as a Norman Rockwell painting. If

I hadn't witnessed the altercation, I wouldn't have believed anything disruptive had occurred.

"Woof."

Bailey used his nose to nudge me back to reality. Even without his excellent nose, the smells coming from the food truck were hard to resist. Besides, Bailey knew Aunt Agatha was a soft touch. I walked over to the back of the truck and made eye contact with my aunt.

Without missing a beat, Aunt Agatha reached behind her, picked up a lunch bag, and handed it to me.

One look inside and a smile spread across my face. There were two hand pies and two frozen cups with vanilla ice cream, as well as two bloodhound-sized dog biscuits and a large frozen cup of something orange, which I suspected was frozen pumpkin pie filling for Bailey.

I loved those fruit-filled pastries that you could hold in the palm of your hand. My aunt knew me and my dog well. "Thank you."

She smiled and continued selling hand pies and ice cream.

I had to jog to catch up to Marcie. I found her heading toward one of the lakes on the massive property. I fell into step beside her, and we walked in silence for a while.

"He doesn't even remember me." Marcie glanced at me out of the corner of her eye. "You don't remember David at all, do you?"

I shook my head. "Did he used to live here?"

"No. He lived in England. His mother was British. He used to visit the US during the summers."

"How is it that I don't remember them?" I asked.

Marcie shrugged. "I guess it's not that unusual. Edward Townsend was so different . . . odd. He didn't hang out with people unless it had something to do with horses. He never brought his grandkids into town to mingle with the Crosbyville kids. Plus, look at this place. It's massive. In addition to the ponds for fishing and boating, there's a pool, tennis and squash courts, horses, and everything else a kid could want."

"Didn't they come into town for food?" I asked.

"Why? They had their own cook."

"Still, I should remember them. I mean, you do."

"You went away to writing camp every summer."

Something registered in my brain. "Did he have a twin brother? I seem to remember there being two of them."

Marcie shook her head. "Cousins, but you'd think they were twins. Edward Townsend had one son, James, and James had one son, David. Edward's brother, Frederick Townsend, had one son, Harold, and Harold had one son, Jonathan. David and Jonathan looked so much alike that it was downright weird." She shuddered. "They looked identical and used to be really close."

"So, what happened to them? I thought David Townsend was the last relative Edward Townsend had?"

"Mary Elizabeth may be a cousin, but David Townsend is the closest relative. At least, that's the news floating around Crosbyville." Marcie stopped walking and thought for a few moments. "James and his wife, Clara, got divorced.

She was a beautiful woman, but well, she had a reputation for being a bit, shall we say, loose."

"Loose?" I asked.

"She cheated on James and got pregnant, and he couldn't forgive her. So, he left and moved to Australia with David."

"That's odd. Usually, the mother gets the kids," I said.

"I don't think she was very stable. Some form of mental illness ran in her family. At least, that's the story I heard. Anyway, James divorced her and got custody of David. She remarried, and I think she died in childbirth."

"That's sad."

"Yeah, it is."

"What happened to her second baby?"

"He stayed with his father. David didn't talk about him much. He saw the boy at school, but I don't think he ever met his stepbrother's father—would that make him David's stepfather?" She asked. Neither of us knew the answer. She shrugged and continued. "Anyway, David didn't talk about him a lot. At least, not to me."

"What about his cousin, Jonathan?"

"Jonathan visited Crosbyville in the summers, too, when he was younger. But, he didn't come often. I barely remember him. How is it that you can recall Jonathan, but not David?" Marcie asked.

"Honestly, I don't remember much about either of them. I think I remember Aunt Agatha talking about them. David loved her blueberry pie. She remembers everything about people when it comes to food. But I don't understand why Jonathan stopped coming to visit his grandfather."

"Frederick and Edward were in business together, but they had a big fight. Frederick left. As far as I know, they never spoke again."

"That's sad. As an only child, I always envied people with siblings. Even the Bennet sisters in *Pride and Prejudice* must have had some good times when they were younger, before Lydia became so boy-crazy and Mary got so serious."

"I know. Me, too. I wanted to be like the March sisters in *Little Women*. I could totally see myself acting out Jo's plays." Marcie squeezed my hand. "Thankfully, I found a best friend who writes and once had a playwriting phase. So, I got to live out my acting dreams."

"Don't remind me. Those plays were horrible. Although, since you're such a talented artist, your scenery made them special."

For a few moments before returning to our original topic, we laughed at the memories of elaborate settings and over-the-top characters who would have made Anne of Green Gables's imaginary friends seem bland in comparison.

"I do remember returning from camp one summer, and all the girls were swooning as if a member of the royal family was in town."

"That's right." Marcie nodded. "I think the last summer David and Jonathan came to Crosbyville, you were at that writing camp at Northwestern." She sighed and looked down.

"What happened?"

"David and I . . . well, we got close." Marcie sighed.

"Oh," I said.

Marcie looked at my face and then burst out laughing. "Pris, not that close. We were only about thirteen."

"Oh, of course. Sure. I didn't mean to imply . . ."

"We held hands and made out." Marcie shrugged. "It was kids' stuff. Nothing serious." She glanced at my lunch bag. "I'm starving. Is anything in there for me?"

I stopped and handed her one of the hand pies and an ice cream. She bit into the pie and groaned. "That's so good."

Bailey drooled by my side until I handed him one of the dog biscuits. He gobbled it down and then turned his soulful eyes back to me until I gave him the other one.

I bit into the remaining hand pie. It was apple and still warm. "Hmm. So, what happened? Did you two break up? And why didn't you tell your best friend about this?"

She shrugged. "Nothing to tell."

"I take it he's the one that ended the relationship. Were you heartbroken?"

"No. I guess that's the problem. It would have been easier if we had broken up. Then I would have cried on my best friend's shoulder and we would have called him names, played sad breakup songs until we were miserable, and ate pints of Ben and Jerry's Cherry Garcia ice cream." Marcie grinned, but the smile didn't reach her eyes. "Instead, it just petered out. Seriously, this passionate crush only lasted one week. How could I possibly have fallen for someone I'd only known for a week?"

"Romeo and Juliet were only together one day." I shrugged. "When you know, you know."

"Thankfully, our encounter wasn't that serious." She laughed again. "We were only thirteen. One week of holding hands, sneaking kisses, and talking on the phone. That's hardly worth committing suicide for. We had some clean fun and then he just left town. Disappeared. No note. No call. Nothing. By the time you got home from camp, I was embarrassed that I'd allowed myself to care about some boy I barely knew who was so out of my league financially. Obviously, he hadn't cared enough to even bother breaking up with me. I guess there was nothing to end. I pushed him out of my mind and vowed I'd never speak his name again."

"And you didn't?" I asked.

She shook her head. "Not until today."

We continued our walk around the lake and ate. The water was peaceful and still and provided a perfect reflection of the tree-lined shore. We ended up at an old, white-washed boathouse. Near the boathouse, there was a bench. We sat, gazed at the water, and finished our snacks.

Canada geese dipped and squawked over the water. Bailey gazed at the geese but didn't chase or howl, even though the look in his eyes indicated he would have liked nothing better than to show those geese who was boss. He was such a good boy. I gave him his frozen pumpkin and he quickly forgot about the geese and licked the container clean. When he was finished, I took off his leash and allowed him to enjoy the smells in this new area.

I kept a close eye on him, while also checking on my

friend. "Were you hoping David Townsend would rekindle your romance?"

Marcie paused and then shook her head. "No. It was hardly a romance. Just a teenage crush. I don't want to date him. I guess I wish I knew what happened. Why he left and never even wrote or called to tell me why." She shrugged. "Closure. Also, I hoped I had been wrong about him, but it doesn't look like it."

Bailey wandered over to the side of the boathouse. He sniffed and scratched at the ground.

"We even scratched our initials into the back of that boathouse," Marcie added.

"Really? Let's see if it's still there." I got up and headed toward the building.

"That was over fifteen years ago," Marcie said, but eventually I heard her coming up behind me.

She eyed the building and eventually pointed at a piece of wood.

D.T. and *M.R.* and a heart with an arrow through it.

"Still there," I said.

Marcie ran her fingers over the engraving and then dropped her hand and shrugged. "I guess no one ever came out here much after that."

I wondered for a moment about Marcie and David as teenagers, but the sound of digging and dirt flying stopped my train of thought. I hurried around the side of the building and found Bailey shoulder-deep in a hole.

"Bailey, stop." I rushed forward and reattached his leash to help pull him away from whatever scent he'd discovered and was determined to unearth. I said a silent prayer that it wouldn't be a dead rodent—or another dead body. It had been six months since Bailey's nose pulled the two of them into a real crime investigation, and I preferred those situations to stay in my children's books.

It took a bit of convincing, but Bailey eventually stopped digging. With any luck, I could replace the dirt and no one would be the wiser. I braced myself and took a step forward to glance into the hole.

"What is it?" Marcie asked.

I leaned forward and pulled out a brown saddlebag. I breathed a sigh of relief. "Just an old bag." I held it up.

Buried in the damp, wet ground near the lake, time had eroded the strap and the bag slipped and fell to the ground. The top of the bag opened, and the contents poured out.

Marcie and I stared, openmouthed. After what felt like an hour, Marcie said, "Pris, that can't be real. Do you think it's real? It can't be real."

I shook my head in disbelief. "It sure looks real. Holy moly."

"What are we going to do?" Marcie asked.

"Rooo," Bailey bayed.

"I'm going to call the police."

Chapter 3

*G*ilbert stared from the bag to Bailey. From Bailey to me, and from me to the bag. Occasionally, he shot a frosty glance toward Marcie, but then he returned his glare to me.

"Tell me again how you found this?" Gilbert frowned into the bag.

"Look, you can stop glowering at us. We were just standing around the boathouse talking when Bailey started sniffing around, and the next thing we knew, he dug up that bag," I said.

"It's real, isn't it?" Marcie asked. "How much do you think it is? Can we keep it?"

"It looks real." Gilbert reached down and fanned through one of the many stacks of bills. "If I had to guess, I'd say there's somewhere between forty and fifty thousand dollars."

Marcie whistled.

"Where did it come from and why was it buried under the boathouse?" I asked.

Gilbert shrugged. "Beats me."

"Maybe it's the money D. B. Cooper tossed from that plane." Marcie said. "I saw a documentary on that case."

"D. B. Cooper?" I asked.

"You know, the guy who threw a ton of money from that airplane, and it was never found," Marcie said.

Gilbert straightened his shoulders. "D. B. Cooper was a criminal who hijacked an airplane in the Pacific Northwest. He demanded two hundred thousand dollars and then parachuted out of the plane—"

"In the documentary, they said they never found the man or the money. So, it's still out there somewhere. And the statute of limitations has expired, so if someone were to find that money, they would be entitled to keep it." Marcie patted Bailey. "Good boy, Bailey."

Gilbert rolled his eyes. "Did you miss the part about the Pacific Northwest?"

Marcie flicked his objection away like it was a pesky mosquito.

I swiped my phone until I found information about D. B. Cooper. "This hijacking took place in 1971." I stared at Marcie with my eyebrow raised.

"So what? The money hasn't changed. Just because it's old doesn't mean you can't still spend it. A kid found some of the money back in 1980."

"It was tattered and disintegrating, and that was nearly

fifty years ago. This money looks practically untouched," Gilbert said. "Plus, that money was found *in the Pacific Northwest*. Not Indiana."

"Could it be counterfeit?" I asked.

Gilbert fanned through the stack a few more times. "I don't know. It looks real, but I'll need to take it in and have someone run the serial numbers. We may get lucky and get a hit."

"And if you don't get a hit?" Marcie asked. "Can we keep it?"

"Then we turn the bag over to the Townsend estate to be assessed with the rest of Edward Townsend's property."

Marcie poked out her lower lip. "Do we have to?"

"Yes. We have to." Gilbert put the stacks of bills back into the saddlebag. Then he took out his radio and called for another officer to join him. When he was done, he told me, "I need to count it, and Officer Rodriguez will be a witness. You're welcome to stick around."

I glanced at the time on my phone. "Sorry, Bailey and I are doing a demo with Crosbyville Search and Rescue at noon and we only have fifteen minutes to get over to the squash court on the far side of the grounds. I glanced at Marcie. "Maybe you should notify David Townsend? I mean, if he is the owner or soon-to-be owner of Townsend Farms, he may want to be here, too."

Marcie narrowed her gaze and frowned.

"Good idea." Gilbert jumped at the idea of getting my chatty friend away from his investigation.

Officer Rodriguez, a thin man with a broad smile, drove

over in the Townsends' golf cart. He climbed out and his eyes widened at the sight of the money.

"Mind if I borrow this?" I climbed behind the wheel of the golf cart without waiting for a response.

"I'm coming with you." Marcie hurried to the passenger seat and hopped in.

Bailey whined.

"Hop in, boy!" I pointed to the back of the spacious four-seater golf cart.

Bloodhounds can be stubborn, so I wasn't sure if he didn't understand or was simply refusing to ride in the back. After a bit of coaxing, begging, and even an attempt at bribery with hand pie crumbs all failed, Marcie gave up.

"Fine." Marcie got out and moved to the back seat.

Bailey promptly climbed into the passenger seat.

I pulled away from the laughter I heard coming from Gilbert and Officer Rodriguez and drove toward the house.

Chapter 4

*A*t more than one hundred acres, Edward Townsend's estate was expansive. Although I've lived in Crosbyville for over twenty-five years, this was my first time going onto the estate. I'd heard my aunt Agatha and some of her friends mention how grand the estate was, but I had never seen it up close and personal. Much of Elkhart County, Indiana, was rural by Chicago and New York City standards, but Townsend Farms was considered rural even by Indiana standards. For miles, the landscape consisted of country roads with corn and wheat fields on either side. During the growing season, it was easy to get lost in the sameness. A sea of tall green cornstalks blocked any structures that distinguished one farm from another until harvest.

The Townsend estate wasn't used for cultivating food, so the landscape was flat and open. The property was surrounded by wooden split-rail fencing, which must have cost a small fortune, given the size of the estate. The main entrance wasn't elaborate but was still impressive, with stone pillars and an electronic gate.

Through the gate, a long winding road meandered around densely wooded trees, a well-stocked lake, and several ponds. There was even a picturesque covered bridge that enhanced the charm and character of the property. The equestrian arena and stables appeared first along the road. Most of the festival traffic stopped here. To the right, one field was set aside for parking. To the left, the festival committee had set up rides, games, and booths. Two uniformed policemen blocked cars from proceeding farther toward the private areas.

On the golf cart, I was able to bypass the guards and head in the direction of the main house. The house was a large brick Georgian manor house that wasn't visible from the road. My jaw dropped open at the sight of the impressive mansion that Edward Townsend had called home. I didn't even realize there were houses this grand in Crosbyville. I parked the golf cart at the side of the house near the garages. There were six.

The front of the house had two wings that extended from either side of the main building, creating a U shape. A low brick wall created a square enclosure with one opening for cars. Inside the opening, a circle was created using bricks that had been laid in a herringbone pattern. The slate-roofed, redbrick manor house was massive, and despite the age of the house, the impression was one of opulence.

"Wow! How big do you think it is?" I asked, getting out of the cart.

Marcie shrugged. "I heard it's about thirteen thousand square feet."

"That's massive. Was it just Edward Townsend living here?"

"It used to be Edward Townsend, his wife, and son. Now, I have no idea." Marcie shrugged. "I'm sure they had lots of staff who stayed, too. Edward Townsend must have had someone who took care of the horses and the grounds. I don't know if he's done a lot of updating. I seem to remember quite a bit of wallpaper. You would hate it."

Having recently bought my first house, an old carriage house that had once belonged to one of Crosbyville's founding families, Marcie had helped me decorate, which included wallpapering several bedrooms. "I forgot you've been here before."

"It was a long time ago." Marcie walked around the back of the golf cart.

Bailey leaped out and we stood staring at the impressive structure for several moments.

The area set aside for the Search and Rescue demo wasn't far away, but I still had quite a hike to get there from the house. I decided to leave the wheels for Marcie and David Townsend to use for the trip back to the boathouse. Perhaps a trip alone in the golf cart would reignite his memory, and maybe something more.

"Pris, I know what you're trying to do, but it's a waste of time. You might as well drive down and—"

"You can't do this. We have a contract!" A voice I recognized as my Search and Rescue colleague's, Hilda Diaz-Sanchez, screamed.

Marcie and I peeked around the corner of the house and saw Hilda Diaz-Sanchez, David Townsend, and Chelsea Baxter huddled near the garage.

"Your contract was with my grandfather, not me, love," David Townsend said in his annoyingly calm Australian accent.

"The fundraiser is in two weeks. I don't have time to find another venue."

"Hmm. I guess you're in a pickle." Townsend paused. "However, I might be persuaded to reconsider for an additional fee."

Hilda released a string of words in a language I assumed was Portuguese, since Hilda was Brazilian, and I knew she spoke Portuguese. Though it might have been Spanish. After an initial burst of anger, she subsided and asked, "How much?"

David Townsend threw out a number that made me gasp.

Hilda nearly choked. Her eyes bulged and she looked as though she was ready to spit fire. Even Chelsea Baxter stared openmouthed at David Townsend for a few seconds before clamping her mouth shut.

Hilda's voice went up two octaves and her Brazilian accent became much more pronounced as she struggled to find the words. *"Escandaloso!* That's illegal. You're a crook.

And you." Hilda turned to Chelsea and pointed a finger in her face. "You're in this, too. You did this."

Chelsea's face was flushed, and she looked ready to have a stroke. She glanced from David to Hilda and then opened her mouth to speak but was saved when David Townsend intervened.

"Look, love. If you don't like the terms, then sue me." He put an arm around Chelsea's waist, turned, and walked away.

"*Eu vou te matar,*" Hilda screamed, and then twisted her hands as though wringing out a cloth. Then she stormed away.

After a few moments, Marcie and I exchanged glances.

"Portuguese is similar to Spanish, and even a decade after my seventh-grade Spanish class, I remember '*matar*' means 'to kill.' You don't suppose she would actually . . ." I looked at my friend.

Marcie shrugged. "Honestly, if she did, I can't say I would blame her. David Townsend is a jerk. He deserves what he gets."

Chapter 5

Hilda Diaz-Sanchez was petite, with thick dark hair, dark eyes, and a fiery temper. Her makeup was always flawless, and even in her typical Search and Rescue gear, which she called SARs, she looked stunning while the rest of us merely looked hot and uncomfortable. The only clue to her age was the fact that she had two grown children and doted on her school-age grandchildren. Marcie joked that she must sleep in a coffin at night, but I didn't attribute her youthful good looks to anything vampiric. She was exceptionally active and must have had great genes because her children, Isabella and Rafael, were both swoon-worthy, too. Hilda had since buried any annoyance from her argument with David Townsend. The only clue that she'd been so angry that she'd actually threatened him were red blotches on her neck. Otherwise, she hid both her anger and her age well.

I was new to Search and Rescue, but Bailey had been a natural and got his SARs certification quickly. I wasn't as skilled as my bloodhound, but like my dog, I was a quick learner. We'd done obedience school in River Bend, the town where I'd lived and worked after college. When I moved back to Crosbyville, I joined the local Search and Rescue organization and went through the training.

In addition to Bailey and me, Hilda had three other members of the Crosbyville Search and Rescue team present with their dogs. The space set aside on the estate for our demonstration was mostly a large, grassy area near the squash court. There were a couple of sheds on the perimeter that were probably used for storing squash equipment. Although, for the life of me, I couldn't tell you what equipment was used for squash. People interested in watching the demonstration stood or sat in lawn chairs. Hilda kicked off the demonstration by introducing each of us and speaking about each of our dogs.

Not much to say about me, except that I was a local children's book author and former teacher at Crosbyville Elementary School. Bailey was much more interesting. Hilda explained to the crowd that bloodhounds had been bred to hunt deer, wild boar, and rabbits. However, since the Middle Ages, they had also been bred to use their superior noses for tracking people. While all canines possess an olfactory ability far superior to that of humans, hounds—and specifically, bloodhounds—were at the top of the list when it came to tracking.

Hilda and her Lab, Teddy, were by far the most skilled

and accomplished handler-and-dog team present. Teddy was cadaver trained, which made him useful at avalanches, earthquakes, and other natural disasters when a search eventually progressed from rescue to recovery. Recently returned from a trip to Teotihuacán, Mexico, they, along with another Crosbyville resident, chief archaeologist Dr. Debra Holt, had participated in a study using search-and-rescue dogs to locate buried human remains from 700 BC at an archaeological site.

Unlike Teddy, Bailey wasn't cadaver trained. Although I firmly believed he was capable, especially considering his last major discovery. Bailey was limited by a wimpy human handler—me.

After the introductions, we showcased our dogs' capabilities. Hilda had arranged for volunteers to leave scent trails and to hide in deep grass, behind outbuildings, and surrounded by a crowd. In each case, the canine-and-handler teams located their target. When it was Bailey's turn, we were given a harder challenge. Due to the superior scent ability of bloodhounds, the trail we were to follow had been created two days prior. A toy used for training was scented by someone Bailey didn't know. We learned that the man's name was Jay Barlow, and neither Bailey nor I had ever heard of him before.

Hilda originally wanted David Townsend to play the role of the missing person. He was new to Crosbyville and she undoubtedly wanted to make him feel welcome in the community. According to Chelsea Baxter, Townsend wasn't interested in participating. Which, given the way things had just worked out between Hilda and David, was probably a good thing. None of the dogs used in search and rescue were aggressive, especially Labs like Teddy. However, I'd seen dogs who are normally quite docile move into attack mode when backed into a corner. Even a well-trained, well-behaved dog might attack if he felt his owner was in distress or danger. All in all, David Townsend was probably safest staying as far away from Hilda Diaz-Sanchez as possible. In light of David Townsend's refusal to participate, Chelsea Baxter had enlisted the aid of Jay Barlow, a close family friend of Edward Townsend's, who was also one of three trustees responsible for the oversight of Edward Townsend's estate.

Bailey was given an article of clothing to sniff. Then he put his head down and went to work. It felt like the search was taking an exceptionally long time, but a quick glance at my watch showed me that he had been working only a couple of minutes. I could tell by the way his ears perched on his head and the sharp wag in his tail, that he wasn't just following the trail of a squirrel or someone eating a hot dog. He was working. Eventually he led me to a shed, where he sat—his alert signal. Mission accomplished.

When I opened the shed door, a body fell to the ground.

There was blue liquid everywhere. A container of blueberries had exploded out of the person's bag and covered the man's body. Bailey's toy tumbled out beside him. After a quick sniff, Bailey started eating the berries.

Someone was screaming, and it wasn't until Hilda Diaz-Sanchez slapped me that I realized I was the screamer. I clamped my hand over my mouth.

This can't be happening.

Who was this man? And how did he end up with my dog's Lamb Chop stuffed training toy?

Chapter 6

Someone escorted me to the kitchen of the Townsend estate.

The kitchen was old-fashioned but still cozy. Unlike modern homes with kitchens that open to the family room, this kitchen was closed off. It was functional with a tile floor, white cabinets, and butcher-block counters. The galley-style kitchen opened up to a larger room with a marble-topped island. An oak dining table sat in an alcove surrounded by windows that brought in lots of sunlight and gave the room a bright and cheery atmosphere.

I sat at the massive oak table and focused on breathing so I wouldn't pass out or hurl the funnel cake, apple pie, and cider I'd consumed that day all over the sparkling clean floor. Even though I was wrapped in a blanket, I couldn't stop shivering. The cook brought me a cup of tea laden with sugar. I preferred holding the cup in my hands and allowing the warmth to defrost my fingers rather than trying to drink the syrupy mixture, but I didn't want to hurt the cook's feelings and felt obliged to take a few sips.

"What happened?" Gilbert squatted in front of me. Chelsea Baxter stood nearby, having followed Gilbert into the house.

"I—I don't know. We . . . I just opened the door and—" I swallowed hard to keep from puking.

"Are you going to be sick?" he asked.

I shook my head and prayed that was the truth. The image of the body on the ground flooded my mind. A dead body covered in blueberry juice and berries everywhere.

"Gilbert, I don't even know who he is. I never met Mr. Barlow before." I glanced around for Bailey. "OMG. Where's Bailey? He was eating those berries." I whipped out my cell phone and quickly googled *Are blueberries poisonous to dogs?*

According to the American Kennel Club, blueberries were a great snack for dogs. In fact, they were a great source of minerals and antioxidants. I breathed a sigh of relief.

"How did you end up using him in the demonstration if you never met?" Gilbert asked.

"Hilda wanted to get a stranger—someone Bailey wouldn't know—for the demonstration. She wanted to focus on the fact that bloodhounds could catch a scent that was several days old. So, she wanted a stranger. Originally, she wanted to have David Townsend, but he refused."

"Humph. Good thing he did, or it might have been him instead of old Barlow lying on the ground with a—"

"Mrs. Davis, we get it." In an instant, Gilbert switched from concerned boyfriend to cop. He was serious, and everything in his voice as well as his demeanor screamed *chief of police*. As a Black woman, I code-switched often, but Gilbert switched into authoritative police chief in a split second.

"Baxter," Chelsea corrected him.

"Sorry. Mrs. . . . um, Ms. Baxter. I'll get your statement in just a minute."

"Humph." Chelsea Baxter folded her arms across her chest.

Chief Morgan nodded for me to continue.

"So, when David Townsend refused, she had to get someone else. That's when Chelsea said she would surprise David . . . um, I mean Mr. Townsend, by getting an old family friend named Jay Barlow to scent the toy and leave a trail. Chelsea came by and got the toy. She was supposed to have Mr. Barlow add his scent to it and then Hilda would hide it." I shot a glance in Chelsea's direction.

"Don't blame this mess on me. I didn't have anything to do with killing that man." Chelsea Baxter paced from one end of the kitchen to the other.

"No one's blaming anyone," Chief Morgan said. "I'm just getting the details."

"Humph." Chelsea paced. "Well, you better not. All I did was get the toy and give it to the old man to touch. That's it. Then, after he'd hugged it for a while, I put it back in that plastic bag and gave it to that Sanchez woman."

Chief Morgan took a deep breath and then stood and turned to look at Chelsea. He pulled out a small tape recorder. He pushed record and then stated his name, the date, time, and everyone present. When he finished, he turned to Chelsea. "When was the last time you saw Jay Barlow?"

"The one and *only* time I saw the old man was Thursday night," Chelsea said.

"How is it that you were helping with the search and rescue? Are you a member of the club?" Chief Morgan asked.

Chelsea snorted. "Not hardly."

"Then how—"

"Listen, Chief, let's get something straight. Just because your girlfriend's gotten herself mixed up in another murder, doesn't mean that I'm the one to blame." She glared.

"Mrs. Davis, I—"

"Baxter. You know I'm getting divorced and going back to my maiden name just as soon as I can get the paperwork approved."

"Sorry, Ms. Baxter. I'm not accusing you or anyone else of anything. I just need to understand what happened and why. I'd appreciate your cooperation in getting to the truth." Chief Morgan frowned. "Now, how did you get enlisted to help with the toy and with Jay Barlow?"

"Well, as half the town knows, I've been going through a very messy divorce, and my good-for-nothing, soon-to-be ex emptied our joint bank account and cut off my credit cards." Chelsea huffed. "Can you believe that? And it isn't just affecting me. I now have my cousin Clarice to feed and clothe." She scowled and marched from one end of the kitchen to the other. "My attorney said he won't help me until I pay up, and I just don't have it. So, I had to get a job."

Chelsea Baxter said the word *job* as though she were being asked to donate a kidney.

As a single parent and the chief of police, Gilbert might have sympathized with Chelsea's situation if she hadn't just acted as though getting a job was beneath her. Instead, he merely waited. The vein on the side of his head had amped up from rumba to cha-cha level, so I knew he was angry. Chelsea Baxter was clueless.

"And jobs that pay well are hard to find, you know. They all want years of experience, and I don't have any. I married Mr. Wrong straight after college. But I majored in marketing, so I offered my PR services to the town council's festival committee to generate publicity. I figured it would be a good way to get my name out there. Then I could start my own business and get paying clients. The festival committee agreed to provide a small stipend for essentials, plus mileage reimbursement. When this whole thing is over, they'll give me a recommendation. Then I'll be on my way." She shrugged. "Anyway, I've been making sure that all the right papers and television stations are here. This year's festival is getting a lot of media attention, especially after Edward Townsend's estranged grandson arrived from Australia after decades away, just before his grandfather died. It was a story that was meant for television, and the networks were eating it up." She looked up in the sky and spread her hand as if she could see an invisible headline. "*Long lost heir returns to Crosbyville.*" She smiled and then turned to stare at us. "You couldn't write anything better than that." She dropped her smile and her arms.

"What happened?" Chief Morgan asked.

"I had reporters from all over the world who wanted to come to Crosbyville to interview the missing heir. They were eating out of the palm of my hand, but when I shared my publicity plans with David, he didn't want anything to do with the media or any other publicity. He absolutely refused to do interviews. In fact, he refused to let the festival take place on his family's estate at all unless I assured him that he wouldn't be forced into the public spotlight." She rolled her eyes.

"I had no idea he was so shy," I said. *So much for his assertion that allowing the festival to continue was what his grandfather would have wanted.*

"Me, either." Chelsea shrugged. "Anyway, I pulled it off, and now this. I barely scraped by with my reputation when my sister, Whitney, was killed. When people find out I'm connected with another murder, none of the *better* companies will want anything to do with me. I'll be lucky to get a job writing obituaries for the *Crosbyville Gazette*."

Chief Morgan took a deep breath and the vein on the side of his head moved back down to rumba level. "So, you were handling the publicity for the festival . . ."

"Right. Well, at first, I was working with Edward Townsend before he passed away, but then he started getting dotty. He—"

"Dotty, how?" I asked.

Chief Morgan shot me a look that made me wish I'd kept quiet, but it was too late.

"You know, mumbling. Forgetful." Chelsea waved her

hand. "He kept mumbling something about allergies." She rolled her finger at the side of her head in the universally accepted gesture for crazy. "Anyway, he wanted to bring in some old geezer who was a trustee, but wanted it kept on the down-low." Chelsea shrugged.

"Bring him in for what?" I asked.

Chief Morgan frowned and I clamped my mouth closed.

Chelsea waved her hand. "How would I know?"

"And the 'old geezer' was Jay Barlow?" Chief Morgan asked.

"Of course." Chelsea looked at Gilbert as though he, too, was crazy. Fortunately, she was wise enough not to suggest it. After a few moments, she continued. "Anyway, Edward Townsend asked me to pick Old Man Barlow up from the airport. I figured, why not? The festival was covering the mileage anyway. So, I picked him up at the River Bend airport on Thursday night and drove him to a hotel in the area. Since I had both that stupid toy and the old guy in the car, well, I just decided to have him touch the toy . . . you know, put his scent on it." She shrugged.

Chief Morgan pinched the bridge of his nose. "That was two days ago?"

"Yes."

"Edward Townsend died on Thursday," I said.

Gilbert glared at me, and I remembered that I was supposed to be quiet.

"Right, so I've been a little busy with all this." She spread her arms wide as though she'd singlehandedly arranged for every aspect of the festival.

"Okay. Thursday, when you picked up Jay Barlow from the airport, was the last time that you saw or spoke to him?" Gilbert recapped.

"That's what I said." Chelsea pulled on her earring and then folded her arms across her chest again. Her gaze was steady and never wavered. She and her sister, Whitney, had been great actresses. Anyone unfamiliar with the two would have believed they were sincere. However, I grew up with the Baxter sisters and knew that they had mastered the art of deception long ago. When it came to looking someone in the eyes and lying through their perfectly capped teeth, they were pros. However, each had a tell, which gave them away, if you knew where to look. For Whitney, her tell had been a smirk. Regardless of how serious the situation was, when she was lying, she couldn't help letting a smirk escape.

For Chelsea, it was an ear tug.

"Who else knew he was here?" Chief Morgan asked.

"No idea."

"Any idea how he got here today?"

Chelsea paused for a few moments. Then she shrugged. "No idea. All I know is that I didn't bring him."

"Thank you, Mrs. Dav—I mean Ms. Baxter." Chief Morgan turned off the small tape recorder. "We'll type up your statement and call when it's ready for your signature."

Chelsea stomped toward the door. She wrenched the door open and turned. "If you're looking for someone who might have killed the old man, maybe you should talk to that so-called lawyer, Natalie Evans."

"Why?" Chief Morgan asked.

"She works with the Townsend estate. I overheard her talking to David. She knew Barlow was here. If you ask me, that common tart is just the type to commit murder. Don't let her expensive clothes fool you. As my grandmother used to say, 'She's as common as pig tracks.'" Chelsea waltzed outside and slammed the door.

Chapter 7

When Chelsea left, the stiflingly hot tension in the room dropped.

"Whew!" I fanned myself. "I don't particularly like Natalie Evans, but that was very harsh."

Gilbert's shoulders relaxed and he set aside his police persona and was back to being my boyfriend. "I have no idea what that means. What is 'common as pig tracks'?" He scratched his head.

"It's a derogatory way of calling someone low or vulgar. It's mean."

"Chelsea and her sister, Whitney, were both 'mean girls.' So it fits, but the big question is, Is she right?"

"Maybe. Of course, she might be jealous."

"Jealous? Chelsea with David Townsend?" Gilbert stared. "She can't have known him more than a few days."

"True, but he's single. More importantly, he's rich—or will be rich soon once his grandfather's estate is settled." I gave Gilbert a knowing look. "You heard her. She's desperate for money."

"For a while, there was even a rumor that she went after Edward Townsend once upon a time."

"Ugh." Gilbert squeezed his eyes shut and shook his head. "But why? Chelsea Baxter is a young, attractive woman. She certainly wouldn't need to marry someone old enough to be her grandfather."

"I guess she was desperate for money." I shrugged.

"Right. She was so desperate she was forced to get a job."

"Exactly."

Gilbert shook his head again, but quickly got back to the business at hand. "Let's get back to your statement." He picked up his recorder and started to give his opening information when the back door flew open.

"Pris, are you okay?" Marcie flung her arms around my neck.

Gilbert turned off his recorder. "How did you get in here? There's supposed to be a policeman guarding the door."

"There was. I told him you asked me to come," Marcie said boldly. "Because I knew you would want me here with Pris."

Gilbert mumbled something that sounded like whoever was on duty outside was looking at a demotion.

"I'm fine now," I said to Marcie.

"You won't be when your aunt Agatha—"

The door flew open again and my aunt flew into the

kitchen. My aunt, who was normally cool, calm, and collected, looked frayed and frazzled. Aunt Agatha was about five feet four with dark skin, light eyes, and curly salt-and-pepper hair that she wore short. Earlier, she'd had a scarf around her hair and her makeup was flawless. Now her scarf was askew. Her runny mascara had created raccoon circles under her eyes, and instead of her normal curls, her hair looked wiry and frizzy, as though she had received an electric shock. The red lipstick she'd worn earlier was also covering her teeth, a sure sign that she had been biting her lips.

Gilbert opened his mouth to complain, but Aunt Agatha gave Gilbert a look that dared him to say one word to her. He recognized the look. He held up both hands in surrender and took one step backward.

Aunt Agatha hurried over and grabbed me by the shoulders and stared into my eyes. "Are you okay?"

I nodded. "I'm fine."

Her gaze searched my soul. When she was sure that I was telling the truth, she pulled me into an embrace that nearly crushed the air from my lungs.

"I can't breathe," I squawked.

She loosened her hold. "What happened?" She fired the question at me like a bullet and then turned her attention to Gilbert. "And why weren't the police doing their jobs, serving and protecting? You can't take two steps on this estate without stumbling over a policeman. *Someone* should have been able to prevent a murder at a public festival." She glared.

Gilbert rubbed his neck. "Miss Bell, I assure you, we're doing—"

"Come on, Aunt Agatha. This isn't Gilbert's fault, and you know it."

The adrenaline that carried my aunt halfway across the estate dissipated and her legs buckled.

Gilbert shoved a chair behind her knees just in time, and she flopped down.

"Are you okay?" Gilbert asked her gently.

"They said Bailey found another dead body." Aunt Agatha sobbed. "I was so worried."

Bailey scooched up to my aunt and placed his head in her lap.

Marcie got a glass and filled it with water and handed it to her.

David Townsend waltzed into the kitchen and stared at Gilbert. "There you are. What in the world is going on? There are police cars, a fire truck, an ambulance, and a full battalion of people trampling all over my property."

"We're doing the job that the taxpayers of Crosbyville pay us to do. There was an accident and we're investigating." He straightened his back and his chief of police mask was firmly in place.

Gilbert was still stewing about that taxpayer comment from earlier.

"Crikey. Who was it?"

I'm going to google crikey. *I'm pretty sure no one really says that word anymore.*

"A man named Jay Barlow." Chief Morgan watched David Townsend's reaction, and he wasn't disappointed.

"Jay Barlow? Hmm . . . I don't think I know—" He snapped his fingers. "Wait. You don't mean Old Man Barlow?" He paused.

"Did you know him?" Chief Morgan asked.

"Not personally, of course. A friend of my grandfather's. Honestly, I'm surprised the old buzzard lasted this long. Was it his heart?"

"Did he have a bad heart?" Chief Morgan avoided answering the question by asking another one.

David Townsend shrugged. "No idea, mate. He was rather old, so I just assumed."

"You know what they say about assuming," Marcie muttered.

"What was that, love?" David Townsend asked.

"Nothing." Marcie sighed. "Just an American saying."

"I just thought of something." Townsend ran his fingers through his hair. "I suppose someone will need to notify the old man's family. Next of kin?"

"Do you know his family?" Chief Morgan asked.

"Me? No idea, mate, but I'm sure Natalie, ah . . . Ms. Evans probably has a way to reach them. She was grandfather's attorney. Would you like me to ask her?" David Townsend turned as though he was planning to leave.

"That won't be necessary." Chief Morgan stopped him. "I have a few more questions for you."

David Townsend turned back. "I don't know that I can

be of any help. I've only been back here a few days. I'm afraid I don't know too many people around here." He stared from Chief Morgan to Marcie to Aunt Agatha, and then his eyes landed on me. "I met this lovely woman earlier when she helped me find my way to the equestrian center." He flashed me a big smile.

Earlier, I'd found David Townsend attractive. Now I struggled to remember what it was about him that I'd liked. That's when I noticed he'd changed clothes. "Weren't you wearing a different outfit earlier?"

Townsend's smile froze. "Yes. I spilled something on my shirt. Plus, after the scuffle with that groom, Hicks, I wasn't looking my best." He adjusted his collar.

Earlier, Townsend had been wearing a linen shirt with caramel brown pants and matching shoes. He still looked stylish but was now wearing dark gray slacks with matching buttery soft leather shoes and a lavender shirt. If I wasn't mistaken, the lavender shirt looked as though it would match Natalie Evans's lavender suit perfectly.

"I hope it wasn't one of my blueberry pies," Aunt Agatha said.

"Excuse me?" David Townsend stared at Aunt Agatha as if she were speaking in a completely different language.

"I'm sure you don't remember me, but I run the Blue Plate Special Café. It's a small restaurant downtown. Your grandfather used to come by every Sunday and get the fried chicken special. We would sit and talk for hours." She paused and looked off into the distance as though she was remembering. Then she snapped back to the present. "Anyway, I was selling hand pies and ice cream. I specifically brought blueberry today. I think that was your favorite."

"I'm sorry, love, but I think you must have me confused with someone else." David Townsend gave Aunt Agatha a condescending smile that seemed to give the impression that she was often mistaken. That was a big mistake.

"I've not lost my memory yet," Aunt Agatha snapped.

You are treading on dangerous ground. If you're smart, you'll apologize and stop talking.

"I'm allergic to blueberries, so you must be misremembering, but I'm sure your hand . . . ah . . . pies are quite delicious, love." David Townsend smiled again.

At twenty-eight, I'll sometimes walk into a room and can't remember why I had gone in there. I've even found my remote control in the freezer once or twice. It wasn't unreasonable to assume that someone in their mid-fifties might be mistaken about a recollection. After all, it had been nearly fifteen years since David Townsend had last been to Crosbyville. However, there was one thing Aunt Agatha was confident about, and that was food. She prided herself on remembering favorite dishes that her patrons enjoyed. If she said David Townsend had liked her blueberry pies, my money was on my aunt.

Aunt Agatha stood to take one step forward, but got her leg wrapped up with Bailey's leash and slipped.

Chief Morgan's quick reflexes kept her from hitting the ground.

An embarrassed flush rose up her neck. She tried to

wave Gilbert's concern away and stand up on her own, but as soon as she tried to put weight on her left leg, she winced.

"Sit back down," Chief Morgan ordered.

The fact that Aunt Agatha obeyed was an indication of the pain that she must have felt. "I'm fine. I just twisted my ankle, that's all."

"You need a doctor. I'll see if the coroner is still here." Chief Morgan pulled out his radio.

"Oh no, you don't! I will not have any coroner examining me until I'm good and dead. No way." Aunt Agatha shook her head.

Chief Morgan opened his mouth, but before he could respond, his radio squawked.

"Chief—" What followed was static and jumbled words.

"Chief Morgan here. Go ahead," Gilbert said.

There was a lot more squawking and static with a few words mingled in. Gilbert's brow furled and he walked to the far side of the room. "Repeat?"

Then the heavens parted, the atmosphere cleared, and for the first time since I started dating a policeman, I was able to clearly hear and understand the radio transmission.

"Chief. You better get out here. The coroner says our corpse isn't dead. This guy's been badly beaten, but he's still alive."

Chapter 8

*C*hief Morgan rushed out the back door, mumbling certain words that I hoped Aunt Agatha didn't hear.

Marcie, Aunt Agatha, and I stared at one another.

"Oh Gawd," David Townsend said. The blood drained from his face.

"Are you okay?" I asked. "Maybe you better sit down before you pass out."

Marcie pulled out a chair for David Townsend, but he just stood staring at the chair as though he'd never seen one before. Eventually, he sat.

"Marcie, get Mr. Townsend a glass of water," Aunt Agatha said.

Marcie marched to the sink and came back with a glass of water and handed it to Townsend.

"Thank you." David Townsend's hand shook as he drank.

He dribbled a bit of water onto his new shirt, then placed the glass on the table. I wondered if he would need to change again. "I suppose I should go out there and see to things. I mean, I am the—"

The kitchen door swung open and Natalie Evans stormed in. "What on earth is going on out there?"

"It's Old Man Barlow," David Townsend said.

"Your grandfather's friend? What happened? Did he have a heart attack or something?" Natalie Evans asked. "Don't tell me he kicked the bucket in the middle of the festival?" Natalie posed the question as a joke, but no one laughed.

"Seems he had an accident," David Townsend said.

"Well, he was old. It had to happen sooner or later." Natalie sighed. "No need to look so bleak. He was an old man. We'll just need to call his next of kin. I'm guessing your grandfather has a number somewhere with someone—"

"That policeman. He said Barlow wasn't dead," David Townsend said.

"What?" Natalie asked.

"He's alive," Townsend said.

"How is that possible?" Natalie glanced at David Townsend but then looked around. Her gaze landed on me. "Someone told me that she found a dead man during her demonstration with that dog." She pointed an accusatory finger at me. I wasn't sure if she was accusing me of killing Jay Barlow. Or if I was somehow to blame for the fact that he wasn't dead, and she'd been given misinformation.

"Originally, they thought he was dead, but the coroner just said he wasn't," Townsend said.

"I suppose they'll take him to the hospital. This town does have a hospital, doesn't it?" Natalie Evans asked.

"Of course we have a hospital. We have electricity, televisions, and indoor plumbing, too." Aunt Agatha glared.

Natalie Evans shot an icy glance at Aunt Agatha but was met with a stare that quickly put her back in her place. After a few moments, Natalie Evans backed down from the stare-off and chuckled. "Sorry, I didn't mean any offense."

Aunt Agatha gave her a look that showed she didn't believe one word of that apology.

"David, if Mr. Barlow's alive, we should probably get to the hospital to see about him. Don't you think?" Natalie said.

"Oh yes. You're right." David Townsend stood. He took a few steps forward but stopped at the back door. He turned. "Thank you, ladies. I'm going to check on my grandfather's friend. Please excuse me." He opened the door and Natalie Evans waltzed out. David Townsend followed her, closing the door behind him.

Afterward, Marcie, Aunt Agatha, and I looked at one another.

"Lawd, have mercy. This is too much." Aunt Agatha fanned herself.

Edward Townsend's cook, a petite woman dressed in blue jeans and a dark shirt, came from the galley area of the kitchen. She patted Aunt Agatha on the shoulder. "Would you like a cup of tea?"

Aunt Agatha jumped. "Good Lord, you scared me."

"I'm sorry," the woman said.

"My nerves are frazzled," Aunt Agatha said. "I think I've sprained my ankle, thanks to Bailey." She glared at my bloodhound, who gave her a sad look in response.

"Aww. Don't be sad, boy. It wasn't *your* fault. I blame Pris. She's the one who left that leash on you, didn't she?" She scratched his ears. Aunt Agatha didn't hold a grudge long. At least, not against Bailey.

"Great. Now what?" I asked.

"Now you need to figure out a way to help me get to the car so you can take me to the walk-in clinic," Aunt Agatha said.

I turned to Marcie. "Where did you leave that golf cart?"

Chapter 9

*A*fter three hours at the walk-in clinic, Aunt Agatha was finally released with a compression boot, a prescription for pain medication, and orders to keep her foot elevated. The final verdict was a fracture. The doctor ordered plenty of rest, but since she hadn't confined her, I wasn't feeling hopeful on that last front.

Marcie, Bailey, and I got her in the car easily, but then the debate started. Where to go?

Aunt Agatha wanted to go home. I couldn't blame her for that. When I'm sick, I want to be home, too. However, her home was a two-story colonial with all the bedrooms on the second floor. No way could my stubborn aunt be trusted to avoid climbing the stairs. My house was an old-fashioned carriage house. Again, the bedrooms were up-stairs. It was a long day, and I was tired. The path of least resistance would be for Bailey and me to stay at Aunt Agatha's where I could keep an eye on her. I drove us to my house first to pack a bag and grab Bailey's food, treats, toys, and other necessities. I pulled up to the house and was pleasantly surprised to see Gilbert's car in front.

I'd sent him several text messages from the clinic to keep him updated. I wasn't surprised that he'd stopped by. I was pleasantly surprised to see that he'd brought a wheelchair. Aunt Agatha had been given crutches at the clinic, but she hadn't mastered the art of using them yet. She was still quite wobbly. I mentioned in one of my messages that I was nervous that she might fall and cause even more damage.

"Hello, Miss Agatha. Can I help you?" Gilbert gave Aunt Agatha his arm and helped her out of the car.

Aunt Agatha took one look at the wheelchair and revved up to argue, but Gilbert was ready for her.

"This chair used to belong to my wife, Sarah. Hannah thought it might make it easier for you to get around if you had a wheelchair instead of crutches. She really wanted you to have it."

The lines on my aunt's forehead straightened out and her mouth softened. "Well, that was sweet. Hannah is a thoughtful little girl." She took a deep breath. "I don't need a wheelchair, but . . . I suppose it won't hurt." She paused a moment but then allowed Gilbert to help her sit in the chair and be wheeled into the house.

When Gilbert passed me, I mouthed, *Thank you.*

He winked and wheeled Aunt Agatha into the house while Marcie held the door open.

"Where is Hannah so I can thank her?" Aunt Agatha looked around.

"She's still at Townsend Farm. Actually, I need a really big favor, and I was hoping that you, all of you, would help me." Gilbert glanced at each of us.

Marcie looked at me for answers, but I didn't have any. I shook my head and shrugged.

"What can we do for you, Chief?" Aunt Agatha asked.

"I'm in a bit of hot water. You see, tomorrow is Mary Elizabeth's birthday. She was invited to bring Clarice and Hannah to a sleepover at Townsend Farm. That was before Edward Townsend died. He assured me the housekeeper and cook would be there. I wasn't thrilled. Hannah begged. Plus, I was planning to make a surprise visit, just to make sure everything was okay, but now I've got to work. Tomorrow, they're supposed to go horseback riding, apple picking, and continue having fun at the festival."

"Will the festival continue?" I asked.

"As much as I'd like to close it down, I can't. It looks like Jay Barlow was hiding in the shed for the Search and Rescue demonstration. He must have slipped and hit his head," Gilbert said. "No foul play."

I shivered.

Gilbert rubbed my arms. "This was not your fault."

"I know, but . . . that poor man." I shook my head.

"No one's seen David Townsend or Natalie Evans since they left to go to the hospital to check on Jay Barlow."

"What about Andrew?" I asked.

Gilbert took a deep breath. "After his altercation with

David Townsend, Andy went out and got wasted. He's sleeping it off in a cell."

"Who's taking care of Mary Elizabeth?" Aunt Agatha asked.

"Chelsea Davis . . . Baxter took them out to get manis and pedis." He shook his head. "Do you know what that costs? What does an eleven-year-old need with a—" He took a deep breath.

"What do you want from us?" Marcie asked, redirecting him.

"Ah, right. Well, Edward Townsend promised me before he passed that Mary Elizabeth and her friends could stay in the main house." Gilbert ran a hand over his neck. "Anyway, Chelsea had agreed to keep all three girls for the afternoon, but she says she can't watch them overnight because she has work to do this evening. With all of the extra folks in town for the festival, we're doing mandatory overtime and stretched pretty thin, so I was wondering—"

"You were wondering if Pris could watch Hannah?" Marcie smiled.

"Well . . . Yes, but—"

"But nothing. Those girls need to have their sleepover. Pris, Marcie, and I can go over there and look after them," Aunt Agatha said. "That's what you had in mind when you came, isn't it?"

Gilbert nodded.

I stared from Gilbert to Aunt Agatha. "But, how? I mean—"

"That house is big enough for half the town to sleep

over. Luellen told Sadie at the diner that the house is over thirteen thousand square feet. With Eddie gone, I'm sure there's bound to be room for a few guests. All three of the girls will want to sleep together in one room and if they're strapped for space, all three of us can share a room, too." Aunt Agatha's eyes were bright and shining, but I wasn't sure if it was excitement or the meds the doctor gave her for pain.

"Us?" I asked.

"Us!" Aunt Agatha said with conviction. "It wouldn't be proper for either of you to stay in the house alone with David Townsend there. Plus, I assumed you wanted to keep an eye on me." She patted her leg. Fractured leg or not, Aunt Agatha wasn't about to let the opportunity to brag to her friends and patrons at the diner that she had slept at the Townsend Farms mansion pass her by.

I caught a look from Gilbert that let me know that he knew exactly what he was doing. I turned to look at Marcie.

Marcie raised a hand. "I'm in. It's not often a girl gets an opportunity to stay in a thirteen thousand square foot house with maids, butlers, and cooks." She turned to Gilbert. "They have maids and butlers, right?"

"Apparently, it takes an army to keep a massive estate running." Gilbert chuckled and used his fingers to count. "Edward Townsend had two maids, a housekeeper, a cook, a chauffeur, Andrew Hicks, whom you've met, a security guard, a lot of people who trained and cared for the horses, and a ton of gardeners."

"But no butler?" I joked.

"He had a personal valet, who sometimes acted like a butler, but no official butler," Gilbert said. After a few moments, he added, "Oh, and there's Natalie Evans, the lawyer, and a private detective, Peter Alexander."

"Does Natalie Evans live in Crosbyville?" I asked.

"She told me she has a townhome in Chicago. Most of what she does is remote. When Edward Townsend needed her, then she would come to Crosbyville. I have learned she usually stayed in River Bend since there's more to do there, but for some reason since David Townsend arrived, she's been staying at Townsend Farms." Gilbert didn't have to alter his facial expression for me to pick up the implication that he thought something was going on between Natalie Evans and David Townsend.

"A private detective? Edward Townsend had his own P.I.?" I asked.

"He hired the detective to help find his grandson."

"All of those people live in that house?" Aunt Agatha asked.

"No, most of the staff don't stay on the grounds at all. The housekeeper, cook, and the valet stay in the servants' quarters in a separate wing. The chauffeur has an apartment over the garage. Andrew and Mary Elizabeth have rooms over the old horse barn," Gilbert said.

"Geez. The *old* horse barn. How many barns did Edward Townsend have?" Marcie asked.

"Several. The old horse barn was smaller. It was replaced by the new horse barn, which is next to the equestrian center. Plus, there's an eighteenth-century stone dairy barn that was on the property before the house." He shook his head. "There's also a cottage near the gates for the security guard. Everyone else who works there stays off the property and comes in for the day."

Marcie whistled. "Wow."

"What about Natalie and the private detective?" I asked.

"Natalie's in a guest room in the main house," Gilbert said.

"Let me guess, Natalie's room is next to David Townsend's room, right?" Marcie asked in a sugary sweet voice that dripped with skepticism.

Gilbert shrugged. "No idea. Does it matter?"

"Not to me it doesn't." Marcie turned away and examined her fingernails as though her polish were the most important thing in the world.

"What about the private detective? Is he staying in one of the guest rooms, too?" I asked.

"I understand there are about ten or so." Gilbert narrowed his gaze and stared at me. "Look, if you don't feel comfortable staying there, it's okay. I can—"

"That's not it. I'm glad to stay overnight at the biggest mansion in Crosbyville with two maids, a housekeeper, a cook, a chauffeur, and a valet." I grinned. "I was just thinking it might provide an opportunity to do a little research for my book."

"Research?" Gilbert asked. "Are you planning to set the next Adventures of Bailey the Bloodhound book at a mansion?"

"No, but I do have a missing person . . . well, a missing

dachshund. Plus, I would love a chance to talk to a real private detective. I'll bet he could give me some tips I could use in the book to make Bailey's role as a detective more authentic."

Gilbert chuckled.

"What?" I asked.

"Nothing. It's just you're writing about a dog who is also a pet detective. What could be more authentic than that?" He grinned.

"You laugh, but kids have expectations. They expect the story to be realistic and for Bailey to behave the same way a real detective would behave. You should hear some of the questions I get when we go to pet-assisted therapy. One little boy wanted to see Bailey's P.I. license."

Gilbert's phone rang. He glanced at it. "This is Hannah. What should I tell her?"

"Tell her that Bailey the Bloodhound and his team will be sniffing for clues in two shakes of a dog's tail," I said.

Chapter 10

It turns out Bailey's overnight bag was the easiest to pack. No discussions about which leash or harness he wanted. He was picky about toys. Lamb Chop was his favorite. Once that went in the bag, he was good. Unfortunately, Marcie and Aunt Agatha weren't quite as easy to please. Not even when they were reviewing my wardrobe.

Marcie followed me upstairs and supervised my wardrobe. "Hmm. I don't think yoga pants and a sweatshirt are appropriate for an overnight at Townsend Farms."

I examined my comfortable go-to outfit to make sure there were no holes or stains. "Why not? We're going to a horse farm." I shoved the outfit into a backpack.

"True, but it's a fancy horse farm." Marcie pulled the sweatshirt out of the bag. "And you certainly can't walk around a million-dollar estate wearing a sweatshirt covered in paint."

"Why not?" I shoved the sweatshirt back into the backpack. "It's not like we're going to some fancy party where we need to dress for dinner."

"True, but I thought you wanted to interview that private detective. You don't want him to think you're some fly-by-night author. You're a bestselling author. I just think you should look the part if you want him to take you seriously."

She was my best friend, and she knew how to get under my skin like no one else. *Darn it.* I pulled the sweatshirt out of my backpack. "Fine."

Marcie smiled and started flipping through the clothes in my closet.

I folded my arms across my chest. "Look, if I'm lucky, I'll probably spend a total of an hour talking to the private detective. The rest of the time, we will be supervising three rambunctious preteens who are going to be riding horses and running around a farm during a festival. There's no way I'm wearing anything special."

"How about this?" Marcie held up a cream cashmere turtleneck and a figure-fitting down vest that I'd purchased from the L.L.Bean catalog but hadn't worn more than once or twice.

"Actually, I love that," I said reluctantly. "I'd forgotten about that vest, but it'll be great for the morning and evening when it's chilly."

Marcie smiled. "Agreed. You could even wear them with your yoga pants and riding boots or perhaps a nice pair of jeans with those red rain boots you bought."

Darn it. She was right.

I shoved the red boots and the clothes into the backpack with my underwear, pajamas, and toiletries. When I looked up, Marcie was holding a denim dress and a pair of ballet flats.

"Just in case," she said.

"Fine." I rolled the dress into a ball and shoved the shoes and dress into the pack. "Now, let's get out of here."

My home had once been a carriage house belonging to Amelia Cooper Lawson, a descendant of Crosbyville's founding family. The extra-large brick structure had also been the town's first post office before a larger, more modern, concrete building had been built. The carriage house remained empty for many years until Amelia Cooper Lawson needed money and agreed to sell. It had a lot of history and charm, and I loved it. The original building housed the Cooper family's carriages and had high ceilings, large doors, and a loft space upstairs where the driver lived. Walls were added over time, which created the four rooms that made up the first floor. There was a living room, a kitchen, a small dining room that I used as an office, and an even smaller powder room.

The biggest downside to the carriage house was that there were only windows at the front of the building. So, light was limited. To brighten the space, Marcie and I had painted the first floor a bright yellow, which made the rooms bright and cozy even without natural sunlight. The color reminded me of sunshine, lemons, and sunflowers.

The upstairs had one decent-sized bedroom, two small

guest rooms, and one bathroom. The walls were in bad shape. One day when I've sold a few more books, I might have the walls professionally replastered. In the meantime, we hid the imperfections with bold floral wallpaper. By far, the best part of the house was the back garden. It was fenced and, thanks to Gilbert's love of gardening, had been converted from an overgrown tangle of weeds into a lovely private oasis filled with shrubs and flowering trees. Bailey loved the space, and apart from a few impudent squirrels that liked to torment him from time to time, it was his favorite space.

Gilbert left to pick up Hannah and the girls from Chelsea Baxter's house. Well, technically, the house where Chelsea had been staying belonged to her late sister, Whitney, and her brother-in-law, Joe Kelley. It was a large house on the outskirts of town. It was expensive. Too expensive for Chelsea Baxter to afford. There was talk that she might sell, but chances were good that any money from selling the house would need to be used to cover Joe Kelley's legal expenses. So, for now, Chelsea and Clarice stayed there.

When Bailey and I were packed, I drove the short distance to Marcie's apartment. Crosbyville, Indiana, was a small town with a population of around thirty thousand. So, it didn't take long to drive anywhere downtown. Crosbyville's Main Street was lined with brick storefronts and a manicured central square in front of a limestone and brick-spired courthouse. I left Marcie to pack and drove two blocks to Aunt Agatha's colonial.

Aunt Agatha yelled orders to me from the first floor.

After my eighth trip up and down the stairs, I glanced at my phone and saw that I had completed more than half of my daily step goal in the last half hour. Eventually, her overnight bag was packed and included outfits for every possible scenario, including unseasonably hot, unseasonably cold, rainy, or windy weather, fancy dinner invites, and unexplained catastrophes that she refused to elaborate on. If I thought packing clothes was hard, it had taken a lot of convincing to reassure my aunt that she did not need to bring groceries because she would not be cooking. I discovered the reason she finally gave up the fight when I pulled up to the security gate and saw the Blue Plate Special food truck ahead, entering the gate. I turned and glanced back at Aunt Agatha, but she refused to make eye contact.

Marcie whispered, "I thought she gave up too easily on the groceries."

"It's almost seven o'clock. If I wasn't so hungry, I might have guessed she was up to something."

The security guard permitted both vehicles to enter. The sun was starting to set and there were still a lot of cars and visitors that followed the path toward the festival. We took the other path that led toward the residence. I was grateful for the mile-long drive to the main house. It was a lovely winding driveway that felt like a trip back through time to a rural estate that would have fit perfectly in my imaginative world of a Jane Austen novel.

"Wow," Marcie said. "Can you imagine growing up in a place like this?"

"No." I shook my head. "It feels bigger than downtown Crosbyville."

"It is bigger than downtown Crosbyville," Aunt Agatha said from the back seat. "We'll all need to mind our p's and q's in a place like this." I wondered, not for the first time, where that saying originated.

We passed rolling lawns, gardens, ponds, an eighteenth-century farmhouse, and an old dairy barn. At the top of a hill sat the manor house. This was my first time approaching from this angle and I was impressed.

I wondered how Edward Townsend would have felt about bloodhounds drooling in his mansion, and cast an eye in my rearview mirror at Bailey. I sent up a silent prayer that he wouldn't do anything that would get us kicked out before morning.

I pulled up to the front of the house behind Gilbert's SUV and parked. Fortunately, the housekeeper and Gilbert met us at the door. The housekeeper directed the food truck to the back. She introduced herself as Mrs. Claymore and then opened the trunk and took out our luggage.

Mrs. Claymore was a small, wiry woman. At first glance, she hardly seemed strong enough to lift a vacuum cleaner. However, when Gilbert went to get Aunt Agatha's bag, she stopped him and told him—nay, ordered him—to get the wheelchair and "help the nice lady into the garage and up the ramp. I'll see to the luggage."

Gilbert hesitated a moment, but then Mrs. Claymore hoisted Aunt Agatha's suitcase out of the back of my SUV as though it were as light as a feather. She marched up the stairs with my backpack on her back and a suitcase in either hand.

We stared at her retreating back until she stuck her head around the door and asked, "Ya coming?"

We didn't dare hesitate longer for fear that she'd toss us over her shoulders and carry us in next.

Inside, we took a few moments to stare. High ceilings and large windows allowed light to infuse the large home. From the front foyer, a broad center hallway ran straight through to the back terrace. Despite its size, the house looked homey. The walls on either side of the center hallway were painted with murals depicting a rural equestrian scene. The wood plank floors bore the scratches and dings of years of use and were topped by a faded Aubusson rug.

We followed Mrs. Claymore through the center hallway to a room that opened from the gallery hall. The focal point of the room was a floating spiral staircase that led to the upper level. The room had old-fashioned black-and-white tile floors that closer inspection showed to be marble. The walls were adorned with yellow-and-white-striped wallpaper. The only furniture was a round table covered with books. There were no paintings. No fancy urns or vases. Just a table with books. Hanging from the ceiling was a crystal chandelier. The fixture looked antique and outdated. The only sign of its value was one ruby red pendant.

"Pris. That's Baccarat," Marcie whispered, and pointed at the pendant.

"Hideous, isn't it?"

I jumped at the voice that broke the silence. "Chelsea? What are you doing here?"

Chelsea Baxter stood in the hall wearing a red dress, Louboutin heels that I'd seen her sister, Whitney, wearing, and a pashmina.

"I have a date." She glanced down her nose at me as though I were the hired help. Which actually wasn't far from the truth, except I wasn't being paid for babysitting three preteen girls.

"And you look ravishing." David Townsend strolled around the corner and smiled.

Chelsea blushed and then swirled around like a five-year-old.

Marcie rolled her eyes and Chelsea scowled.

David then turned his attention to me and Marcie. "Well, well. I didn't realize this was a museum!" He grinned as his gaze moved from me to Marcie to Chelsea. He looked at us like pieces of meat hanging from a hook at a butcher's shop.

"What?" I asked.

"I must be in a museum because you two . . . I mean, three, ladies are truly works of art."

Chelsea giggled.

I calculated whether I had enough time and clothes to take a shower. I suddenly felt dirty. Marcie rolled her eyes. "Eww. That is one of the worst pickup lines I've ever heard." Marcie walked away and leaned against the wall. She folded her arms across her chest and scowled.

If she thought her reaction would faze David Townsend,

then she must have been sorely disappointed because he simply threw his head back and laughed.

Chelsea glared and then struck a pose. "Well, I, for one, am ready to paint the town red."

David looked her up and down and then stuck out his arm.

Chelsea hooked her arm in his and strutted to the front door.

Bailey was lying in front of the door like a large bloodhound rug. When the couple approached, he gave an uncharacteristic growl.

David Townsend lifted his leg, and for a minute, it looked as though he intended to kick my dog.

That's when something snapped. The blood rushed to my head. My vision went red, and for the first time in my life, I felt a growl develop in my stomach and rise up my throat. "If you kick my dog, so help me, God, I will rip your leg out of its socket like I used to do with my Ken and Barbie dolls."

Townsend froze. His leg was pulled backward and still in the air. After a few seconds, he lowered his leg to the ground.

Chelsea turned to face me. "Whitney was right about that beast. He's a menace and needs to be put down."

Whitney had practically made a career out of irritating everyone who wasn't part of her clique, which included Marcie and me. Bailey was the sweetest dog, but when someone stepped on his tail, as Whitney had once, then he reacted instinctively.

A new voice piped up. "Keep talking and I'll take this boot and put it up your—"

"Aunt Agatha." I turned to find my aunt had made her way into the foyer.

"Now we see where you get your charming personality," Chelsea mumbled.

"What's going on?" Gilbert came into the small foyer followed by Hannah, Clarice, and Mary Elizabeth.

Seeing the girls, Bailey got up from his position in front of the door. Tail wagging, he pranced over to the girls and proceeded to lick each one while his tail swished dangerously close to the table covered with books.

Chelsea rolled her eyes. "That's so unhygienic."

"I believe you were on your way out?" Aunt Agatha paused a beat and then added, "Then, you best get to stepping."

David Townsend frowned. After a moment, he shrugged and flashed a smile. "Come on, love."

Chelsea and David left and closed the door behind them a bit harder than was necessary.

"Now let's get this party started," Aunt Agatha said. "How about we make some pizzas?"

"Yay!" The girls cheered and rushed to the kitchen, followed by Aunt Agatha and Bailey. That left Gilbert, Marcie, and me in the foyer.

"What did I miss?" Gilbert asked.

Marcie and I exchanged glances. After a few moments, I shrugged.

"Nothing. Chelsea's dressed for the hunt," Marcie said.

"The hunt?" Gilbert repeated.

"Bear hunting," Marcie clarified.

"I still don't understand." Gilbert tilted his head to the side.

"Bears are one of the largest land mammals. Based on how she's dressed, I'd say Chelsea's set her sights on taking down a big bear—a billionaire," I said.

"Ah . . . David Townsend's the bear."

"I hope she gets her prey. They deserve each other." Marcie marched out of the room.

Chapter 11

*A*unt Agatha sat in the wheelchair and supervised the pizza production like a boss. Each of us was given a pizza crust covered with sauce and was allowed to put on whatever toppings we wanted. Hannah was going through a vegetarian phase and loaded her crust with a mountain of fruit and vegetables, then piled it high with cheese. Clarice followed suit but took her pizza to another level by eliminating the cheese and going vegan. Mary Elizabeth's pizza was loaded with pepperoni. The adults all stuck to more traditional options, sticking with pepperoni, sausage, cheese, and the usual vegetables.

Edward Townsend's kitchen had a pizza oven that made short work of seven pizzas. Each one came out of the oven and looked amazing, thanks to Mrs. Green, the cook. At first, I worried that Aunt Agatha and Olivia Green wouldn't get along. In my limited experience, two cooks working in the same kitchen was a disaster waiting to happen. However, from the moment Aunt Agatha rolled into the kitchen, both women practically fell over each other in their attempts to accommodate the other. Flattering phrases were thrown back and forth like a volleyball.

"I defer to your experience, Olivia. It's your kitchen."

"Oh no, Agatha. You're the professional with your own amazing restaurant."

Back and forth, the two women fawned over each other.

"There's so much sugar I feel my teeth rotting," Marcie whispered.

"What's going on?" A thin, bald man waltzed into the kitchen.

Based on the description I'd gotten from Gilbert, I knew he was Peter Alexander, the private investigator whom Edward Townsend had hired to find his heir. This man was slender, but muscular. He had the body of a man who worked out. Even his neck muscles were defined, and his arms were solid.

I had been excited about the opportunity to talk to a real private investigator. I wanted to pick his brain for ideas that I could use in my books. However, in the bright lights of the Townsend kitchens, talking to a *real* detective for help with a children's book featuring a dog seemed trivial. My tongue stuck to the top of my mouth, and I couldn't come up with words that didn't sound ridiculous. I was spared speaking for a few moments when Clarice, Hannah, and Mary Elizabeth all started talking at once.

"Pizza!"

"That looks delicious," Peter Alexander said. He didn't look anything like Sam Spade, the fictional character created by Dashiell Hammett and played by Humphrey Bogart. He was my inspiration when I wrote Bailey the Bloodhound. Peter Alexander looked like an accountant or an insurance salesman, not someone who would take on criminals.

"Is something wrong?" the private detective asked.

That's when I realized I'd been staring and pulled my eyes away. "No. Nothing."

Olivia Green stepped forward. "Are you hungry, Mr. Alexander? I can make you a pizza or I can heat up something else if you'd prefer."

"No need." He waved her away.

"Dad, you promised you'd get the tent from the attic and set it up," Hannah said.

"There are enough bedrooms in this house, why do you need—" Gilbert took one look at the three preteens and gave up. "Fine. I'll get the tent from the attic and set it up, but then I've got to get back to work." His last comments were barely audible over the girls' whoops and cheers. He allowed himself to be dragged off.

Peter Alexander pulled out a chair across from me and sat. I could feel his gaze on me, and I forced myself to focus on avoiding his eyes. However, try as I might, my eyes kept rising from my empty plate. Eventually, I pulled my gaze up from the table and met his.

The detective smiled. "Anything bothering you, Ms. Cummings?"

"Yes. I mean, No. Nothing's bothering me. It's just that I was wondering if you wouldn't mind answering a few questions." I took a deep breath. "If you're not too busy."

"I'm not busy. How can I help you?"

"I'm Priscilla Cummings, but you already knew that." I paused. "How did you know that?"

"Well, I am a private detective."

It took a few moments before I noticed the gleam in his eyes. Eventually, I caught on and he chuckled.

"I wish I could say that finding out your name required a great deal of investigative work, but I was talking to the security guard, and he told me the names of the house guests."

"Oh." I tried to hide the disappointment in my voice, but I failed.

"See, people are far more impressed when they think I've used mad detecting skills to get information. Sadly, the reality of being a detective is very boring." He shook his head.

"Pris is a bestselling author." Marcie, who had walked over to the sink with her empty plate, now stood behind Peter and made faces indicating that I should get on with it.

"How interesting. What do you write?"

I overcame the desire to lean forward and whisper like the kid played by Haley Joel Osment in *The Sixth Sense* who had to tell Bruce Willis that he saw dead people. "I write children's books."

"Fascinating."

Marcie continued to motion behind the detective's back for me to hurry up.

"Actually, I was wondering if you would consider allowing me to interview you. I'm sure you're very busy, but it won't take a lot of time. I'd just like to talk to a *real* detective, because my books involve a bloodhound who's also a detective." Once I started speaking, the words tumbled out of my mouth like cement in a mixer. Once the word vomit started, I just kept spewing out more and more. "Of course, a dog detective may be nothing like a real detective, but I like to make my stories as realistic as possible and—"

"Yes."

"What?"

Peter Alexander grinned. "You can ask me questions. I might even answer them," he joked. "Seriously, I would be happy to answer your questions, as long as it doesn't require me to divulge any client confidential information."

"No. I'm sure there won't be anything confidential. I just want to ask general questions about what it's like being a private investigator," I said.

"Great. You two talk P.I. stuff and I'm going to go upstairs. There's a theater room with a real popcorn machine." Marcie left.

"Popcorn?" Peter Alexander asked. "There's usually popcorn at a sleepover, but I've never been to a sleepover that had a theater room and a real popcorn machine. It's been decades since I crashed an all-girl sleepover." He chuckled.

"Things haven't changed much. There will be lots of junk food. Lots of giggling and lots of talking about boys."

"Are you sure you don't want to join your friend? I hate

to disappoint you, but that's probably going to be a lot more entertaining than the life of a private detective."

"I'm sure it will be fascinating. I'm looking forward to this. Do you mind if I take notes? I don't want to miss anything."

He nodded his consent to notes. "Now, I know you're going to be disappointed. I'm not being modest when I say it's boring. No peering through windows and taking photos or tapping into phone lines and listening in on private conversations. It's mostly a lot of surfing the web and going through public records."

"Oh." I tried to keep the disappointment out of my voice. I could tell by the expression on his face that I wasn't successful.

"Sorry to disappoint you. Maybe if you ask some specific questions, I can tell you more."

"I'm not disappointed," I lied. "Maybe you could tell me whatever you're able to share about this case. Edward Townsend hired you to find his grandson, but you—" I could feel the blood rushing up my neck as I remembered that Natalie Evans had been the one to locate David Townsend, not Alexander. I swallowed the rest of the sentence, but he guessed what I was going to say.

"It's okay." He shrugged. "I was hired to find an heir."

"My current book involves a missing person . . . well, a missing dachshund, but maybe you could tell me what steps you followed to locate a missing person," I said hopefully.

He thought for a minute. "There's lots of information

on the Internet. You've probably seen those ads for services that will provide background information about people."

I nodded. "I thought those sites were scams to get your credit card information."

"Most of them are, but there are legitimate sites where you don't need to pay. It's all public information, you just have to know where to look and what to look for. There are also sites that you do pay for that basically just make it easier by consolidating the information for you. So you only have to go to one website instead of ten or twelve. Everything in one place."

"But how do you even know where to start?"

"In a case like this, you have to ask a lot of questions. *When was the last time you saw the person? Where were they living? What job did they have? What were some of their hobbies?*"

"Why hobbies?" I asked.

"If someone likes to sail or go deep-sea fishing, then they probably have a sailboat and a fishing license. I get as much information as I can. Edward Townsend gave me a lot of information on his family tree. You know, aunts, uncles, cousins, anyone who might be alive. I try to get as many family photos as possible. You'd be amazed how helpful old family Bibles are in cases like this."

"Seriously?"

"Oh yeah. Those mammoth-sized Bibles with a list of births and deaths are great resources. Then I start looking through public records."

"Like?"

"Death certificates, court records, property records, stuff like that. That's how I figured out Mary Elizabeth was Edward Townsend's cousin."

"So, the rumors are true? Mary Elizabeth is related to Edward Townsend and may be an heir?" I asked.

He nodded. "Her maternal great-grandmother and Edward Townsend's mother were sisters. Apparently, the sisters had a falling-out years ago, but there's no doubt that they're related."

"What about Andrew Hicks?" I asked.

Peter was shaking his head before the words were out of my mouth. "Nope. Mary Elizabeth's father, Jefferson Hicks, married Annabelle Burnside when he was only eighteen. Annabelle was older and already had a son—that's Andrew. Annabelle died a few years later. Then Jefferson Hicks met and married Amanda Stallings and they had Mary Elizabeth."

"When I was teaching, I met her parents a couple of times. They were both very nice, but I know they spent a lot of time traveling. Where are her parents now?"

"Jefferson Hicks is pretty high up in the State Department. He's finishing up some assignments in the Middle East. Edward Townsend wanted to meet Mary Elizabeth, but her parents weren't able to come here and there was no way they were willing to let her come alone. They were concerned for Mary Elizabeth's safety, so when Andrew got the job working for Edward Townsend, they agreed to let her stay here with Andrew. He's as big of a horse fanatic as Edward Townsend was. The two hit it off immediately, which is how he came to work and live here. Edward Townsend hired Andrew Hicks and Mary Elizabeth begged her parents to let her stay with her stepbrother instead of being carted off to a private boarding school in Connecticut. Surprisingly, Edward Townsend agreed. He promised he'd see that she was well taken care of until they could get back to the States."

"Interesting. Do they know Townsend's dead?"

"Yes. They're working to get here as quickly as possible, but Mary Elizabeth is fine. Andrew is around, and they know I'm keeping an eye on her. Plus, it's not like there was anything suspicious about Edward Townsend's death, so . . ." He shrugged.

"Okay, that seems pretty straightforward, but what about David Townsend?" I asked reluctantly.

Peter Alexander paused for several moments. "He had a passport, birth certificate, and other documents that identified him as David Townsend."

"Were they authentic?" I asked.

"Hard to tell. They appear to be valid. I have no reason to believe that they aren't valid." He paused. "After ten years in law enforcement I've learned not to trust anyone or anything. I've seen documents so perfect they could fool Saint Peter and get Lucifer himself through the Pearly Gates. Not all private detectives are created equal. Some P.I.s are sloppy, but I was a cop for ten years. I make sure that I meticulously work to confirm the identity of anyone that I bring forward." He gave me a hard stare that spoke the words he wasn't saying.

"And you couldn't confirm David Townsend's identity?"

He shook his head and took a deep breath. "He knows the right answers, answers only the real David Townsend could know. That attorney, Natalie Evans, is convinced and she seems to have been very thorough."

I wondered for a split second about Natalie Evans's thoroughness. However, I didn't want to let my mind think about it. Instead, I forced myself to go down a different path. "But how? I mean this is the twenty-first century. Couldn't you just run his fingerprints? Or do a DNA test? One of the teachers I used to work with wanted to find out her heritage and she just paid a hundred and thirty dollars to one of those genealogy places she saw advertised on TV. They sent her a test tube and all she had to do was spit in it and send it back."

"Generally speaking, yes. But there are a few complications in this instance. First, David Townsend's fingerprints aren't in the United States database. Remember, he was raised in Australia. I reached out to a friend of a friend who knows someone with the AFP."

"What's the AFP?"

"Australian Federal Police."

"What about Interpol?" I asked, jotting down notes. "I thought they kept track of international things like that."

"Interpol runs an international fingerprint database, AFIS—"

"What's that stand for?" I scribbled the initials down in my notepad.

"Automated Fingerprint Identification System. But, AFIS

is only going to identify someone if they were involved in a crime and their fingerprints were on file." He spread his hands.

"Surely a DNA test could tell if David Townsend is Edward Townsend's grandson or not. I saw a commercial about having your dog's DNA tested if you want to know about your dog's lineage. Plus, I saw a documentary about scientists who have been able to use DNA to identify King Tut's parents. Those mummies have been buried for thousands of years."

"I planned to have DNA tests run. I had just managed to convince Edward Townsend to do it, but . . ."

That's when it hit me. "But he died."

Chapter 12

Peter Alexander and I stared at each other for a few moments. Then he nodded. "Right. I talked to the trustees, but I don't think they will bother to confirm his identity further."

"Why not? As trustees, aren't they responsible for making sure they get the right person? I mean, there's a lot of money at stake. Isn't there?"

Peter nodded. "Edward Townsend was a billionaire. He owned real estate, businesses, stocks, bonds, and lots of assets. His estate is probably worth somewhere around two to three billion dollars."

I whistled. "Given that much money, I'd expect a fleet of attorneys and accountants who would want every type of verification imaginable. Who are the trustees?"

"Edward Townsend didn't like lawyers. He said they

were a necessary evil when it came to business dealings, but in everything else, they just made things more complicated than they needed to be so people would have to pay them to explain it all. He had three trustees. He ticked them off one by one. Natalie Evans, his attorney. Jay Barlow, an old family friend and successful businessman. And his accountant, Carla Taylor."

"I know Carla. She's great. But Jay Barlow's in the hospital. That just leaves Natalie Evans, and she hardly seems objective."

"What's that supposed to mean?"

I cringed at the shrill voice, and I knew my face was burning with shame. I did a quick mental recap and didn't remember saying anything too embarrassing. I turned around and came face-to-face with a haughty Natalie Evans.

Both arms folded across her chest, Natalie Evans looked down her nose and tapped a peacock blue Manolo Blahnik with a crystal-cut buckle accessory and four-inch heels that she hadn't been wearing earlier. In fact, she'd changed into peacock blue satin skinny-leg pajamas with a long silky tunic that was sheer and left nothing to the imagination. It appeared that Natalie Evans was dressed for hunting, too. I couldn't help wondering if she, too, was in search of a billionaire bear.

"Natalie. I didn't know you were here," I said.

"I'll just bet you didn't."

The best offense is a good defense. "I was interviewing Peter for my book."

"Humph. Yeah, right. You're a terrible liar. You were

implying that I did something wrong. Well, you better be careful because if you continue talking about things that you don't know anything about, you're going to find yourself faced with a big, fat lawsuit for slander."

I gulped and tried to recall what I'd said.

"Ms. Evans, I think you're overreacting. Ms. Cummings didn't say anything slanderous that would be cause for legal proceedings." Peter Alexander paused and narrowed his gaze. "I don't think anyone wants to find themselves in court, especially the Townsends."

"What's that supposed to mean?" Natalie asked.

"Edward Townsend struck me as an extremely private individual. When I suggested putting advertisements in city newspapers for information on locating his heirs, he was vehemently opposed."

"What does any of that have to do with me?" Natalie asked.

He shrugged. "It would be impossible to have a case for slander without bringing in the surrounding details about David Townsend. I just don't believe that would be in alignment with Edward Townsend's wishes. That's all." He gave her an innocent look.

I glanced from Peter Alexander to Natalie Evans. Peter looked completely blank, as though he had no idea that he had just scored a major takedown. Natalie Evans, on the other hand, seethed. A red patch of molten lava moved up her neck. Her countenance changed completely. Her lips curled. Her eyes narrowed and her nostrils flared. She looked feral.

Gilbert walked into the room. "Pris, I've got to go. Is there—" Gilbert stopped. The tension in the room was thick as molasses. He glanced from Natalie to Peter and then to me. "Did I interrupt something?"

I swallowed the lump in my throat and tried to speak, but no words came.

Natalie Evans slid her mask back in place. If I hadn't seen the transformation with my own eyes, I wouldn't have believed it. I merely shrugged. His radio squawked and he rolled his eyes. "I really have to go. Do you need me to pick up anything for dinner tomorrow?"

"I'm fine, and the weather is fair to middling." I grinned.

As a policeman, Gilbert was always concerned about personal safety. He had security phrases that he'd taught his daughter, Hannah, to use if she needed help, but wasn't able to or comfortable about asking. If she was in trouble, she could tell him that she'd forgotten her textbook and needed him to bring it to her. If she was okay, she was to say the weather was fair to middling. Gilbert was a city boy, born and raised in Chicago, but his late wife, Sarah, had been raised in rural Indiana and used the phrase often.

He even had a code to be used in the event of a serious emergency. Since Hannah hated brussels sprouts and beets, if a request was made for either of those, then he knew that Hannah was in real danger. After a recent incident, I'd learned that requesting either of those root vegetables would indeed bring in a SWAT team. I wasn't fond of brussels sprouts or beets, either, so those security words worked for me as well.

Gilbert reluctantly walked to the back door. "Call me if you need anything." He walked out.

"Now, maybe we can get down to busi—" Natalie Evans turned as the back door opened again.

I assumed Gilbert had forgotten something and returned. I was surprised that instead of seeing my boyfriend, in walked David Townsend.

David Townsend smiled broadly. "Isn't this cozy." His glance ravished Natalie Evans's body like a hungry dog with a steak.

If he thought Natalie would appreciate the appraisal, he was sorely mistaken. Natalie scowled and folded her arms across her chest.

Confused, David Townsend asked, "What's wrong?"

"I just overheard Nancy Drew and Scooby-Doo over there talking about me. Talking about us," Natalie said.

"Really? What could they possibly have to say about either one of us? I'll confess to being a sinner, but you, my dear, are as pure as the driven snow." David Townsend grinned mischievously.

"According to these two, you're an impostor masquerading as the grandson of Edward Townsend, intent on getting your hands on his money." Natalie glared.

"Tsk. Tsk. Tsk." David Townsend chuckled. "And you? What are they accusing you of?"

"I'm an accessory and complicit in assisting you to perpetuate the fraud. According to her—"

"That's not true," I said. "I didn't accuse you of anything. I merely said—"

"No. You merely implied that I assisted in the commission of fraud, false impersonation, and grand larceny of Edward Townsend's estate, that's all." Natalie turned to David Townsend. "I guess that makes you a grifter."

"I did no such thing," I said.

Natalie waved away my protests. "I was just explaining to our little amateur detectives that I would sue them for every penny they had if they continued their vicious, slanderous lies."

"Actually, Ms. Cummings was interviewing me for her book. During the course of our conversation, she asked me how I go about locating missing persons. Naturally, the current situation springs to mind, and I shared some of the steps that I went through in locating Edward Townsend's heirs," Peter Alexander said. "Ms. Evans interrupted our conversation and jumped to an erroneous conclusion. The question is *why*."

Natalie Evans was revving up like a Formula One race car, but David Townsend held up a hand. He gazed at Peter Alexander, tilted his head to the side, and tapped his chin as if he were trying to remember something. "Now, what's that old saying, about people in glass houses not throwing stones?"

Peter Alexander's eyes flashed. "What's that supposed to mean?"

"I think you know."

The two men stared at each other like prizefighters standing in the middle of a boxing ring, each one playing a psychological mind game to intimidate the other. Natalie and I watched to see who would blink first. Despite his size, I would have bet every dime I had that Peter Alexander, former law enforcement officer, would have outstared David Townsend. But I would have lost. Peter Alexander turned away. I was close enough to see the blood rise up his neck.

The shift was small, but I saw it. Advantage David and Natalie in this matchup. Natalie saw it, too, and she smirked.

Peter Alexander may have been ready to concede, but I wasn't. "I don't know what glass houses you're referring to, but if you're truly who you say you are, then why not submit to a DNA test?"

Natalie Evans unfurled her claws and lunged at me. "Why you—"

David Townsend's reflexes were quick. He wrapped his arms around Natalie's waist and held on for dear life.

Based on the string of expletives that Natalie spewed out, she must have spent quite a bit of time hanging out on the docks with sailors. Her vocabulary was limited but she was thorough in her attacks against me and Peter Alexander.

Even though David Townsend had a firm hold on her, Peter stood and moved in between Natalie and me. It took a few moments, but felt like hours. Eventually, Natalie's rage was spent, and she collapsed like a deflated balloon.

Marcie rushed into the kitchen. Aunt Agatha hadn't fully mastered the wheelchair, but she followed close on Marcie's heels. Both women entered and abruptly stopped to take in the situation.

"What on earth is going on? It sounds like two barn owls in here," Aunt Agatha asked.

Natalie's legs were rubber bands, and she was only able to stand because David Townsend was holding her up. She bawled hysterically. She had raccoon circles under her eyes and one eyelash was lying on her cheek like a spider.

"This is a house, not an alley," Aunt Agatha said.

Natalie howled even louder.

"And stop all that noise," Aunt Agatha ordered.

To my great surprise, Natalie Evans took one look at Aunt Agatha, hiccupped, and clammed up. I guess she recognized the voice of authority when she heard it.

Having dealt with Natalie, Aunt Agatha turned her attention to me. "Now, Priscilla Renee Cummings. What is the meaning of this? You were raised to know better than to come into someone else's home and fight like a common alley cat." She glanced at Natalie as though she wasn't sure if Natalie had been raised to know better or not. Then she turned her attention back to me. "What is going on here?"

Even in my late twenties, I felt the same way that I had when Aunt Agatha scolded me when I was five years old.

"It wasn't my fault," I said. In my head, I heard the reggae rapper, Shaggy, singing, "It Wasn't Me."

My aunt's expression indicated that she couldn't care less whose fault it was. She wanted an answer, and she wanted it now.

I looked from Natalie to David. *Where do I even begin? How do I explain this?*

Peter Alexander came to my rescue. He explained once again about the interview and how he was merely sharing information about how he or any other detective located missing people. "Ms. Evans overheard a piece of the conversation and misunderstood."

"I didn't misunderstand anything. She was talking about me. I know it." Natalie sniveled. She wasn't a pretty crier, and her face was red, puffy, and distorted. I couldn't hold that against her. I didn't look pretty when I cried, either, but she looked completely different.

I opened my mouth to defend myself. The back door opened, and Gilbert walked in. He stopped for a minute and took in the situation. It was clear that he was here as Chief of Police Morgan. "Jay Barlow's dead."

We gasped. My mind flashed back to the scene from earlier today, opening the door and finding him on the floor of the shed, covered in blueberries. "That's horrible. I had hoped he would have recovered from his injuries."

"He didn't die from his injuries. Jay Barlow was murdered in the hospital."

Chapter 13

Murdered? In the hospital? How was that possible?

My brain went into pinball mode. Tilt. Tilt. Tilt. I felt dizzy and must have blacked out. When I came to myself, I was sitting in a chair with my head between my legs, and Gilbert was kneeling in front of me. I sat up.

"You okay?" he asked.

I nodded. "That poor old man. Are you saying that someone deliberately visited him and—"

"Don't think about it," Gilbert said.

"Drink this." Aunt Agatha hadn't been idle during my episode. She'd wheeled herself over to the sink, filled a glass with water, wheeled back to the table, and handed the glass to me.

My hand shook as I drank the water and Gilbert had to

help steady my grip. His help was partly from concern, but partly from the fact that I had already managed to slosh water onto his uniform.

When I finished, Gilbert put the glass on the table.

"How?" I asked.

His head shake was so subtle, I barely noticed.

"Geez, mate. That's awful." David Townsend ran his hand through his hair. "Surely, there must have been some kind of mistake. He couldn't have been murdered. It had to be something to do with his age. He was really old, after all."

"Help me understand what being old has to do with murder." Aunt Agatha turned her gaze to David Townsend.

Uh-oh. I recognized that David Townsend was headed into a trap. Whenever Aunt Agatha started a sentence with, *Help me understand*, she was already upset. She wasn't yelling, but she was mustering up for a fight, and Aunt Agatha quiet was worse than if she were yelling. David Townsend was about to be handed his head on a silver platter. If he had any sense of self-preservation, he would simply apologize and be quiet. If I liked him better, I might have tried to help him. Warn him that there was danger ahead. But I clamped my mouth shut. I wasn't inclined to help him avoid it. Besides, he should have been able to recognize the warning signs by the tone of her voice. Gilbert wasn't even family, but I could tell by the gleam in his eyes that he knew there was danger ahead.

"Do you think reruns of *Lost in Space* aired in Australia?" Marcie whispered.

I had been so caught up in watching the drama unfold, I hadn't even seen her make her way over to sit by me.

Marcie and I loved old sitcoms. *Lost in Space* originally aired in the 1960s, well before our time, but, thanks to the wonders of syndication and streaming, we both watched the outdated show many times and enjoyed laughing at the technology that had probably seemed cutting-edge when it first came out. I picked up her reference immediately, and could easily imagine the Robot in the room with us, waving his accordion arms with lights flashing, repeating, *Danger. Danger. Danger, Will Robinson.*

"Beats me, but even if *Lost in Space* never aired in Australia, I think even Stevie Wonder could see that he's stepped on a nerve and needs to tread lightly," I said.

"Well, the old man was ancient. It was only a matter of time before he kicked the bucket." David Townsend tapped his chest. "Probably a bit loco, with a bad ticker. Getting coshed on the head was probably the last straw. Tough old bird, but . . ." He shrugged.

"Wow. Just when you think it can't get any worse, he managed to make it worse. She's going to eat him alive." Marcie scootched her chair closer.

"Young man, I'll have you know that just because someone is older, doesn't mean they're senile and with one foot in the grave. As you have so deftly demonstrated, youth isn't always an indication of mental capacity, or we wouldn't be having this conversation. Age also doesn't indicate cardiac issues. Now, before you stick the rest of your foot in your mouth, let me help you understand a few things. First—" Aunt Agatha held up a finger and was ready to give Townsend an education. Before she was able to get into third gear, the door opened, and in walked Carla Taylor.

"Good grief. Who invited you?" Natalie Evans asked.

"She must be feeling better," Marcie whispered to me.

"Why?" I asked.

"If she's well enough to throw shade at Carla, then she must have recovered from her meltdown," Marcie said.

"Good point."

"I invited her," Chief Morgan replied to Natalie.

"A bit presumptuous, wouldn't you say, old chap?" David Townsend flashed a cocky smile.

"You have no right to invite anyone here. This house belongs to David. He's the legal heir." Natalie Evans was gunning for a fight. She would probably have been taken more seriously if she hadn't still looked like a raccoon, but her nasally voice was almost back to its annoying fingernails-on-chalkboard level. "This isn't a Holiday Inn. It's a home."

Carla Taylor was tall, dark, and stunningly beautiful. She was a confident Black woman and no wallflower. She stepped forward. "First, this is the estate of *my* client Edward Townsend. As an attorney and a trustee, you are well aware that Edward Townsend's *heir* has yet to be officially identified, and until that happens, then David Townsend is also only an 'invited guest' in this house." She paused.

Natalie rolled her eyes and stared at her nails as though her fingernails were the most important things in her life.

"I love it when she gets all sassy on folks."

I was so absorbed in watching Carla take down Natalie, I didn't see Tabby slip in. Tabitha, Tabby to her friends, was Carla's partner. She was also my stylist at The Big Tease salon in town. When we met, the right side of her head was buzz-cut and dyed magenta while the left was dyed in a rainbow and gelled to stand up in spikes. She still sported the buzz cut on the right, but today, she'd eliminated the gelled spikes. The left side was smooth and swooped over her eye. One of the coolest things about Tabby was that her hair was rarely the same two days in a row.

Tabby hugged me, pulled out a chair, and turned to watch the entertainment. "We need popcorn."

Natalie was clearly flustered. "I was Edward Townsend's lawyer, and I don't need some . . ." She struggled to find the right word.

"Oh, this is 'bout to get real good." Tabby leaned forward.

"I suggest you choose your words carefully." Carla put a hand on her hip and raised one perfectly arched brow.

A red flush rose up Natalie Evans's neck and her face was a blotchy, red mess. "I don't need some accountant telling me how to do my job." She flicked her hand as though she were swatting away flies.

"Two points to Natalie for the quick save. I feel confident 'accountant' wasn't the first word that crossed through her mind," Marcie said.

"She's still down about fifteen points, so I'll grant you the two," Tabby said.

Chief Morgan gave us the same look that librarians give to loud patrons.

"Shush." I turned to Marcie and then to Tabby.

"As trustees over Edward Townsend's estate, I asked Ms. Taylor to come to help me with my investigation," Chief Morgan said.

"I don't understand. What's the death of an unrelated old man got to do with my grandfather's estate?" David Townsend asked.

"Obviously, Chief Morgan is grasping for any police work to do. Just because two old men are dead, doesn't mean they were murdered. Old people die every day," Natalie said.

"What's with the raccoon eyes?" Tabby asked.

Chief Morgan turned around and flashed another look at Tabby.

She ran her finger across her mouth, indicating her lips were zipped.

Natalie Evans's hearing must have been better than we thought, because she walked over to the oven and glanced at her reflection in the glass door. "I look a hot mess. Why didn't someone tell me?" She went to the counter and got a paper towel, ran it under the faucet, and then proceeded to clean away some of the excess mascara from under her eyes.

"Honey, I thought you already knew you were a hot mess." Aunt Agatha paused for two beats. "Oh, and your eye shadow is jacked up, too."

Tabby snorted. I swallowed the laugh that bubbled up in my chest, but nearly keeled over from a coughing fit.

Natalie stopped long enough to cast a withering glance in Aunt Agatha's direction, but she should have saved her energy. Her disdain slid off Aunt Agatha like eggs on a Teflon pan.

"Can we please get back to business?" Chief Morgan asked.

"Yes, what investigation? Jay Barlow was mugged or he tripped and hit his head and died. There's no murder and nothing to investigate, mate," David Townsend said.

Chief Morgan's jaw was clenched and the vein on the side of his head was pounding. "Jay Barlow was murdered. I've initiated a—"

"Really, Chief Morgan, I have to agree with David. I think you're grasping at straws here. Who could possibly want to murder an old man like Jay Barlow? Only a handful of people in Crosbyville even knew him aside from Edward Townsend, and he's already dead." Natalie scrubbed the mascara off her face and pulled off the eyelash that remained. Without the eye makeup and false lashes, her eyes looked small and her face looked average. For a brief moment, I wondered what she looked like before her *Real Housewives of Orange County* transformation. I wondered if she might have been someone that I would have liked.

"I think you're just wanting to create drama to boost your career and give your girlfriend some additional publicity for her ridiculous children's books."

Nope. Not someone I would have liked.

"Irregardless, I don't see how that gives you the right to invite anyone to this house."

I closed my eyes and put a hand over my right eye to stop the twitching. Marcie rubbed my arm to comfort me.

"What's wrong? You look like you're having a stroke," Tabby whispered. "Please tell me you're not having a stroke. I'm not sure what you're supposed to do for that. Am I supposed to slap her? Or hold her tongue and give her a wallet to bite on?"

"She's not having a stroke. It's just an allergic reaction to the mangled use of the English language." Marcie patted my arm. "Pris, let it go."

I blinked and shook my head like Bailey after a bath or a tumble in the grass. "What did she say? I missed everything after 'irregardless.'"

"Your aunt Agatha just threatened to put her boot up Natalie's—"

"Tabby, do you mind?" Chief Morgan gave Tabby a look that probably left many a criminal shaking in their boots.

Tabby giggled and this time she not only indicated that her lips were zipped, but she tossed the key over her shoulder.

He glared at her for a few beats before continuing. "As I was saying, based on a cursory investigation into Edward Townsend's financial accounts by Ms. Taylor"—he turned and nodded at Carla—"I have reason to suspect criminal activity, including embezzlement. Jay Barlow was here at the specific request of Edward Townsend and within days of his arrival, both men are now dead. So, this is now an official murder investigation into the death of Jay Barlow. I have also requested an autopsy of Edward Townsend's body, so until I'm satisfied that his death was due to natural causes, I've placed a block on all of his accounts—"

"You can't do that. You don't have the authority to do that," Natalie said.

"You're right." Chief Morgan paused and then reached into his pocket and pulled out a letter. "I don't have the authority, but this is a court order granting me the authority." Gilbert held up the paper.

Natalie stood with her mouth open like a fish.

"You better close your mouth or you're gonna catch flies," Aunt Agatha said.

"How on earth did he get a court order at this time of night?" David Townsend looked at his watch. "It's close to nine o'clock."

I'd been wondering the same thing, so I looked at Gilbert for clarification.

"Crimes don't just happen between eight and five. Crimes take place at all times of the day and night and the police have to be able to do our jobs. Judges are available twenty-four/seven, three sixty-five in case we need a court order or a warrant. I simply called Judge Elkins and presented my evidence, and she signed my order," Gilbert said.

Natalie Evans may have been silent, but her brain had still been working. "Edward Townsend hated and distrusted lawyers, courts, and all forms of government bureaucracies. He had his trust drawn up in such a way that it wouldn't get bogged down by probate, taxed to the hilt, or any other courts. In the event of his death, only the trustees have the authority to dictate what happens to the estate. Carla Taylor is one trustee and I'm the other one. It would take two-thirds of the trustees to agree to the disbursement of the estate. Now that Jay Barlow's dead, we—"

"Now that Jay Barlow's dead, the alternate trustee takes his place," Gilbert said.

"Alternate trustee? What alternate trustee?" Natalie asked. "I was Edward Townsend's lawyer. I would have known if he had assigned an alternate trustee."

"Ooh, plot twist," Marcie whispered.

Chief Morgan pulled another paper from his pocket. "I had Judge Elkins give me permission to open Townsend's safe deposit box. Before he died, Edward Townsend named an alternate trustee and an executor for his estate."

"He did what?" Natalie's shrill, nasally voice became even shriller and more nasally.

Moments earlier, David Townsend had been flushed. Now the blood drained and he looked about two shades paler. "Who?"

"His alternate trustee and executor—or should I say, executrix—is Miss Agatha Bell." Gilbert turned to face Aunt Agatha.

Chapter 14

*W*ay to go, Miss Aggie." Tabby clapped.

"Wow! I didn't see that coming," Marcie said.

"Neither did I." I turned to look at my aunt. Based on her deer-in-the-headlights expression, she hadn't seen it coming, either.

"What do you mean? I don't know anything about any trusts or wills," Aunt Agatha said.

"He left this for you. Maybe it'll explain things." Gilbert passed an envelope to my aunt.

Aunt Agatha glanced at the envelope that had her name on it and paused. "Eddie was a kind man and a good friend." She sniffed.

I went over and hugged her.

She patted my arm and then pulled herself together

and opened the envelope. She glanced at it, but then passed it to me. "I'm a bit of a mess right now. Maybe you could . . ."

I took the letter and began to read it out loud.

"'Dear Oracle, I guess this is it.'"

"He always called me that—Oracle." She chuckled. "He used to say I was wise, like that woman in *The Matrix*." She cried softly.

Marcie passed her a tissue and hugged her tightly.

I continued.

"'If you're reading this letter, then I've cashed out. Now, don't you go getting sappy on me. I had a good run. We're both old enough to know that eventually, everybody has to close out the books and give an account to the Head Auditor. Now, you know how I feel about lawyers. Accountants are only a step higher up on the ladder.'"

Carla sniffed.

"'But, they're a necessary evil. Anyway, I have my money arranged in a trust with a lawyer and an accountant. Both are young women with sharp minds. They're good at what they do, but there's no love lost between them. That's okay. They keep each other in line. But they need a third person who can keep the peace between the two of them. That's where my friend Jay Barlow comes in. Jay's a good man—a good businessman. He's made nearly as much money as me, which is no easy feat. Jay's not a young man, but his mind is as sharp as a meat cleaver. Don't be fooled by his dopey ways. He knows his onions. Plus, he's been a good friend for more years than either one of us wants to own. Most important, I trust him. Funny, the older I get, the more important it is to me to have people around me that I can trust. That's just one of the reasons I spent so much time with you, my friend. You've always been honest. You aren't afraid to tell it like it is. If I was making a fool of myself, you said so. I respect that. I didn't always like it, but I respected it. That's why I'm naming you as my alternate trustee in the event that one should become necessary.'"

"That crazy old fool," Aunt Agatha said. "I don't know anything about trusts. I'm just an old woman who likes to cook."

"'You may not have a college degree, but you have something most of these lawyers and CPAs don't have—common sense. My sweet mother used to call it Mother Wit. I'm asking you to use that wit to help an old friend. I've lived a good life, but it isn't without regrets. I think you know my biggest regret.'" I stopped and glanced at Aunt Agatha.

"Crazy old fool," she whispered.

"'I'll miss sitting in the diner eating your fried chicken and listening to the pearls of wisdom you dropped my way.

"'Yours affectionately and forever, Eddie.'"

There was a pregnant pause.

"That's a lot of bullsh—"

"I see you're as eloquent as ever, Natalie." Andrew Hicks stumbled into the kitchen.

At least, I think it was Andrew. His face was covered in cuts, dried blood, and bruises, and his eye was so swollen that his face looked deformed. He slumped down into a chair near me and rested his head in his hands.

"Andrew? What on earth happened?" I asked.

"Good to see you, too." Andrew tried to smile, but it came out looking more like a grimace. The effort of curling his lips must have hurt because he winced.

"Good Lord, you look awful," Aunt Agatha said. "Were you hit by a truck?"

"Sure. A big ugly truck with large fists." He tried to laugh, but the effort had him doubled over in pain and coughing.

"Carla, see if you can find Mrs. Claymore. Tell her we need a basin of hot water, a washcloth, and several towels. Pris, get a pot and fill it with ice. Gilbert, you and Peter get him to a bed." Aunt Agatha threw out orders at the speed of sound. If anyone thought of ignoring her, they were smart enough not to say it out loud.

Everyone sprang into action.

Gilbert and Peter gingerly helped Andrew Hicks to his feet. Hicks cried out in pain and promptly passed out.

Gilbert hoisted Hicks in his arms and carried him while Peter held doors and cleared a path. They ran into Mrs. Claymore in the hall, who directed them to a nearby bedroom.

Gilbert deposited Hicks on the bed and was promptly ordered out of the room while Aunt Agatha and Mrs. Claymore tended to his injuries.

Before closing the door, Mrs. Claymore called down the long hallway for Hudson, Edward Townsend's valet, and told him to fetch Dr. Williams.

"If you hurry, you should be able to catch him on the property. He was coming by to check on one of the foals."

Mrs. Claymore turned her back, confident that her wishes would be carried out.

Hudson grabbed a jacket and hurried out without a backward glance. It was as if she'd told him to fetch a cup of sugar or a can of green beans. Hudson was a thin man of few words, but he did what he was told. After a few minutes, he returned with a stocky man wearing glasses. They knocked at the door and then entered.

Those of us not involved in tending to Andrew Hicks's wounds hovered outside of the door for a few moments before returning to the kitchen. Carla, Tabby, Marcie, and I sat at the kitchen table sipping cold tea. David Townsend leaned against the counter, and Natalie Evans paced. Peter Alexander and Gilbert whispered together in a corner.

"What kind of doctor makes house calls at this time of night?" Carla glanced at her watch.

"Veterinarians," I said.

Tabby had taken a drink of tea and snorted it out of her nose. She broke into a coughing fit. When she could talk, she asked, "Are you serious?"

I nodded. "When Bailey's vet, Dr. Briton, was on vacation, he filled in."

"Weird." Carla sipped her tea.

Hannah, Clarice, Mary Elizabeth, and Bailey heard all of the commotion and came down to see what was going on. At first, Mary Elizabeth wanted to go to her stepbrother but was convinced by Carla and Tabby that she needed to wait. Mary Elizabeth dropped her head on Marcie's shoulder and cried.

Hannah and Clarice cried tears of support on Tabby's and Carla's shoulders.

The mood in the kitchen was somber. Bailey placed his muzzle in my lap. I petted his ears and scratched the spot behind his left ear that made his leg jiggle.

David Townsend broke the silence. "I've heard stories about police brutality in the States, but—"

"What?" It was only one word, but the ice in Gilbert's voice would have sunk the *Titanic*. He wasn't just Chief of Police Morgan, he was "Go Ahead, Make My Day" Chief Morgan. "Mr. Townsend, I'm the chief of police in this town, and I take accusations of police brutality very seriously. So, if you have something to say, say it."

"Well, no one is accusing you of anything, mate. You were here, but the last I heard, Andrew Hicks was locked up in your jail. So, I assumed—"

"Andrew Hicks was released over an hour ago. He wasn't under police surveillance, but he was last seen heading into Kelly's Bar, which is located less than one block from the hospital where Jay Barlow died. I've got men at the bar and the hospital getting statements and I assure you that I will get to the bottom of this. However, if you have a specific complaint, then I suggest you make it or keep quiet." Chief Morgan waited.

David Townsend had paled when Aunt Agatha was reading the letter from Edward Townsend, but the color had returned to his skin with a vengeance. His ears were so red, they looked as though he had a fever. He clamped his mouth shut.

Chief Morgan waited a few beats. "Nothing? Good." He wrenched open the back door and marched outside.

Tabby whistled. "I've never seen him that angry before."

"Me, either." I hopped up and hurried after him.

Outside, after looking for him for a minute, I heard a loud crack. There was a pause and then another crack. I followed the sound and discovered Gilbert with an ax. Both hands gripped the ax. He swung it high overhead and then brought it down hard, splitting the wood log that now lay in two pieces on a tree stump.

I watched him wrench the ax from the stump, toss the pieces on top of a pile of firewood, and pick up another log. He repeated the process several times. When the force used to split the wood decreased, I asked, "Do you want to talk about it?"

"Not really."

His jacket lay nearby. I picked it up, slid my arms through the sleeves, and wrapped it around myself. It smelled of Old Spice soap and Gilbert.

"Are you mad at the entire world or just the forested parts of the earth?" I asked.

He split about five more logs before stopping.

He wiped a bead of sweat from his brow. "Neither."

Bailey circled twice and then curled up in a ball by my side.

"You do realize that David Townsend's an idiot, right?"

It was dark, but I could see his smile. "The dispatcher at the station said he's 'hot.'"

"Miranda Lynn is sixty-five and blind as a bat."

"She just got new glasses." Gilbert laughed.

"Glasses only work if you wear them. She's so vain, she takes them off when any men are near and walks around bumping into walls just like Marilyn Monroe in *How to Marry a Millionaire*."

Gilbert walked up to me. "I take it you're immune to David Townsend's charm?" He wrapped his arms around me.

"What charm? I hadn't noticed anything except an annoying Australian accent that sounds phony, a big mouth that doesn't keep up with his brain, and a roving eye."

"You noticed that?"

"Kind of hard to miss."

He kissed me long and hard. When we came up for air, I had to take a moment to remember where we were. I shivered.

"Are you cold?" He pulled the collar of his jacket closer around me and zipped it.

"Actually, I'm rather hot and bothered, if you want the truth."

"Good." Gilbert chuckled.

"What's really bothering you?" I asked.

"I don't like old men getting murdered in my patch. Or young men getting the tar beaten out of them after being released from police custody."

I ran a finger along the side of his jaw, which he had clenched so tightly a vein bulged along the side of his head. "Andrew Hicks was no angel. Betty Wilson said he spends a lot of time at the Dew Drop Inn."

"Gossip at the hair salon?" Gilbert grinned. "What's

the owner of The Big Tease doing at the Dew Drop Inn? I thought she only went there with Joe Kelley, and he's still locked up."

"Betty moved on. She's been keeping company with Leonard Freemont."

"Leonard Freemont?" Gilbert frowned.

"Dr. Leonard Freemont, principal of Crosbyville Elementary School."

"And your former boss."

I nodded.

He raised an eyebrow. "Interesting pairing."

"I guess there's no accounting for taste. Betty's too good for him."

He chuckled.

"Anyway, word around The Big Tease is that Andrew Hicks had lost a lot of money at the casinos and on the horses. Plus, more than one of the women he was . . . *entertaining* at the Dew Drop Inn was married. So, what happened to him may not have anything to do with the Crosbyville Police or any of this."

"I don't suppose you've got any names of these women to share with local law enforcement?"

"Sorry, I wasn't paying careful attention, but I'll bet Tabby could give you a few names if you ask nicely."

"I'm always nice."

I glanced at the pile of firewood. "Maybe I should do the asking."

"Listen, I don't want you and Bailey getting mixed up in any of this." Gilbert pulled away, holding me at arm's length.

"Promise me, you and Bailey will stay out of it and leave the investigating to me."

"Scout's honor." I held up three fingers.

"I'm serious. This is dangerous."

"So am I. I have a manuscript due in just a few weeks. We have no intention of getting involved in your investigation. Right, Bailey?" I turned to glance at Bailey, who was still curled up by my leg.

On hearing his name, Bailey lifted his head and looked from me to Gilbert and then back to me. He gave a quick "Woof" and returned to his nap.

"See, even Bailey agrees."

Gilbert shook his head. "I'm not sure that's what he was agreeing to, but I'm going to trust you."

Chapter 15

*G*ilbert and I headed back toward the house. Before we reached the back door, I stopped. "Gilbert, what do you know about Peter Alexander?"

He gave me a long look before answering. "Not much. Why?"

"Nothing. It's just something odd that happened when he and David Townsend were talking earlier." I shared the conversation and my impression that Peter Alexander and David Townsend had been verbally sparring.

Gilbert shrugged. "Townsend's been sparring with just about everybody, except Natalie Evans."

"Up to that point, Peter Alexander had been winning."

"Not surprising. David Townsend isn't exactly a Rhodes scholar," Gilbert said.

"I know, but something shifted."

"What?"

I thought for several minutes and then gave up. "No idea. It was just a feeling. It was like David knew something, and Peter knew he knew."

"I'm going to need more than a feeling."

I shrugged. "That's all I've got, but you mark my words, there's something between those two."

Gilbert reached for the doorknob but hesitated when we heard a commotion inside. He listened for a few moments and then rushed inside.

In the kitchen, David Townsend held Mary Elizabeth tightly by her wrists, while Hannah and Clarice pummeled his back and legs. Marcie, Carla, and Tabby tried to pull the girls off.

"Quiet," Chief Morgan ordered.

The silence that followed was abrupt.

"You have two seconds to let her go, or I'll have you in handcuffs so fast it'll make your head spin." Chief Morgan's gaze drilled into David Townsend's like a laser.

For a split second, David Townsend looked as though he might not comply. However, the second passed and he came to his senses and gently let go of Mary Elizabeth, stepping back. Marcie quickly grabbed her.

"Now, will somebody tell me what's going on here?" Chief Morgan asked.

"That little hellion attacked me," David Townsend whined, and pointed at Mary Elizabeth.

"He deserved it. He said a lot of nasty things about my brother," Mary Elizabeth said.

"I believe he's your stepbrother. Hardly someone Edward Townsend would have wished associated with his family in any way whatsoever." Natalie Evans sipped a beverage that didn't look like the tea we'd been sipping earlier.

Mary Elizabeth stuck her tongue out at Natalie, who in a childish moment returned the gesture.

"Can someone tell me what's going on?" Chief Morgan asked.

"David was spouting off about how Andrew was likely responsible for all of this trouble," Carla said.

"That's a lie. Andy would never hurt anyone," Mary Elizabeth said.

"I was merely exercising my rights. You Yanks are so proud of your rights, freedom of speech and all that. Anyway, that's when the little devil attacked me," David Townsend sneered.

"He had no right to say those things about Andy," Mary Elizabeth said. "Besides, I know for a fact that he's the one responsible for everything. I heard him."

"Liar!" David Townsend said.

"Quiet," Chief Morgan yelled. "Mary Elizabeth, what do you mean, you heard him?"

"Surely, you're not going to believe the word of a child over that of Edward Townsend's grandson—it's ludicrous. You can't possibly—"

Chief Morgan shot Natalie Evans a look that froze the

words on her tongue. When he'd silenced her, he squatted down and motioned for Mary Elizabeth to come to him.

Mary Elizabeth walked over and stood in front of him. Her shoulders were back, and her head was held high.

"Now, what did you hear Mr. Townsend say?" While talking to Mary Elizabeth, Gilbert put Chief Morgan in the background. He was parental, Hannah's dad.

"It was after the fight where Andy gave him a bloody nose. I spilled blueberry tart all over my white top and I needed to change before my next competition. Mrs. Claymore said she'd soak my top so the stain wouldn't set. I had just come up to the house when I heard them arguing."

"Who?" Gilbert asked.

David Townsend stepped forward. "Chief Morgan, this is ridiculous. You can't honestly believe—"

Instantly, Chief Morgan was back in charge. He held up his hand like a traffic cop rerouting cars in heavy traffic.

David Townsend stopped.

Mary Elizabeth had worked herself into an emotional frenzy. Her face was red, and she was starting to hyperventilate.

"Maybe we should go someplace quieter." I moved over to Mary Elizabeth, who rushed into my arms.

Gilbert, Mary Elizabeth, Bailey, and I walked out of the room. When David Townsend and Natalie tried to follow, Chief Morgan stopped them.

"Wait here," Chief Morgan ordered.

"I have a right to hear what she says," David Townsend argued.

"And I'm his lawyer. My client has a right to face his accuser and to—"

"Ms. Evans, we both know that only applies in a court of law. We're dealing with an eleven-year-old kid. Now, I said wait here and I mean it," Chief Morgan said.

For a moment, Natalie looked as though she would continue to argue, but the chief of police wasn't in the mood. He turned and walked away.

We went into a room that must have been Edward Townsend's library. Double doors opened into a room covered completely in rich mahogany. The coffered wood ceiling was adorned with a large crystal chandelier in the center. The large plank hardwood floor was covered with a thick Aubusson rug. A spiral staircase unobtrusively located in a corner provided access to an upper story. The second floor had been opened up to create an upper alcove with intricately carved wood details including columns, pilasters, and bookshelves. A mahogany rail with decorative iron pickets encircled the elevated space. Bookshelves lined the lower level, which also contained a red marble–tiled fireplace. A massive mahogany desk sat in front of a window. In front of the fireplace were a large leather sofa and two chairs.

My heart skipped a beat as I entered my dream space—a room filled from floor to ceiling with books. Feeling a bit like Belle from *Beauty and the Beast*, I resisted the urge to check out the book titles while breaking out in song and dance. Instead, I made my way to the sofa and sat next to Mary Elizabeth.

Even though Bailey wasn't wearing his vest that signaled

he was a working therapy dog, he must have sensed that he was needed. He walked over to Mary Elizabeth, placed his head in her lap, and gazed up at her.

Mary Elizabeth stroked his head, and I could see the calming effect that he had on her. The tears slowed and soon stopped. Her breathing slowed down and she no longer seemed on the verge of a meltdown.

When I thought she was calm enough to answer questions, I gave Gilbert a nod.

"Okay, Mary Elizabeth. Take your time. Can you tell me what you heard?"

She hesitated, but took a deep breath and started to talk. "I heard him, David Townsend."

"What did he say?" Gilbert asked.

"He said, 'You're a liar and a thief. You stole that money and I want it back. All of it. You'll see to it, or you're going to find that I can be a very dangerous enemy.'"

Chapter 16

Do you know who he was talking to?" Gilbert asked.

"No. I just heard him. That's all." Mary Elizabeth shook her head.

She was a little too quick and too adamant in her denials. Mary Elizabeth knew something. Gilbert must have picked up on it, too.

"It's okay. You don't have to be scared. Nothing bad is going to happen to you. I promise," Gilbert said.

"But I didn't see who he was talking to." She hopped up from the sofa. "Can I go now?"

"Sure. You can go," Gilbert said.

Bailey rose to follow her. He stopped at the door and looked back at me.

"It's okay, you can go with her," I said.

It was only then that Bailey left. He'd keep Mary Elizabeth safe. Bloodhounds weren't known for being aggressive. They also weren't known to have strong protection instincts like Rottweilers, Doberman pinschers, and German shepherds. However, Bailey had shown that if push came to shove, he would do what he needed to do to protect his humans. I shivered at the thought that Mary Elizabeth might need protecting.

"Cold? We have plenty of firewood if you want me to build a fire in this thing." Gilbert pointed to the fireplace.

"No. I'm not cold. I just . . . Do you think Mary Elizabeth is in danger?"

"Do you think that's why she won't say who she heard David Townsend talking to? Do you think she's afraid?"

I pondered that question for a few minutes. Eventually, I gave up. "No idea. She's scared of something, but I don't know what. Or whom."

*W*e returned to the kitchen and the next few minutes were chaos. David Townsend denied saying anything remotely close to the words Mary Elizabeth reported. Natalie Evans threatened to sue Mary Elizabeth, Gilbert, the Crosbyville Police Department, and pretty much everyone else who'd been there that night. This continued until Aunt Agatha came into the room along with Dr. Williams.

"How is Andrew? Can I interview him now?" Gilbert asked.

Dr. Williams was a stocky middle-age man who looked more like a rock musician than a doctor. He had long hair that he wore pulled back in a ponytail. His arms were covered in tattoos. He also had soft brown eyes and a big smile. Bailey loved him and started wagging his tail on sight.

"Not now. I gave him a strong sedative and he'll be out for several hours," Dr. Williams said.

"What happened to him?" I asked.

"He got beat up pretty badly. It's a wonder he was able to walk. In addition to the bruises you saw, I suspect he has several cracked ribs. He really needs to go to the hospital and get X-rays, but before he passed out, he refused to go to the hospital." He shrugged. "So, I patched him up the best that I could. However, I've left strict instructions that if he seems worse, then he may have internal bleeding and should get to a hospital."

Mary Elizabeth gasped. She looked as though she had been put through the ringer. I doubted if she had any tears left or she might have broken down again.

Aunt Agatha frowned at Gilbert and Dr. Williams. "I'm not sure what all this is about, but whatever it is, it can wait until morning. It's almost midnight and these children need to be off to bed." Neither her tone nor her facial expression was open to discussion.

It wasn't until Aunt Agatha mentioned the time that I realized how tired I was. Everyone else must have felt it, too, because everybody agreed and headed off to their respective rooms.

Aunt Agatha looked at Tabby and Carla. "You two are welcome to stay. There's plenty of room." She glanced at Mrs. Claymore, who had been standing quietly by the door.

"I've already asked Hudson to light a fire in the east bedroom. I've turned down the bed and everything's all ready." Mrs. Claymore smiled.

Tabby and Carla exchanged glances.

Tabby's eyes asked a question and Carla responded with a shrug. "Honestly, I want nothing more than a hot bath and a good night's sleep, but I'm exhausted." She turned to Mrs. Claymore. "Okay, lead on."

They collected their belongings and followed Mrs. Claymore out of the room.

Aunt Agatha and Marcie escorted Mary Elizabeth and Clarice out of the room. She turned to Hannah. "Say good night to your father. I'll be in to tuck you in shortly."

Gilbert turned to me. "I'm sorry, but with most of my officers working the festival, I'm short-staffed for a murder investigation. I have to go."

"It's okay, Dad. I've got Pris, Miss Agatha, and Bailey the Bloodhound. I'll be fine." Hannah gave her dad a hug and said good night.

Gilbert's eyes held a sadness that hadn't been there earlier. I often saw it whenever he had to leave Hannah alone. However, he quickly pulled down the mental shade that shielded his emotions from view and was all business once again. He turned to Dr. Williams, who was putting on his jacket. "Could it have been an accident? Could he have been hit by a car?" Gilbert asked.

Dr. Williams shook his head. "Not unless the car was fitted with a bumper made of brass knuckles. Whoever did that to him was thorough. He might feel as if he'd been hit by a car, but I seriously doubt it, based on the abrasions and bruises on his face."

"I don't suppose he mentioned who beat him up?" Gilbert asked with the slightest glimmer of hope in his voice, but Dr. Williams squashed that hope as if it were a bug on his windshield. The doctor promised to swing by to check on his patient tomorrow morning when he came to a nearby farm to check on a mare who was expecting a foal any day now.

After Dr. Williams left, Gilbert and I were alone in the kitchen.

"How about you? You okay?" Gilbert asked.

"I'm fine and don't worry about Hannah. Between Aunt Agatha, Marcie, me, and Bailey, she's got an army looking after her."

He stared into my eyes. "Are you sure? I honestly don't want to burden you with looking after Hannah in the middle of all of this. I—"

I held up a hand to stop him. "It's okay. Hannah's fine. I'm fine. We're both fine. Watching her isn't a burden and you know it. I love Hannah."

He grinned and raised a brow. "Just Hannah?" I spent the next few moments showing him how I felt rather than telling him. We were interrupted when his cell phone rang.

Gilbert growled as he answered. "This better be important."

He listened to the caller, and I took a few steps back to cool off.

One glance at Gilbert's face told me that his call had indeed been important.

He disconnected. "I need to go."

"What's wrong?"

"I asked for a toxicology panel on Edward Townsend before he was embalmed."

"Why? I thought Edward Townsend died of natural causes," I said.

"Call it a hunch." Gilbert shrugged. "I don't believe in coincidences. Edward Townsend asks his friend Jay Barlow to come to town, but then both men are dead within days of each other. That's just too many coincidences. Then, with the alleged fraud, I wondered if there might be something we missed." He took a deep breath. "Edward Townsend was poisoned. Now I've got two murders on my hands."

Chapter 17

*G*ilbert didn't have any additional information, although he probably wouldn't have shared it with me even if he did. He gave me a quick kiss and then rushed out.

I tossed and turned most of the night until a frustrated Bailey hopped down from the bed, found a quiet corner, and curled up to finish his night's sleep.

"Softie," I muttered.

Bailey didn't bother looking up. He merely shoved his muzzle under his paw and continued getting his beauty sleep.

I pondered everything that had happened and examined each detail from every angle imaginable. Eventually, I sat up and pulled out my notepad. The only way that I could sift through all of the data was to write it down.

What did I know for sure?

Bailey may not have wanted to stay on the bed while I tossed, but he would listen while I talked. At least, I think he listened. "Edward Townsend was poisoned. Knowing the type of poison used might help determine when he was killed. I suppose it's possible to poison someone slowly over time. More than likely, he was given a lethal dose recently." I thought for several minutes. "That seems more probable, but I think if I were going to poison someone, I would rather do it slowly."

Bailey glanced up at that.

"What? If I do it slowly, then there should be less chance of getting caught."

Bailey snorted.

"Don't worry, I'm just talking out loud. I'm not planning to poison a bloodhound, no matter how stubborn he can be."

Satisfied with my response, Bailey closed his eyes and returned to his dreams.

"Regardless of the type of poison used, Edward Townsend was dead. And he had been killed first. I wonder if that matters?"

Bailey didn't respond.

Edward Townsend was a successful businessman. He might have made a lot of enemies over the years as he was building his fortune. "I suppose there may have been hundreds of people who wanted him dead. Would someone really want to murder the kind, elderly man simply because of a business deal?"

Bailey opened one eye and stared at me as though to say, *Really?*

"You're right. People have killed just because someone cut them off in traffic."

Satisfied that I had finally gotten the revelation, he put his head down.

A quick Google search on my phone took me to a site that listed the top four reasons for murder and grouped them so that they all started with the letter *L*.

Lust, love, loathing, and loot.

"Hmm. I consider myself a creative person, but I can't imagine anyone killing either Edward Townsend or Jay Barlow because of lust. Can you? I mean, you can't judge a book by its cover, but lots of people do. I get emails all the time from kids who tell me your covers were the reason they picked up your book. Everyone loves your covers." I stared at Bailey.

He stared back at me.

"Still, neither man struck me as the type who would ignite a murderous lust in someone. What do you think?"

Bailey stood up and shook himself.

"Me, either." I crossed *lust* off the list.

"Love?"

Bailey yawned.

"You're right. It's possible, but highly unlikely." I crossed that off the list.

"Loathing?"

Bailey gave a short, quick bark. Lying on his side, he

stretched his legs and shuddered. Then he lay still with only his side lifting with each breath in his sleep.

I watched his chest lift with each breath and wondered if he was chasing squirrels or some other woodland creature in his dreams. After a few moments, I got back to my list. "Now, we're getting somewhere. There's bound to be someone who hated either or both men."

"Loot." Definitely. I thought for a few moments and then jotted down my list of suspects.

"First place has to go to David Townsend." I wrote down David's name. "He certainly had a good motive." After Edward Townsend's death, David Townsend stood to inherit a massive fortune from the estate.

"He was here, so I suppose he had the opportunity and the means to kill him, but, again, that will depend on the type of poison used."

I took a few moments and pondered other people who might have had a motive to kill Edward Townsend. David Townsend headed the list, but if I was fair, there were probably a host of other people who stood to gain by Edward Townsend's death. I made a note to get more details about the will that Edward Townsend left. It would be natural for a wealthy man like Edward Townsend to have left bequests for faithful servants, good friends, churches and charitable organizations, and a host of other recipients. It might even be millions of dollars. Even if it wasn't millions, depending on circumstances, hundreds or thousands could have made a huge difference in people's lives.

My mind immediately switched to Andrew Hicks. He

was a gambler and had made someone angry enough to beat him within an inch of his life. I didn't have proof, but if I were to hazard a guess, I'd say that Hicks could have used the money. He got in a fistfight with David Townsend. He'd demanded to be paid for his contract. Of course, that's no proof. Few people are willing to walk away from money they feel is owed to them, but that made two people on the list of suspects. Andrew Hicks and David Townsend.

"Why do I keep coming back to David Townsend, Bailey?"

Hearing his name, Bailey opened his eyes, yawned, and stood. He stretched and did a nearly perfect downward dog pose. Then he walked over to the bed and placed his large head on the mattress. He gazed up at me.

I scratched his floppy ear. "If I'm completely honest, I have to admit that I don't like David Townsend. He's cocky, arrogant, and acts as if he's God's gift to women everywhere. Not to mention what he did to Marcie. Although, to be fair, it was fifteen years ago and I probably wouldn't be pleased at the way I acted at thirteen, either." I sighed and continued to scratch. "But, it's not just Marcie. I despise the way he looks at women as though he has X-ray vision." I shuddered. "He's creepy. And he stands to inherit a lot of money from the trust. So, he stays on the list, right, boy?"

Bailey's eyes were rolling back in his head from the ear scratches, but I felt sure we were on the same page where David Townsend was concerned.

"The trust. That's another area that I need to investigate." I wondered if trustees get paid. Even if they don't get paid, they would still have access to the money in the trust, wouldn't they? In Edward Townsend's case, that could amount to a lot of money.

I could ask Carla. She was a trustee. Carla was a trustee, just like Natalie. I couldn't add Natalie to the list just because I didn't like her. If I added Natalie, then I'd have to add Carla, too.

"Darn it. I don't want to add Carla. I like Carla."

I slowed my scratching and Bailey nudged my hand.

Talking about Carla struck a chord. "Hadn't she mentioned something about missing money when she came by yesterday? I wonder how much money was missing. Could that be the money that was in the satchel you found?" I absentmindedly continued to scratch Bailey.

"I don't even know how someone goes about embezzling money. Do you?"

Bailey lifted his leg and began to lick himself.

"Eww. That's disgusting."

Bailey looked up for a moment and then continued to groom himself.

I returned to my list. "Is it possible to get large amounts of cash? Or, maybe now, everything is done electronically? If the Townsend family's loot was the motive for the murders, then who has access to the trust? The trustees could be potential suspects. Carla and Natalie are trustees. Both would get paid by the trust, if the trustees got paid. I wonder. Are they paid?" That's when it hit me. Natalie and Carla weren't the only trustees.

Bailey finished bathing himself and climbed back up

on the bed. He turned around three times and then curled himself into a ball.

"Aunt Agatha is now a trustee. Will she be a suspect?" My heart froze. The blood pounded in my veins, and I had to take several deep breaths to slow down the sound of the blood rushing to my head and the dizziness that followed.

Breathe in. Breathe out.

Several rounds of deep breathing helped put everything back in perspective. "Geez. What am I nervous about? Aunt Agatha just became a trustee a few hours ago. She couldn't possibly have had a reason for wanting Edward Townsend or Jay Barlow dead. She hadn't even known that Edward Townsend had named her as a trustee and his executor. Plus, it's Aunt Agatha. There's no way my aunt would have killed anyone.

Bailey lifted his head and gazed at me.

"But, what if Edward Townsend was murdered so that the killer could get access to his money? And what if the way the killer plans to access that money is through the trust? Could that be the reason that Jay Barlow was murdered?" A cold shiver went through my body. My heart rate increased, and I could feel the dizziness returning.

"If that's the case, Aunt Agatha could be in danger."

Chapter 18

I tried to shake off that crazy idea, but no matter what I did, it wouldn't go away.

I didn't want to think about this anymore. I didn't want to think about suspects, motives, or murder. I didn't want to think about trusts. And I absolutely didn't want to think that my aunt could be in danger.

So, I stopped. I stopped writing in my notepad. I ripped out the paper that I'd been writing on and tore it up into tiny pieces. If I'd had a match, I would have burned it, but I didn't have matches. Instead of fire, I decided water would be the next best thing. I got up and went across the hall to the toilet. I wrapped the torn paper in toilet paper and prayed it wouldn't clog the drain. Then I flushed the handle and watched while the toilet paper and tiny pieces of note paper swirled around in the bowl and then washed out to . . . wherever sewage went in the country.

I was determined not to think about murder, but theories on killers and trust funds bombarded my mind. I tried to get some sleep, but if I stayed in my room alone, I was afraid I'd be buried under an avalanche of negative thoughts. I glanced at the time. It was four a.m., and the sun hadn't started to rise. The harder I tried to push negative thoughts down and sleep, the more negative thoughts assaulted my mind. Eventually, I gave up trying to sleep. I got up and dressed to search for coffee and anything that would distract me. I needed something else to think about.

Books. That's what I needed. I could go downstairs and get lost in Edward Townsend's library. With any luck, there would be an Agatha Christie or Rex Stout novel that could distract me for a few hours until everyone else woke up.

I walked into the kitchen for coffee and was startled to find that it wasn't empty. Carla sat at the table with her face buried in a large mug of coffee.

"Good morning. Any more of that?" I asked.

Carla grunted and pointed toward the coffeemaker.

I opened the back door and let Bailey out to take care of his business. I prayed that he wouldn't catch a scent trail that might require me to put on a coat and boots and chase him down. Luckily, it was early, very early, and Bailey wasn't a morning dog. If there were scent trails, it was too early for him to care what animal had left them. It was autumn, and the temperature had dropped to the low twenties and upper teens overnight. A frost covered the ground. It was cold, and Bailey hadn't had breakfast. He wasn't interested in following trails. Not yet. He quickly took care of the necessities and hurried back inside.

I rummaged through cabinets until I found a mug and filled it with coffee. There was a bottle of creamer in the fridge and a sugar container on the table. I helped myself and sat down.

Carla didn't look as though she wanted to talk and that was fine with me. We sat and sipped our coffee in silence. We finished one pot, and Carla made another. It wasn't until she had finished her third or fourth cup that I felt brave enough to speak.

"Are you human yet?" I asked.

Carla grunted. "Barely, but I'm getting there."

"Where's Tabby?"

"Jogging."

"Really? I wouldn't have taken her for a runner."

"Starts at four thirty every day. Rain, sleet, snow, or hail, she has to get in ten miles." Carla sipped. "Says she wants to run a marathon."

"That's dedication."

"That's nuts."

"I take it you aren't into physical fitness." I hid my smile behind my mug.

"Not running, and certainly not at some ungodly hour like four thirty in the morning." Carla turned her head and looked at me. "You don't strike me as an early-morning person, either. What has you up this early?"

"I couldn't sleep."

"I take it your hunk of a police chief wasn't keeping you entertained?" She grinned.

I felt the blood rush to my face. "Gilbert left right after everyone went to bed last night."

"Something else must be bothering you, then." Carla waited a beat. "You look like you want to ask me something. Better do it before you lose your courage."

"I do have a couple of questions."

"Fire away. I'm almost fully caffeinated by now, so you stand a good chance of getting a logical answer."

"First, about Edward Townsend's trust. Do the trustees get paid?" I didn't want Carla to think I was prying into her finances, so I quickly added, "I was wondering about Aunt Agatha. Will she get paid for being a trustee for Edward Townsend?"

"Whether or not a trustee gets paid depends on the way the trust is written. In this case, the answer is yes. Edward Townsend had a large estate, and the trust is huge. All the trustees share one-half of one percent of the trusts," Carla said.

"One-half of one percent shared by all three trustees? Oh, well, that's okay." I released my breath.

"You seem relieved." Carla's lips twitched.

"I am. I had this crazy idea that someone might try to kill—I mean someone might want to harm Aunt Agatha to get to Edward Townsend's trust."

"I mentioned that Edward Townsend had a large estate, right?"

I nodded.

"My firm is still valuing all of his assets, but I feel safe in saying that with real estate, businesses, stocks, bonds, certificates, art, and well, everything, the Townsend estate will likely be valued at somewhere between two and three billion dollars," Carla said.

I had taken a sip of coffee only seconds before, so when the magnitude of what Carla said finally struck me, I spit out my coffee and started coughing. It took a few moments of Carla pounding on my back before I was able to talk. "But, that's . . . that would be more than ten million dollars."

She nodded.

"Even split three ways, that's . . ." I picked up my cell phone and pulled up the calculator app.

Before I could punch in all the numbers, Carla said, "Depending on the final valuation, the total is somewhere between ten and fifteen million dollars. Divided by three, each trustee would get between three to five million each."

"Holy moly." I gawked.

"If the person who killed Jay Barlow wanted the money he'd get from the trust, then that's certainly a big chunk of motivation."

Chapter 19

I needed a moment to catch my breath and process everything Carla had just told me. But I was struggling to wrap
my brain around that much money. "But how?" I mean, even
if the killer did want to get access to the trust, I don't see
how killing a trustee would do that."

Carla sighed. "Again, a lot of this depends on how the
trust was set up."

"You're a trustee. Don't you know?"

"I'm a CPA, not a lawyer. Natalie Evans will be your
best bet for understanding the legalities of the trust." Carla
took one look at the expression on my face and threw her
head back and laughed. "You look like you'd rather walk
over hot coals than ask Natalie Evans about the trust."

"Barefoot. I'd rather walk over hot coals barefoot."

"Natalie's a pretentious, stuck-up snob. She'd sell her

grandmother to human traffickers if she thought it would advance her career, and I don't trust her any further than I can pick her up and throw her."

"Why don't you tell me how you really feel?"

"It's the truth. I know it. She knows it, and Edward Townsend knew it."

"If he knew that about her, why did he keep her on? Why appoint her as a trustee of his estate? I know he didn't like lawyers, but surely he could have found one good, honest, trustworthy attorney."

"Natalie Evans is as sharp as a whip. She knows her stuff and she's ruthless. And we all know that Edward Townsend was a decent man, but he was also a tough businessman. The business world can be cutthroat. Dog-eat-dog doesn't even scratch the surface. If Edward Townsend was in a fierce negotiation, he wouldn't hesitate to use any weapons at his disposal. And he wasn't trying to maim or slow down the opposition. He was going for the jugular. Natalie Evans brought the weapons. She was like one of those Roman gladiators. If she was going into a sword fight, she'd have a dagger hidden in her boot and she wouldn't think twice about using it if her enemy got too close."

"Yikes. So, how do you work with someone like that?" I asked.

"Honey, I'm a gay Black woman trying to make it in a world built for straight white men." Carla looked me straight in the eyes. "My skin is as tough as an elephant's hide. I'm smarter than I look. Plus, I've got a few weapons up my sleeve, along with an exit plan." She tilted her head to the side and looked as if she were sizing me up. "Before you take on Natalie Evans, I recommend you get yourself a dagger—something sharp that will pierce her right through the heart."

"We are talking figuratively, right?" I chuckled to lighten the mood.

Carla shrugged and sipped her coffee.

I didn't consider myself a fighter. I certainly wasn't in Natalie Evans's, or, apparently, Carla's league. But I loved my aunt. After my parents died, she and my grandmother raised me. Now that Grammy Bell was dead, Aunt Agatha was the only family I had. I loved her. I would never stand by if someone tried to hurt her. But am I cutthroat enough to protect her from this? Could I go for the jugular?

"What if you're not really into close-combat fighting?" I asked. "I'm not sure I could stab anyone, even metaphorically speaking."

"Then you'd better make sure you never turn your back on Natalie Evans and don't let her close enough to stab you, because I guarantee she won't hesitate to take you out if you get in her way."

Chapter 20

My conversation with Carla left me feeling confused and more than a little bit frightened. I needed to think through everything she'd said.

Tabby entered the back door dripping with sweat. She was decked out in tight running pants that fit like a second skin, and a sweat-wicking shirt. The only deviation was a small backpack that was strapped to her body like a sling. She entered and dropped the backpack on the floor. "Good morning."

Bailey bounced up from his nap to greet her.

"Hey, Bailey." Tabby dropped to her knee and gave him a scratch while he licked the sweat from her neck.

"Any coffee left?"

Carla got up and poured a cup of coffee and handed it to Tabby. "What's in the pack?"

"Since I was out, I ran by the house and picked up clean underwear and a change of clothes." Tabby sipped her coffee.

"I love you," Carla said.

Tabby grinned. "I know."

Carla went to shower and dress. Tabby sat down to finish her coffee, and Bailey and I went to the library in search of a good book.

It was still early, and the house was quiet. I hadn't expected anyone to be up yet, so I was surprised when I entered the library and ran into Peter Alexander.

Literally. I bumped right into Peter coming out of the library while I was going in.

"I'm sorry. I didn't—"

Peter wasn't interested in apologies. He rushed past me and up the stairs.

I watched his back and wondered what had happened. Yesterday, he had been completely different. Yesterday, he was friendly and open. Today, something had upset him.

"Are you going to stand there all day, gawking after him?"

I turned and came face-to-face with Natalie Evans.

"Sorry, I didn't see you."

"Then, you might need to get your prescription checked."

"Prescription?"

"Contacts? You're wearing them, aren't you?"

"Yes, but . . ."

"How can I tell? It's the dimples." She pointed to the area on either side of the bridge of my nose. "It takes a long time to get rid of the indentations that glasses make on people who have worn them for a long time."

I forced my hand to remain down and not to reach up and touch those indentations. *How did she know about the indentations made by glasses anyway?* I stared at her nose.

"And you can stop staring. I haven't worn glasses in over a decade."

"Sorry."

"For what?"

"I didn't mean to interrupt your conversation with Peter."

Natalie folded her arms across her chest. "You shouldn't apologize so much. It makes you look weak."

"I'm sor—" I swallowed yet another apology. I wasn't aware that I apologized a lot before now, but I'd issued three in less than a minute. Well, two and a half. I wondered if Natalie was right. Did apologizing too much make me seem weak?

"Did you want something?"

Natalie's question snapped me back to reality. "A book. I couldn't sleep. So, I thought I'd check out the library." I wasn't apologizing, but for some reason, I'd substituted overexplaining in place of apologies. Natalie didn't own Townsend Farms. She was a trustee, but that didn't give her the run of the mansion. At least, I didn't think it did. I knew I was merely an invited guest.

"Well, knock yourself out." Natalie waved her arm wide. "I'm sure it'll be okay for you to borrow a book. God knows, Edward won't be needing them, and David doesn't strike me as the bookworm type."

"I hadn't thought about asking permission. I couldn't

sleep and thought maybe I'd borrow one to read. Maybe I should wait and ask . . ." *Who? Who could I ask?*

"I'm sure it's fine. You are playing this true to type, aren't you?"

"I don't know what you mean."

"Crosbyville's children's book author and local celebrity perusing a luxury library? All you need is a photographer to take your picture sitting in front of the fireplace with your faithful bloodhound curled up by your feet." She rolled her eyes. "It seems a bit passé, if you ask me."

"Good thing I'm not planning a photo shoot. Just looking for a good book." I walked to the bookshelf and glanced at the titles.

The books were mostly bound leather with embossed gold lettering on the spines. They reminded me of a set of expensive encyclopedias Grammy Bell bought when my mom and my Aunt Agatha were in high school during a fundraiser for their local Girl Scout troop. The full set of encyclopedias with color photographs had been expensive. I loved those books. As a kid, I spent many days flipping through the pages and reading up on everything from Argentina to walruses. If ever I asked a question, Grammy Bell would say, "Go look it up." All the answers were in those books. It was in those books that I researched the village in Africa where my parents had lived, worked, fell in love, and died. Aunt Agatha still had the collection.

"Earth to Priscilla." Natalie Evans waved a hand in front of my face.

"Oh, sorry. I was just . . . thinking." *Darn it. I apologized again.*

"I was just wondering if your boyfriend is done wasting everyone's time and has finally arrested Andrew Hicks for trying to kill that old man?"

Interesting dilemma. Do I shut down her attempts to pry information about the investigation out of me, first? Or, do I pump her for information and then shut her down?

"What makes you think Andrew Hicks killed Jay Barlow?" *I chose the latter.*

"Anyone with half a brain cell could see that Andrew Hicks is nothing more than a lowlife thug. Edward Townsend knew he was no good."

"Really? Why'd he hire him and let him stay on his estate?"

"Just because Andrew Hicks was a liar, a drunk, and a two-bit gambler doesn't mean he wasn't good with horses." She leaned back in the large executive chair and put her feet on the desk.

It was a position I felt confident Edward Townsend wouldn't have permitted, but Edward Townsend was dead. Clearly, Natalie was establishing her position in the new order.

"I'm sure Edward Townsend would have no trouble finding someone with fewer vices to look after his horses."

"Of course, but Edward was an old man. The older he got, the more adamant he became about finding legitimate family and tracking down his heirs." She scrunched her nose and stared at Bailey as though he had something to do with digging up all of Edward Townsend's heirs.

"Seems natural to me. Edward Townsend built an empire. The older he got, the more important family became to him. He needed his own flesh and blood to leave his legacy."

"That's just a lot of baloney. Where was his family all this time?"

I felt sure that was a rhetorical question, but I couldn't let it pass unchallenged. "Isn't the rest of his family dead?"

Natalie was quiet for such a long time, I thought she wasn't going to answer. As a former teacher, I knew that silence was a good tool to have in your arsenal, especially when dealing with a student with a guilty conscience. An extended silence always felt much longer than it was. Most people couldn't let it hang in the air like a wet blanket. They were compelled to fill it. Natalie Evans was no different. "Edward's only son, James, is dead. He died in a plane crash. Edward's brother, Frederick, was a no-good thief."

"What?"

"Didn't you know that? Frederick Townsend stole from his brother. When Edward confronted him, he lied. They had a huge fight. Edward never spoke to him again. His son, James, wasn't much better. He was a weakling who married a tart named Clara. Eventually, he divorced her and moved to Australia, a country populated by criminals."

"Australia was not populated by criminals. It's true that Australia was a penal colony used by the British more than three hundred years ago, but—"

"Save the history lesson for someone who cares." Natalie waved her hand as though swatting away a bothersome fly.

It took all my willpower to maintain my composure. The look on Natalie's face told me that she knew exactly what she was doing. She knew she'd sized me up and knew exactly how to get under my skin. *Darn it.*

"No family's perfect. Everybody's got a black sheep."

"I'll bet you think I'm the black sheep in my family." Natalie threw back her head and cackled. "Well, you'd be right, except for one thing." She paused, took her feet off the desk, and leaned forward. "My family's full of black sheep. My grandmother was Evelyn Frechette. Ever heard of her?" She paused.

I shook my head.

"Grandma Evelyn wasn't as well known as her husband, John Dillinger." She grinned. "I'll bet you recognize that name."

I was too shocked to do anything except nod.

"No one knew Grandma Evelyn had Dillinger's baby. The family kept it on the down-low. They were afraid of retribution from the police." She rolled her eyes. "Changed the family name to Evans and avoided the limelight. But, what's that British saying, 'Blood will out?' Anyway, in my family, I'm the only good one."

Well, that's scary.

"No matter how you try to hide or change, what's in the blood will eventually come out." Natalie laughed. "There's another saying about blood being thicker than water."

"What does that even mean?" Natalie asked.

"It means that people will do anything to protect their family." I was thinking about Aunt Agatha.

"Oh, how right you are. Some people would even cheat, steal, and sacrifice everything to protect a family member."

Something in Natalie Evans's voice made me ask, "Are you speaking in general terms? Or are you referring to someone in particular?"

Natalie's eyes gleamed. If she intended to look coy, then she failed. She was a bad actress. "Actually, I was talking about your private detective friend."

Whatever I had been expecting, that wasn't it. "Peter? What does he have to do with any of this? He wasn't related to Edward Townsend, was he?"

"Of course not. I was thinking about what you said about every family having a black sheep. Even work families—including the police department." Natalie tossed that comment in my lap, but I couldn't figure out what to do with it now that I had it.

"Yes, I'm sure they do."

She rolled her eyes. Obviously, I'd missed the point. "Right, so what do you do when you're a cop and one of your family members is on the wrong side of the law?"

It was early and this mental Ping-Pong match with Natalie Evans was wearing me out. I wasn't picking up on whatever clue she was putting down. "I give up. What do you do?"

"Ugh. You're clueless." Natalie stood up and marched to the door.

"Wait, what's the answer?"

"Ask your P.I. friend."

Natalie left me staring after her as she left the room. *What was she talking about?*

Bailey poked me with his nose.

I glanced down at my friend and gave his ear a scratch. It was barely daybreak and I was mentally exhausted. Sparring with Natalie Evans wasn't for the faint of heart. "I thought the Baxter sisters had been mean girls, but neither Chelsea nor Whitney had anything on Natalie Evans." For a brief moment, I entertained the idea of who would win in a WWE-style grudge match between the late Whitney Kelley and Natalie Evans.

"I've known Chelsea and Whitney for most of my life and I've only known Natalie Evans for two days. What do you think, boy?"

Bailey gave a short "Woof."

"Yeah, my money's on Natalie, too."

Suddenly, I felt tired. Whether due to the sleepless night or exhaustion from trying to keep up with Natalie Evans's mental gymnastics, I couldn't say. But I no longer wanted to read.

I glanced at my watch. If I hurried, I could probably sneak in a nap before breakfast.

Chapter 21

I headed back to my bedroom, but was waylaid by the aroma of bacon, coffee, cinnamon, and sugar. I stopped and, like a bloodhound on a scent, I followed my nose to the source of the delicious smells.

Aunt Agatha was sitting at the kitchen table sipping coffee and chatting with Olivia Green.

"Do I smell bacon?" I looked around.

"I told Olivia that the scent would draw you here like a moth to a flame." Aunt Agatha hid her smile behind a cup of coffee.

"Seriously, is there bacon?" I glanced around.

"Normally, I fry it, but your aunt suggested I bake it." Olivia Green rose from the table and moved to the oven. "I have to say, you were right, Agatha."

"Lifting the meat onto that rack helps to keep it from sitting in the grease. And you can't go by the look. Don't wait until it looks done. Four hundred degrees for about fifteen minutes should be plenty of time," Aunt Agatha said.

"Well, they say it's never too late to teach an old dog a new trick." Olivia laughed.

"So, the bacon isn't ready?" I asked.

"Not quite, but you can help yourself to one of these delicious cinnamon rolls that Olivia made." Aunt Agatha slid her plate in front of me. "I've already eaten three. If I stay here much longer, I'll be as big as a house."

She chuckled and the praise fest between the two cooks continued while I ate the sweet roll. It was flaky and soft, with just the right mix of sweet and spice. I tasted the cinnamon and the sugar frosting, but there was something else. I looked up and found both women staring at me.

"What? Do I have frosting on my face?"

"How is it?" Aunt Agatha asked.

For a moment, I wasn't sure how to respond. The cinnamon roll was good, but cooks could be temperamental. I wasn't sure if admitting that I liked the cinnamon roll would be a slap in Aunt Agatha's face. Enjoying baked goods from someone else didn't mean that I didn't love my aunt's pastries. To lie or not to lie? That was the question.

Bailey nudged my arm.

I looked into his face, which was always so open and honest. That face was a reminder. Honesty was always the best policy. "Sorry, boy. This is mine." I finished chewing and turned to face the women. "That's got to be the best cinnamon roll I've ever eaten. It's light, flaky, and gooey. It's sweet and cinnamony, but there's something else." I thought for a moment. "Orange?"

"I told Olivia the same thing." Aunt Agatha grinned.

"You really like it?" Olivia Green asked.

"I do. In fact, are there more lying around?"

Mrs. Green brought a tray to the table and slipped two more onto my plate. Then she went back to the alcove and continued to prepare breakfast, leaving Aunt Agatha and me to talk.

"Olivia's a natural cook." Aunt Agatha glanced around the kitchen. "She's clean and keeps a clean kitchen." She nodded her approval.

"You two have really hit it off," I said.

"We have, and that's saying a lot. Two cooks don't usually get along too well when it comes to sharing the same kitchen, but Olivia's easygoing and takes suggestions well."

"You sound like you're interviewing her for a job."

Aunt Agatha glanced around. "Well, that's one thing that I wanted to talk to you about. I was thinking about offering her a job at the diner. What do you think?"

"It's your diner. What do *you* think? Business has been good. Do you feel like you need the extra help?"

"I've been thinking about it off and on. I'm not getting any younger, and I could use an extra pair of hands in the kitchen, especially now." She patted the compression boot.

"Plus, I'll be taking on extra work now as a trustee. That's bound to take more of my time." She took a deep breath. "Olivia's honest and works hard, but she learned how to cook by cooking. She didn't go to no culinary college and doesn't have a degree. Edward Townsend didn't care about that, and neither do I. We shared an appreciation for good food. But now he's dead, and Olivia has to think about her future."

"She doesn't think that David Townsend will keep her on?"

"Who knows? That fly-by-night peacock don't think about nobody but himself. As soon as he can get his hands on Eddie's money, he'll be on the first thing moving to get back to Australia." Aunt Agatha pursed her lips.

"That's awful. I hadn't thought about what would happen to everyone who works here. Olivia, Mrs. Claymore, Hudson, and the others." I paused.

"I can tell you it's running through all of their minds. They're good people, but good people need to eat and pay their bills, too."

I turned to my aunt. "Maybe you can do something. You're a trustee and Edward Townsend's executor. You could make sure they continue to get paid."

"And I intend to, but that will only be good until David Townsend fires them and sells the house. It's hard out there for people who are a bit beyond their sell-by dates and don't have college degrees. The two maids will be fine. They've already got interviews lined up at the new hotel chain they're building along the toll road. But Hudson, Mrs. Claymore, and Olivia won't find it so easy."

I reached over and squeezed her hand. "I think Mrs. Green will be a great addition to the Blue Plate staff."

"So do I." She smiled.

"Maybe you should have a talk with David Townsend. Given the size of his inheritance, he might be inclined to be . . . generous."

"Don't count on it," Aunt Agatha said.

"I thought you liked David Townsend. You said that when he was a teenager, he was nice and well mannered. Was that just because he liked your blueberry pies? Or has he changed that much in the past fifteen years?" I teased.

"He was a nice boy." She clicked her tongue. "But people change. He lost his parents, and you know that isn't easy."

I hadn't thought about that. She was right. I knew exactly what it felt like to grow up without either one of your parents. It was hard. Sometimes, kids could be cruel. Whitney and Chelsea Baxter had certainly been cruel to me. Suddenly, I felt horrible for all the unkind thoughts I'd had about David Townsend. I was blessed to have had Grammy Bell and Aunt Agatha to love and teach me right from wrong. Maybe David Townsend hadn't had anyone to teach him how to treat women with decency and respect. Or, how to behave like a gentleman.

"Australia must have been rough on him. I tell you, I don't even recognize the man he's become. All that 'crikey,' 'mate,' and 'love' is enough to make me want to put David Townsend across my lap and spank him."

"Careful. He'd probably enjoy it."

I spit out my coffee and turned around to see who'd delivered that comment. That's when I noticed Chelsea Baxter enter the kitchen wearing nothing but the purple shirt David Townsend had worn yesterday and a large smile.

Chapter 22

"Chelsea, what are you doing here?" I grabbed napkins from a holder and mopped up the coffee that I'd just spit across the table.

"David called last night. He said the house was over-flowing with kids, angry women, incompetent detectives, and old people." She gave Aunt Agatha a long meaningful glance. "That's when he invited me to come over and help keep him . . . entertained." She grinned, leaving no secret about the reason for the call.

"I think they call that a booty ca—"

"Aunt Agatha!"

I felt the heat rise up my neck, but Chelsea merely laughed. There was no shame in her game.

"Call it what you want. David and I have gotten . . . close."

"Coffee?" Olivia Green brought a mug and a carafe of steaming hot coffee.

"Thank you." Chelsea accepted the coffee and sipped it with a big grin on her face. "I could easily get accustomed to this."

"Don't get too accustomed to it. You're not staying." Natalie Evans entered the kitchen and glared at Chelsea.

Olivia Green filled a platter with bacon and filled another platter with hot, fresh-out-of-the-oven cinnamon rolls. She set the platters on the kitchen table.

Before she could turn to leave, Chelsea set down her coffee cup, picked up the platters, and headed out of the room. "Thanks. We'll just take these. Gotta keep up our strength." She flashed a big smile at Natalie and turned to leave.

Unfortunately for Chelsea, to leave the kitchen, she had to pass by Natalie Evans. Natalie subtly stuck out a leg and Chelsea tripped. Chelsea's arm flailed as she tried to keep her balance to prevent herself from falling flat on her butt.

The plates shot out of her hands. Aunt Agatha reached out and grabbed one of the platters before it crashed to the floor. Olivia Green caught the other. As if in slow motion, the bacon and cinnamon rolls continued their momentum, flying into the air before falling onto the floor.

Normally, Bailey was a good, well-behaved dog, even in the kitchen when surrounded by food. Although he was certainly tall enough to help himself to anything on the counters, he never did. It had taken a lot of training, but he never pilfered people food.

Over the years, we'd established a special set of what I referred to as Kitchen Rules. Kitchen Rules meant any food on the table or on a counter was strictly off-limits. However, any food that hit the floor was fair game. The look in his eyes as the bacon and cinnamon rolls landed on his turf was laughable.

The veterinarian Bailey saw before Dr. Britton told me once he believed that dogs couldn't smile. If he could see Bailey's face at that moment, he would definitely amend that opinion. Bailey turned his head and gave me a look that reminded me of a kid on Christmas morning who just realized that Santa Claus had brought presents.

I couldn't have denied him that treat even if I wanted to. "Go for it, buddy."

Bailey gulped down the food in record time, as though he was afraid I would change my mind.

Chelsea managed to keep her balance, but when she was upright and steady, she turned her fury toward Natalie.

"Oops. Did I do that?" Natalie gave Chelsea a *Sorry-not-sorry* look.

"You did that on purpose!" Chelsea narrowed her gaze and lunged at Natalie.

In all the confusion, I hadn't noticed that Peter Alexander had entered the kitchen. Fortunately, his reflexes were quick. He grabbed Chelsea around the waist and held her back.

Good sportsmanship should have prevented Natalie from attacking once her opponent was immobilized, but Natalie was a gladiator, and gladiators weren't known for sportsmanship. Natalie snatched the empty platter out of Olivia Green's hands. She lifted her arms overhead and would have clubbed Chelsea, but David Townsend entered from the hallway door just as the back door opened and Gilbert came through.

He quickly assessed the situation, switched into police mode, grabbed Natalie around the shoulders, and pulled her toward the corner of the room. A split second later, David Townsend removed the platter from Natalie.

Chelsea and Natalie flung insults at each other like bullets.

Finished licking the frosting from the floor, Bailey barked along.

"Quiet!" Aunt Agatha yelled.

To my surprise, Natalie, Chelsea, and Bailey obeyed.

"Have you two lost your ever-loving minds?" Aunt Agatha asked. "Fighting like two alley cats in heat?" Aunt Agatha took the platter from David Townsend and placed both on the counter, well out of reach of both women.

"What on earth is going on?" Chief Morgan asked.

Both Chelsea and Natalie started talking at once, and Chief Morgan put his fingers in his mouth and let out a whistle that would have been perfect for hailing a taxi on New York City's busiest street. It worked to restore the calm in Crosbyville, too.

"One at a time." Chief Morgan turned to Chelsea. "Perhaps we can start with you, Mrs. Davis—I mean, Baxter."

For the first time, I realized that Gilbert's use of Chelsea's married name was a deliberate tactic to disarm her and not a result of a short memory. *The little devil.*

Chelsea rolled her eyes before sharing her side of the incident, which grew from a simple tripping incident to a malicious attack intended to do bodily harm. Chelsea demanded that Chief Morgan arrest Natalie for assault and attempted murder.

Natalie denied everything and promised to not only sue Chief Morgan, but the Crosbyville Police Department and the city of Crosbyville for false arrest if he even thought of detaining her.

Chief Morgan rubbed the back of his neck. He knew Chelsea was exaggerating, but he also hated being threatened. He turned to glance at the crowd now gathered in the kitchen. "I take it you were all witnesses to this *alleged assault.*"

"I saw the entire thing, and the only real crime was wasting perfectly good food." Aunt Agatha glanced from Chelsea to Natalie. "A pound of bacon and cinnamon rolls and the only one who got to enjoy them was Bailey."

Bailey licked his lips and wagged his tail.

Natalie wrenched her arm away and turned to glare at Chief Morgan. "May I leave?"

Chief Morgan nodded.

"I'll deal with you later." Natalie gave David Townsend a withering glance and then turned and marched out of the room.

David Townsend's eye showed definite signs of bruising

from his fight with Andrew Hicks, but he didn't let it hinder his lecherous ways. He moved closer to Chelsea and placed an arm around her waist. "Come on, love. I've got just the thing for your bruises."

Chelsea gave David Townsend a sappy look, and the two waltzed out of the kitchen.

Marcie and Carla entered. Stopped and looked around.

"Was that Chelsea Baxter prancing out of here wearing nothing but a man's shirt?" Marcie asked.

"Her poor mother would roll over in her grave if she saw that girl prancing around this house half-dressed and fighting as if she didn't have any home training." Aunt Agatha grunted.

"Fight? What fight?" Carla asked.

"We missed a fight between Chelsea and Natalie?" Marcie turned to frown at me. "I can't believe you didn't call me. You're supposed to be my friend."

"Marcella Rutherford!" Aunt Agatha yelled.

"Sorry, but come on, Pris. What happened?" Marcie asked.

"We just saw the first round in the Battle of the Mean Girls, gladiator style," I said.

"Really? Who won?" Carla asked.

I raised a brow and gave Carla a look that asked, *Really?*

"Stupid question. Natalie won," Carla said.

"That's no surprise, but why do you look worried?" Marcie asked. "It's not like you and Chelsea are friends."

"I guess I'm a little worried," I said.

"Why?" Marcie asked.

I turned to Carla. "Earlier, you told me never to turn my back on Natalie."

Carla nodded. "I remember."

"Chelsea Baxter made the mistake of turning her back on her when she didn't have a sharp dagger." I looked at Carla, who gave a quiet whistle.

Chapter 23

I don't know what all of this fuss is about, but wasting food like that really should be a crime." Aunt Agatha clucked her tongue and gave Gilbert a look that implied that this was somehow his fault.

"I'm sure Bailey doesn't consider the food wasted." I glanced at my happy bloodhound. Now that the excitement was over, he was still licking frosting from his paws.

"That was a pound of bacon. I've got more in the freezer, but it'll take time to defrost," Olivia Green said.

"I couldn't help but notice that you have plenty of sausage. How about I whip up a couple of breakfast casseroles while you make some more of those delicious cinnamon rolls?"

The plan was agreeable to Mrs. Green, and the two women moved over to the business end of the kitchen and got to work.

Carla made a fresh pot of coffee, and the rest of us sat at the table. We drank coffee and went back through the morning's entertainment.

Gilbert shared that he was now investigating the murders of both Edward Townsend and Jay Barlow. "Has the doctor been here yet to check on Andrew Hicks? I need to talk to him."

Hudson entered the kitchen, saw the crowd, and turned to leave, but was stopped when Chief Morgan said, "Wait. I want to talk to you, too."

Chief Morgan got up and followed the valet out of the room.

Carla, Marcie, and I sat at the table talking, but all conversation stopped when Mary Elizabeth, Clarice, and Hannah burst into the room. Tabby followed at a slower pace.

"Can we get our hair dyed?"

"Tabby said she would dye our hair."

"Please! Please!"

"Hold up." Tabby held up her hands. "I said I would give you a little color, but you all had to get permission."

The girls jumped up and down in excitement. "Please!"

I glanced at Tabby, who was drinking a cup of coffee.

"And before you crucify me, it's just a nontoxic spray-in color that comes out with soap and water after one shampoo," Tabby said to the adults.

"Please, Pris?" Hannah begged. "Clarice and Mary Elizabeth are both getting streaks. I'll be the only one with dull brown hair. I want a rainbow, just like Miss Tabby's. If you say it's okay, then my dad will say it's okay."

I turned to Tabby. "You're sure it'll come out?"

"Positive." She took a finger and crossed her heart.

"In that case, I'm sure your dad will be okay—"

I barely got the words out of my mouth when the whoops and cheers started.

Gilbert came back into the room. "What's all the excitement?"

Hannah jumped up and down. "Pris said I could get my hair dyed."

Gilbert shot me a look that made me think he was questioning my sanity. "Really?"

"Oh, Dad. All of the girls are getting it," Hannah said.

Part of me wanted to hop up and explain. After all, I wasn't Hannah's mother. I had no right to make an important decision like this. Perhaps I should have asked Gilbert before agreeing, but Hannah seemed so happy. Plus, he left me in charge when he asked me to babysit the sleepover. In most things, Gilbert trusted my judgment, especially when it came to what he referred to as *girl things*. Would he trust me to make a sound decision in this case?

Gilbert glanced down into his daughter's eyes. "Okay, but how will I recognize you?"

Hannah threw her arms around her father. "Oh, Dad. It's just a little hair dye."

"I thought you were going horseback riding today?" Marcie asked. "You better get dressed if you want to ride."

The girls, followed by Bailey, rushed out of the room to get their riding clothes on.

Gilbert leaned against the counter, folded his arms

across his chest, and stared. "Any other changes I need to know about? Piercings? Tattoos?"

For a brief moment, I thought he was serious until I noticed his lips twitching.

"I told her she had to wait until she was ten before I'd even consider tattoos," I joked.

"I better get my tools together." Tabby finished her coffee and placed her cup in the sink. Then she walked out of the kitchen. After a moment, she stuck her head back in the door. "I promise, it comes out after one shampoo." She winked and then left.

"I've got work to do. If you need me, I'll be going through the trust documents in the study." Carla hoisted herself up and walked out.

"It's been years since I rode a horse. I'm going to take some aspirin in preparation for the pain to come," Marcie said as she left.

Peter Alexander stood quietly in the corner. Then he put down his mug and headed toward the door.

"Ah, Peter, do you have a minute?"

The private detective forced a smile that didn't reach his eyes. "More questions for your book?"

"Not exactly." I glanced at Gilbert and tried mental telepathy to convey that he needed to question Peter, but my telepathic powers weren't working this morning.

Peter moved back into the kitchen and glanced at me.

My earlier conversation with Natalie Evans flashed through my mind. *What was it she had said?* It had something to do with black sheep, blood being thicker than water, and families. I wasn't sure exactly what she had been hinting at, but I caught a glance at my aunt Agatha from the corner of my eye and got an idea.

When I was a kid, I thought Aunt Agatha was clairvoyant. I was convinced that she knew everything that happened during my school day. She could take one look at my face and get me to confess. I was well into my teens before I realized that I was wearing my guilt like a neon sign. *Guilty! Guilty! Guilty!* One look at my face was all it took to let her know that I'd been up to something. One look was all it took, and I folded like a house of cards whenever she said, "I already know all about it. Do you want to tell me your side?"

Peter Alexander was carrying guilt and something else that I couldn't identify around like a backpack filled with bricks. It was weighing him down. I could help him get rid of the burden he'd been carrying, just like Aunt Agatha had helped me.

"Earlier, Natalie Evans hinted at some history of yours. It wasn't her story to tell, and I suspect she didn't do it justice." I glanced at Peter. He was buying it. "Over the years, I've learned there are always two sides to every story. Would you like to tell us your side? What happened with your family during your time as a cop?" I waited.

Peter Alexander stared at me for several moments. "Yeah. I think I'd better." He released a heavy breath and sat down at the table.

Chapter 24

*H*e stared at his hands for several excruciating moments. Eventually, he inhaled. When he exhaled, out came his story.

"I come from a long line of policemen. My great-grandfather, my grandfather, my dad, and both of my uncles had all been cops. All I ever wanted was to carry on the family tradition and join the force. As soon as I hit twenty-one, I joined the academy." He smiled and his eyes shone with a light as he remembered. Then a dark shadow passed over his face.

"Gary, my younger brother . . . he never wanted to join the force. But we pressured him. I pressured him. He needed to uphold the family tradition. Wear the uniform. Serve and protect." He frowned. "I shouldn't have pushed him. I knew Gary wasn't cut out to be a cop. Anyway, he followed the tradition and joined the academy. One day, he had an accident. He climbed up a fire escape to get a toddler who'd climbed out of the window onto a balcony. It was on the fourth floor. The fire escape was old and rusty. Gary fell and hurt his back. The doctor said he twisted on the way down to protect the kid from hitting the concrete. He wrenched his back. That's when he started taking pills for the pain. He was never the same after that." He spread his hands wide. "You can guess what happened."

"He got addicted?" Chief Morgan asked.

Peter nodded. "He tried to stop. He'd be fine for a day. A week. A month. But he would go right back to the pills. As if that wasn't bad enough, he started on alcohol. Then his wife got fed up. She packed up the kids and left. He fell to pieces." He paused. "They say cops have the highest divorce rate in the nation."

"Actually, that's an outdated report," I said.

"What?" Peter looked at me.

I could feel Gilbert's eyes on me, and the heat rose up my neck. I never meant for him to know that I'd been reading studies about divorce rates for police officers. "I saw a magazine article somewhere that said police officers used to have the second-highest divorce rate, between sixty and seventy-five percent. Recent data shows that the divorce rate among law enforcement is two percent *below* the national average."

"I didn't know that." Peter chuckled. "I guess Miriam didn't know it, either. Or, maybe she did know it and just didn't care. I don't know. Anyway, she said it was bad enough being married to a cop and not knowing one day to the next when he left in the morning if he'd come home at night. Add a cop addicted to pain pills and liquor on top of the stress, and she'd had enough."

"A lot of people get divorced. And a lot of people are addicted to drugs, alcohol, or some other vice. What's that got to do with you?" Chief Morgan asked.

"I was doing a rotation—helping out on vice outside on the South Side of Chicago. We'd just made a major bust. Over thirty million dollars' worth of cocaine, ecstasy, and fentanyl was confiscated."

Chief Morgan dropped his head. "I think I know where this is going."

"Before the case went to trial, close to a third of the pills were missing."

"Your brother?" Chief Morgan asked.

Peter nodded.

"I'm sorry for your brother, but what does this have to do with you?" I asked.

"Internal Affairs wanted me to turn on my brother." He choked. "Funny, we talk about fellow cops as brothers, but Gary really was my brother. My flesh and blood. I couldn't do it. Because of my family's years of dedicated service, I was offered a deal. Gary resigns from the force without a mark on his service record. In exchange, I also quit the force."

"What about your service record?" I asked.

Peter shook his head. "Records were supposed to be closed, but . . ."

"But Edward Townsend wouldn't hire a private detective without having his pit bull, Natalie Evans, investigate him first."

"I thought you said the records were sealed," Chief Morgan said.

"They were supposed to be, but enough money can reveal even the best-kept secrets." He shrugged. "Anyway, I went to talk to the old man about David Townsend. I still had some friends on the force—friends who knew the truth. Anyway, I told him there just wasn't enough proof that David Townsend was his grandson. I tried to get him to agree to some tests. At a minimum, I suggested he consent to a DNA test before he turned over a fortune to him."

"I take it Edward Townsend didn't agree," Chief Morgan said.

"Natalie Evans had fed him some cock-and-bull story about my being bitter because I hadn't found David, she did."

"What difference would that make?" I asked.

Peter gave me a hard stare. "Because of the finder's fee. Whoever found Edward Townsend's heir stood to get two million dollars."

My jaw dropped. "Seriously? Two million dollars?"

Peter nodded. "I thought you knew."

Chapter 25

So, if Mary Elizabeth is declared Edward Townsend's heir, then you would stand to receive two million dollars?" I asked.

"Wait, where did this come from?" Chief Morgan asked.

I explained that Mary Elizabeth was a distant cousin of Edward Townsend's, which is why Edward Townsend hired Andrew and why Peter brought her here. "So, Mary Elizabeth could inherit everything if David Townsend isn't the heir."

"But, if David Townsend is the heir, then Natalie Evans gets the finder's fee?" Chief Morgan asked.

"That sums it up."

"Did Edward Townsend believe that David was his grandson?" I asked.

Peter hesitated. "He seemed to. Natalie brought David

Townsend here about a week ago. At first, he was ecstatic and declared that David was exactly who he claimed him to be. He'd asked him questions, personal questions. Family questions. Things he said only a member of the family could possibly know. He was satisfied. A few days ago, he was different. Something changed. He didn't seem quite as sure as he had once been."

"Do you know what happened?" Gilbert asked.

Peter shook his head. "No idea. Whatever it was, that's when Edward must have arranged for Jay Barlow to come."

"How was Jay Barlow going to resolve things? I mean, wouldn't the best course of action be to have the DNA test done and go from there?" Chief Morgan asked.

"I don't know. On Thursday night Edward Townsend sent me a note apologizing for some of the things he'd said to me and asking me to come to his room later that evening."

"Did you go?" Gilbert asked.

"I did. That's when I found him. He was dead."

"You were the one who found him?" I asked. "I didn't know that."

"Yep. So, if you're looking for a suspect, I'm probably going to be at the top of your list. Natalie had gotten into his head, and Edward Townsend called me a dirty cop." He pursed his lips. "No one will believe that I wasn't. Forget all that malarkey about 'innocent until proven guilty.' The moment word gets out that evidence . . . drugs were discovered missing on my watch, *and* I left the force under suspicious circumstances, I'll be tried and convicted in the court of public opinion before you can finish processing my paperwork." He frowned and continued to tick off everything against him. "I had an argument with the victim earlier that day. And as far as motive goes, I had two million of them. Depending on how he died, chances are good that I had the means." Peter glanced at Chief Morgan. "If I had to guess, I'd say he was poisoned."

Chief Morgan nodded.

"Great. Oh, and just in case the evidence against me isn't damning enough, I took a look around for anything suspicious when I found him, so my fingerprints are going to be all over his bedroom."

Chapter 26

Chief Morgan didn't ask Peter Alexander if he killed Edward Townsend, but he did ask him not to leave the county without talking to him first.

Peter Alexander nodded and left.

When he was gone, the energy in the room felt the same as that of a funeral.

Aunt Agatha took the seat vacated by Peter Alexander. "Well, that man has certainly had his fair share of problems."

I filled Gilbert in on the weird conversation I'd had earlier that morning with Natalie Evans.

"Pris, that sounds a lot like you were investigating, and you promised me you wouldn't get involved in this investigation." Gilbert turned in his seat to face me head-on.

"I'm not investigating. I just went in the study to get a book and ran into Natalie. I would have told you about it, but I didn't have a chance. But I'm out of it. I'm going horseback riding and, hopefully, I'll get caramel apples and funnel cakes at the festival."

Clarice, Hannah, and Mary Elizabeth rushed back into the kitchen like three small tornados of energy. "Pris! Pris! Pris!"

"Miss Cummings," Gilbert corrected.

"Sorry, Miss Cummings, can I be the volunteer?" Hannah raised her hand.

"It's my birthday. *I* should get to be the volunteer," Mary Elizabeth said.

"You get all the fun because it's your birthday. I want to be the volunteer." Clarice pouted.

"Wait. What are you talking about?" I asked.

"The festival. According to the schedule online, Bailey the Bloodhound is going to be doing a demonstration for the R.E.A.D. program soon." Clarice scrolled through her cell phone until she found the schedule and then turned it around for me to read.

"I completely forgot." I glanced at the time. "Holy moly. We have just enough time to get over to the area where Bailey and I are scheduled to do the demonstration for R.E.A.D." I glanced at my watch. "In twenty minutes."

I hopped up from the table, gave Gilbert a quick kiss, and hurried out of the kitchen. "Bailey!" He followed close behind me. I kept Bailey's harness in the car, so I was able to grab it and quickly rush to the area set aside for our demonstration.

Bailey was a busy dog. Not only was he involved in

Search and Rescue, but he was also a registered therapy dog. Therapy Dogs International provided tests and certifications, clearing dogs to make visits to hospitals, nursing homes, and schools. Before I retired from teaching, I ran across an article about pet-assisted reading programs. An empirical study showed that children who struggled with reading showed significant improvements when reading aloud to a dog compared to children who read to a teddy bear or even to adults. I tried it in my classroom at Crosbyville Elementary School and found the improvements were considerable.

After retiring from teaching, I didn't want to give up working with children. With the financial help of Amelia Lawson-Cooper, a member of Crosbyville's school board and a descendant of one of the city's founding families, I helped to file the paperwork to create Crosbyville Reading Education Assistance Dogs (C.R.E.A.D.), the newest chapter of R.E.A.D. The program, which had originally started in Salt Lake City in 1999, was now an international program with chapters all over the world, including Italy, Sweden, the Netherlands, and now Crosbyville, Indiana.

Normally, children picked a book and read to Bailey for fifteen to thirty minutes in private one-on-one sessions. However, since C.R.E.A.D. had been selected as one of the festival's grantees, we were merely going to do a quick group reading at the Crosbyville Public Library's booth.

Clarice was a good reader. So, I let her demonstrate the benefits of R.E.A.D. by reading aloud from *Bailey the Bloodhound, Pet Detective*. All in all, it was a successful event. The kids all loved Bailey, and the parents asked questions about how they could sign their children up to read to him. Bailey did an excellent job, and I treated him to some of his expensive liver treats.

Afterward, we went horseback riding and then sampled far too many of the festival's assorted food offerings. Finally, the girls went back to the house with Tabby, who had purchased several bottles of washable hair dye, including neon green and hot pink, for the girls to streak their hair.

The walk back to the house for Marcie and me was considerably slower than the initial leg of our journey.

"Given the horse did the majority of the work, you wouldn't think I would be as sore as I am," Marcie said.

"I should have taken aspirin before the ride, too."

Marcie shook her head. "It didn't help."

"I just want to go home and soak in a nice hot tub until my skin shrivels up like a prune," I said.

"Normally, I wouldn't think prune-shriveled skin was a good thing, but I completely agree." Marcie stopped and looked at me. "Hey, did Gilbert say anything more about the money we found?"

"You mean the money *Bailey* found?" I grinned.

She dropped to one knee and gave Bailey a scratch. "Bailey found the money, but he's such a good boy, and he loves his Aunt Marcie, don't you?" She talked baby talk and scratched until she got him worked up into a lather and he howled in delight.

"Are you two done?" I laughed.

She stood up and Bailey shook himself.

"Gilbert hasn't mentioned the money, but I wouldn't hold out much hope that Bailey or any of his friends will see a dime," I said.

"Why not?" Marcie asked. "Whatever happened to 'finders keepers'? Aren't there laws about that?"

"I think those laws only apply in elementary school." I pulled out my phone and swiped. "I suppose it depends on where the money came from in the first place. If it was stolen, then it belongs to the original owner."

"That makes sense. Darn it!"

"Why do you want the money?" I asked. "Do you need money because—"

"I don't *need* the money, although who couldn't use an extra fifty thousand dollars? It would just be nice to have some funds so the next time the school board considers eliminating art and music programs, and you know there will be a next time, I can just waltz out of the classroom without a care in the world." Marcie put her head up, stuck out her chin, and took a few steps as though she were a model walking a runway in Paris.

"I know what you mean," I said.

"Do you?" She stopped. "You're a bestselling author. You were able to quit teaching and follow your dreams."

"Hah! Don't let that *bestselling* title fool you. Writers don't make a ton of money, at least debut authors writing children's books featuring a dog who's a pet detective don't. Plus, I only get paid twice a year."

"I forgot about that. Do you need money because—"

"I'm fine. Plus, I could always sign up to do substitute teaching or do a bit of waitressing at the Blue Plate for Aunt Agatha. I used to do well when I waitressed on the weekends in high school." I shrugged. "But, things are good. I make enough to keep a roof over our heads and Bailey in liver treats."

Bailey heard the L-word and turned and put his paws up on my shoulders.

"Down, boy. You're starting to pack on a few extra pounds. We're going to need to cut back on your snacks." I scratched his ear. One glance in his eyes, though, and I caved in and slipped him a small liver treat. "Okay, you can't just stop cold turkey, can you? We'll work on scaling back."

Marcie and I walked on toward the house.

We ran into Dr. Williams on our way and hurried to catch up to him.

"Dr. Williams, I'm sure you don't remember me from the chaos last night, but—"

"You're Bailey's mom." He bent down and greeted my dog. When he and Bailey finished, he stood up and grinned. "I'm terrible with faces and names, but I remember dogs."

"You got the important one." I extended my hand. "I'm Priscilla Cummings, but please call me Pris."

Marcie introduced herself.

The doctor smiled. "I'm afraid I won't remember, but please call me William." He shook hands with each of us.

"William? I'm sorry. I thought Williams was your last name," I said.

"It is." He grinned. "My parents had a wicked sense of humor. William Williams."

"That was wicked. I hope you didn't get teased too much in school. Kids can be brutal," Marcie said.

"They were until I introduced them to my pet snake." He grinned.

"Please tell me you don't still have it." I stopped and stared.

"I have three, but they're all at home." William grinned.

I shuddered.

"If you're on your way to see Andrew Hicks, maybe you won't mind if we walk with you," Marcie said.

"Certainly. It's not every day that I am accompanied by two beautiful women and a celebrity." He glanced down at Bailey.

"I was amazed that you actually came out to the house last night. Human doctors don't make house calls. Your patients are lucky to have such a dedicated physician," Marcie said.

Dr. Williams blushed. "It comes with the territory when you specialize in large animals and livestock. Much easier for me to visit the animals than it is to get them to my clinic."

"Was it very difficult working on a human patient?" I asked.

"Well, it's not often that my patients can tell me what's bothering them in a language that I can understand," he joked. "But the basics of medicine are the same. Honestly, I didn't do much. He really should have gone to a hospital, but I knew he wouldn't."

"Why not?" I asked.

"He never does."

I stopped. "What do you mean? Have you been called to help Andrew Hicks before?"

"Oh yes. This wasn't the first time. Sadly, it probably won't be the last, either. I'm not really at liberty to talk about it, but if you want to know, I'd suggest asking Hudson. He's the one to tell you what's really going on."

Chapter 27

D r. Williams couldn't or wouldn't share more. I didn't think that veterinarians were bound to client confidentiality, but then again, I wasn't authorized to ask questions. In fact, I wasn't involved. I wasn't investigating. I'd promised Gilbert that I would stay out of this, and I intended to keep that promise.

Marcie, Dr. Williams, and I walked back to the house together, but once we were there, I decided that the library might be a good place to write. So, I went upstairs, grabbed my laptop, and headed back to take up residency in the book lovers' paradise.

On my way to the library, I passed a drawing room. It was a quiet room with comfortable chairs and an excellent view. Carla was there, sitting at a small writing desk near the window. She was talking to David Townsend. Based on the frown on her face, it wasn't a pleasant conversation.

"Look, I'm not accusing you of anything." Their voices floated into the hallway, and I felt myself slow down to listen.

"Then, I don't see why I can't get an advance to help cover some of my expenses. According to Natalie . . . ah, I mean Ms. Evans, it's not an unusual request. Most trusts don't even have to go through probate."

"True, but Edward Townsend's estate was substantial. Plus, there are . . . discrepancies with some of the accounts. I'm requesting an official audit of all of Edward Townsend's accounts. Given the size of his holdings, that could be a lengthy process."

"But, surely, you can release some of the money now. I mean, what do you expect me to do? It's *my* inheritance."

I peeked into the room, where Carla had raised an eyebrow at David. "Mr. Townsend, it's my understanding that your claim hasn't been confirmed. You have to prove that you are Edward Townsend's heir and therefore entitled to any of the funds held in the trust. And, until such time, I don't know what to tell you."

"Love, are you implying that I'm not related to Edward Townsend? Because if you are, I take exception to that." David Townsend flashed a crooked smile.

"No. That's not what I'm saying."

"Good, because I would hate to think that you don't believe me." He laughed.

Carla didn't laugh. She removed her glasses and looked at David Townsend as though she were examining a specimen under a microscope. "Mr. Townsend, I'm a CPA. My job is to audit accounts, and I'm good at what I do. I—"

"Now hold up, love, I wasn't implying that you—"

Carla held up a hand to halt the barrage of words. "Permit me to finish." She paused a beat and then continued. "I've discovered several discrepancies. To date, I've discovered at least twelve million dollars that can't be accounted for. Someone has shifted large sums of money across multiple accounts. I'll get to the bottom of it. There's always a trail and I'm on that trail. Until I can track this down, no money is leaving Edward Townsend's trusts."

"What are you saying here, mate?"

"I'm saying that someone has embezzled funds. But even if there wasn't any question of embezzlement, now that Edward Townsend's death is being investigated by the chief of police as a potential murder, everything will be out of my hands. The courts will freeze all his assets until the police can finish their investigation. So, it may be quite some time before any money will be paid to anyone, including you . . . *mate*."

Chapter 28

*I*f looks could kill, Carla would have dropped dead on the spot. Molten lava flooded David Townsend's face, highlighting his bruised face and soon-to-be-black eye. He sputtered for several moments and then turned and stormed out of the room, past me, and down the hallway.

Carla glanced up and saw my face. Of all the responses I might have expected, laughter wasn't in the top one hundred, but that's what she did. "Boy, was he furious."

"Aren't you worried? I mean, he looked hopping mad, as Aunt Agatha would say."

"What's he going to do? I'm just the messenger. Sure, I found the embezzlement, but it's the courts that will be holding up the funds." She rubbed her hands. "This is what I love about accounting."

"Are you serious?"

"It's just like those mysteries you love to read. It's a puzzle. I just need to follow the trail to the missing money." She slipped her glasses back on and glanced down her nose at me. "And make no mistake about it. I will find the money. That's the real fun part of accounting." She laughed and then turned back to her laptop.

I suppose there was a grain of truth there, but it certainly wasn't my idea of fun. I shrugged and continued to the library.

At the entrance, I had a moment of déjà vu when I was nearly bowled over at the entrance again. Unlike last time, Peter Alexander wasn't the culprit. This time, Hilda Diaz-Sanchez was the person storming out of the library. Also, unlike last time, Hilda stopped and apologized.

"Priscilla, *lo siento*. I didn't see you there."

"It's okay. Are you okay?"

I'd noticed her accent was much more pronounced when she was upset or angry, and she often interspersed her English with Spanish. Or was it Portuguese? Hilda's face and neck were flushed.

"*Sí. Sí.* It's just frustrating. I wanted to talk to David Townsend *una vez más*. Just one more time. I wanted to appeal to him about the fundraiser for the Search and Rescue event," she said. "But he wasn't available. So, I met with that *abogada* . . . that lawyer, Natalie Evans."

I took a deep breath to brace myself for Natalie's response to Hilda's request. "I take it she refused to consent to the original contract signed by Edward Townsend?"

"Actually, she agreed to honor the contract at the original price, *if* I would pay cash." She shrugged. "That's *muy bien* . . . that's fine, as long as I can get a receipt."

"Cash is unusual, but . . . that's great, right?" I tried to hide my surprise. "What's the problem?"

"*El problema* is that Edward Townsend was donating *la comida* . . . the food, beverages, waitstaff, and security. This lawyer, she said the new heir would be getting rid of all the staff, and I'd have to hire my own." She took a deep breath. "I suppose I should be grateful that I don't have to look for another venue. There's no time for that. However, I also don't have the time or *el dinero* to get caterers, waiters, food, and security. I mean, we don't need the same level of security that he has for the festival, but somebody needs to man the gates and help with parking."

I thought for a few moments. "I'm sure Aunt Agatha will cut you a deal on the food. And she may be able to provide some help with the waitstaff, depending on how much you need."

"*Dios mio.*" Hilda's eyes lit up. "Do you really think she would? It's short notice and her diner is always so busy."

I grinned. "I think she's considering adding additional staff, so there's a good chance that she can help out. Let's ask."

We didn't need Bailey's superior olfactory receptors to track down Aunt Agatha. Hilda and I just followed our own noses. Sure enough, she was in the kitchen baking along with Olivia Green.

I explained the situation to Aunt Agatha, and she agreed to provide the food at cost. Since Aunt Agatha had only two full-time employees, and even with Olivia's help and any of the other Townsend staff who were willing, she couldn't guarantee enough people for a full sit-down meal. So they agreed on a buffet instead.

"That way, we just need to have a few people around to make sure the food stays hot and the buffet is stocked," Aunt Agatha said.

"I wonder if Gilbert could help with security?" I mused.

"Pris, that would be wonderful."

"I can't promise anything, but I'll ask Gilbert."

"Ask me what?" Gilbert walked through the back door.

"Speak of the devil," Aunt Agatha said.

I quickly explained the situation.

He scratched his chin, which was developing a five-o'clock shadow, a sign that he had been working late. "The budget is tight, but I've got a couple of young cops who are always excited about overtime, especially for a fairly cushy event like this one. Sitting in a booth and directing traffic with virtually no chance of getting shot is a cakewalk. I'd volunteer myself if it meant I could get out of wearing a tuxedo." He grinned.

"Oh no, you don't. You're not getting out of wearing a tuxedo that easily. Besides, it's already rented." I gave his arm a playful punch.

"Can't blame a guy for trying." He turned to Hilda. "Seriously, I'm sure I can provide a couple of guys for a few hours. No problem."

Hilda beamed. She threw her arms around his neck and hugged him. Then she looked around at everyone. "You are all wonderful. I am so glad I ran into Pris today."

Gilbert and I left Hilda with Aunt Agatha and Olivia Green discussing the menu in the kitchen.

Once we were alone, I grabbed the collar of his jacket, pulled him close, and kissed him thoroughly. His response was immediate and passionate. After a moment, I pulled away. We were both breathless.

"Wow. What was that for?" he asked.

"Just my way of saying thank you."

"You're welcome, and for what?"

"For helping with the fundraiser. You could have said no. I would have understood."

"It's a good cause. I'm glad to help. But feel free to *thank* me like that anytime." He grinned. "In fact, if you want to thank me more, I'd be happy to—"

His cell phone rang and I didn't get a chance to find out what he would be happy to do, but I had a pretty good idea, and the thought brought a smile to my face.

When he finished, he reached for me again. "Now, where were we?"

The time while he was on the phone reminded me of my earlier conversation with Dr. Williams. I needed to make sure Gilbert talked to the vet before I forgot. So, I brushed him off gently and told him about the conversation.

Gilbert wasn't thrilled by the information. The vein on the side of his head was pulsing at high speed, a sure sign that he was angry, but restraining himself.

"I thought we agreed that you weren't getting involved."

"I'm not involved. Marcie and I were walking back to the house, and we ran into Dr. Williams."

"And you decided to pump him for information about the case that you're not involved in."

"I did not *pump* him for information. I was being a good neighbor and asked how Andrew Hicks was doing." I stepped back and folded my arms across my chest.

"Fine."

"What does that mean?" I asked.

"It means fine."

I glared. "That's not how you said it."

"How I said it? You've got to be joking. Pris, I'm agreeing with you. You were just being a good neighbor. Can we please not have a fight about this and get back to the part where you were just *thanking* me?" He reached for me, but I stepped out of his reach.

"You don't believe me. You think I'm butting into another murder investigation."

"That's not what I said. I said 'fine' because I accept what you're saying."

"No, you don't. Not when you say it like that."

"Like what?" Gilbert rubbed his neck.

"Like you don't believe me, but you're saying you believe me to get me to shut up so we won't get into a fight."

"How did you get all of that from that one word?"

"I'm a writer. Words matter."

"What word should I use to say, 'I accept what you're telling me'? I want to make sure you don't misinterpret me."

"I don't think you need to be concerned that I'll *misinterpret* anything else," I said softly, and turned to go.

"Pris, wait—"

I didn't wait. I hurried out of the house as quickly as I could.

My car was parked out front, so I opened the back door for Bailey and then hopped inside and drove away.

Chapter 29

I didn't pay attention to the time, but the sun was moving lower in the sky and there was a nip in the air. I drove without any clear plans and let my anger and frustration simmer like a pot left on the stove too long.

Gilbert called, but I wasn't in the mood to talk to him. I was angry. "He doesn't trust me. How are we supposed to have a meaningful relationship without trust?" I glanced in the rearview mirror at Bailey, but he didn't have any answers.

"I told him that I wasn't getting involved. And I wasn't involved. In fact, I wouldn't even be here if he hadn't involved me by asking me to watch Hannah."

Bailey yawned.

Driving always had a soothing effect on me. I was able to think, put things into perspective.

"Gilbert is a good man who treats women with dignity

and respect. Not like David Townsend, who ogles every woman he sees." I shuddered at the thought of being involved with a man like David Townsend. "He may be rich, or he *will* be rich when Edward Townsend's estate is settled, but there isn't enough money on the planet to make me want to be with someone who doesn't respect me."

I drove to downtown Crosbyville. I was on automatic pilot, not really paying attention to where I was going. My car turned into the park near the town square. It was one of Bailey's favorite places to walk, and he got excited when he realized where we were.

I parked, put Bailey's harness on, and hooked up his leash. Then we walked.

"Trust is important. How could he not trust me?"

The back edge of the park had a walking path that was popular with joggers. We avoided it like the plague. I still had nightmares of runners who thought they could merely jog by a curious bloodhound. More than one runner has ended up in a pileup with Bailey's leash wrapped around their legs and a hundred pounds of dog sniffing their sweat-soaked skin.

The middle section of the park had benches, a fountain, and a well-trimmed hedge maze, which was Bailey's favorite. He loved following human and animal scents through the maze. The city employed a great team of workers who did a wonderful job maintaining the park. In addition to the green hedge maze, they planted colorful flowers that they changed out seasonally. Bailey bypassed the flowers and headed straight for the maze's interior. I was thankful that the begonias that had graced the garden had now been replaced by mums. Given what—or *whom*—Bailey had dug up in the begonias a few months ago, I couldn't even look at the plants without hyperventilating. Nothing bothered Bailey. He was fearless. He put his nose to the ground and sniffed.

My phone vibrated. I glanced at the screen, prepared to ignore it if Gilbert's face popped up. It wasn't. Instead, I was pleased to see a picture of Hannah.

Tabby had given her a graduated purple that went from dark to light stripes. She'd parted her hair into two sections. The top of her hair was left its normal brown color, braided and wrapped around her head. Hannah called it mousy brown, but it was actually a deep chestnut. As she got older, I knew it would thicken and she would be a stunner. For now, she was a cute kid. The bottom section that hung down to her shoulders had been dyed different shades of purple and curled. Tabby had added the color so that if Hannah took down the braid, her natural hair covered the purple dye, making it invisible. She looked amazing. The colors looked great, and her smile brightened her entire face. It was contagious, and I couldn't help smiling, too, as I looked at the picture. I immediately replied with several heart emojis.

More vibrations.

The next picture was of Clarice. Her natural hair was blonde and much longer and thicker than Hannah's. Her thick hair was pulled back into a high ponytail that was dyed a vibrant pink. Clarice's hair wasn't just pink. It was glow-in-the-dark, neon pink. The next picture showed that when the lights were turned off, Clarice's hair did, indeed, glow. It looked great. Still, I couldn't help wondering what Chelsea would say when she saw it. I reminded myself that Tabby had promised the color would wash out.

The final picture was of Mary Elizabeth. Like Hannah, she had brown hair, although her hair was a deeper color and longer than Hannah's, flowing down well past her shoulders. Mary Elizabeth had chosen streaks of a vibrant red that framed her face. It was more subtle than the other two girls but suited her perfectly. She had accessorized with feathers and barrettes.

All three girls looked wonderful. Tabby had done a fantastic job, and I fired off a quick reply offering to pay for the girls' hair. She had put in quite a lot of time doing this. She deserved to be compensated for her time, expertise, and creativity.

Tabby declined my offer of payment, replying to my text:

Wish all clients let me go wild with color. Hint. Hint!

I wondered what Gilbert would think of Hannah's hair. Gilbert.

He loved Hannah. He was a great dad, even though his job meant he didn't get to spend as much time with her as he wanted. It wasn't easy being a single parent. He didn't trust Hannah with just anyone.

"He had trusted me to look after her."

Bailey glanced back at me. If ever a dog's facial expression said, *duh*, Bailey's did.

His nose drove us deeper into the hedge maze, toward the center.

"I was just inquiring after Andrew. The poor man had been beaten to a pulp," I told Bailey. Inside, I felt justified for getting upset with Gilbert. "I was just being neighborly."

My conscience prickled. Gilbert wasn't perfect, but who was? "He is a cop who serves the citizens of Crosbyville. He is willing to put his life on the line for us.

"He doesn't have a drinking or a drug problem, either." My mind immediately went to thoughts of Peter Alexander's brother. He'd gotten hurt in the line of duty. He'd ended up addicted and ultimately lost his wife and family.

I walked in silence while a knot of guilt gnawed at my insides.

My thoughts turned to Andrew Hicks. I'd peeked in on him earlier in the day, and he had looked awful. He was battered and bruised. His eye was swollen so badly his face looked deformed. Whoever beat him up had done a thorough job of it. He was lucky he hadn't been killed. I shivered. That would have been horrible, especially for Mary Elizabeth.

We walked in silence for a few additional moments, which gave my brain too much time to think. I wondered who could have beaten another human being to that extent. Were they able to sleep at night knowing they'd nearly killed a man? I figured they were. The type of people capable of delivering a beating like that wouldn't have any scruples about beating a man.

"Dr. Williams said it wasn't the first time, either." I shuddered. Alcohol, gambling, and horses. That's what the folks at The Big Tease had called Andrew Hicks's vices.

Bailey pulled me deeper and deeper inside the maze. I couldn't judge. Everyone had their vices. Besides, alcoholism was a disease.

Gilbert wasn't perfect, but he worked hard, took care of his daughter, and he had cared for me. Well, he had up until today.

"Maybe I overreacted." I stopped walking, and Bailey turned to stare at me when he found that forward progress had halted.

"I've been a fool, Bailey."

He sat and stared up at me.

"Don't look at me like that. I'm not the only one who's overreacted from time to time." I bent down and scratched his ears. "I seem to remember you going a bit overboard the other day, just because a rabbit had the audacity to come through your yard."

Bailey wasn't listening. He was completely absorbed in his ear scratches.

"So, maybe I owe Gilbert an apology. What do you think?"

Bailey rolled over on his back, exposing his belly for better scratching coverage.

"Oh, taking his side, are you? You males all stick together, don't you." I scratched more furiously and threw in a belly pat for good measure.

"All right, let's go back to Townsend Farms. If I've got to eat crow, then I might as well get it over with."

"Is there enough crow for two?"

I looked up and into the dark, soft eyes of Gilbert Morgan.

"Gilbert, what are you doing here?"

"Look, I believed you when you said you weren't interfering in the investigation and I'm sorry for whatever I said that made you feel like I didn't believe you. I just want you to be safe. I—"

I pulled Gilbert's collar close and kissed him long and hard. When he pulled away, he gazed into my eyes. "Does that mean you forgive me?"

"There's nothing to forgive. I'm sorry. I overreacted. I shouldn't have—"

Gilbert pulled me close and this time he kissed me until my knees were weak and I felt as if I were drowning. After an eternity, I pulled away. "Wait, how did you find me?"

He grinned. "I'm a trained police officer. Don't tell me you're doubting my ability."

I stared.

"Okay, I was downtown at the police station taking care of some paperwork, and I saw your car when I passed by the park. Now, can we continue apologizing?"

I reached up and kissed him again, but I experienced a sense of déjà vu when his cell phone rang.

Gilbert swore under his breath. "I'm tempted not to answer it."

I pulled away. "You have to answer. You're the chief of police."

He answered and listened for several beats. "When was the last time anyone saw him?" His brow was furled, and his eyes were no longer the soft, brown liquid pools that I'd stared into moments ago. Now they were cold, hard granite. "I'm on my way."

One look at his jaw and I knew something was terribly wrong. "What happened?"

"David Townsend's missing."

"Maybe he just went out for a breath of air." The words had barely left my mouth, but I knew Gabriel wouldn't be this upset unless something was very wrong.

"His car was found abandoned half a mile from the estate. His cell phone and wallet were found on the ground nearby. And there was blood on the steering wheel and the driver's seat."

Chapter 30

We both drove back to Townsend Farms in our own cars. Gilbert was the first to arrive. In the police car, he had an advantage. He sped through red lights with sirens blaring and flashing lights. I followed the traffic rules until I got into the country. Then I put the pedal to the metal and drove as quickly as road conditions allowed.

I arrived and was surprised to see Hilda Diaz-Sanchez and her lab, Teddy, dressed in their SARs attire. I pulled up next to her truck.

"Pris, great. You and Bailey will be needed." Hilda looked at my outfit.

"What's going on?" I asked.

"David Townsend's missing. I thought you knew."

Under normal circumstances, Bailey and Teddy would have been playing chase and rolling in the grass together.

However, Teddy had his working vest on and was all business. Bailey sniffed his friend, and then sat patiently. He knew it was time to work.

"I did, but I didn't know they had asked for search dogs."

"I just got the call." She held up her phone.

My cell phone vibrated.

"That'll be my text to the group asking for volunteers. You'd better go up and change into some boots and grab a warm jacket," Hilda said.

I left Bailey with Hilda and hurried upstairs to change into jeans. Technically, my yoga pants would have been fine, but I wasn't the most graceful of searchers and had fallen and scraped too many body parts to forgo the additional safety of denim. I was glad I'd packed my red rubber boots. They would keep my feet dry and would still look stylish.

By the time I got back downstairs, most of the other members of the Crosbyville Search and Rescue team had arrived.

Hilda passed out the small handheld radios that we used when we were working. We tested them to make sure they all worked. Everyone also had cell phones and we had all the team members' numbers saved in our contacts. But we can't rely on cell phones when we're on a mission. We couldn't risk getting into a dead spot without cellular service or with run-down batteries. Reliable communication could mean the difference between life and death. We also had compasses and even a few paper maps. Officer Rodriguez joined our group and distributed the maps he was carrying to each of us.

Chief Morgan came out of the house followed by Chelsea. Gilbert carried one of David's shirts.

Chelsea's face was streaked with tears and her eyes were red and puffy. She looked genuinely miserable.

Marcie came outside and stood beside me. "She looks awful. I actually feel sorry for her."

"I know. Me, too. I guess she really cared for David."

"Hard to believe, considering they've known each other for such a short time, but I suppose when you know, you know." She shrugged.

Gilbert held up a hand for attention. "I've pulled every available officer that I can spare. I'm asking that each officer pair up with one of the canine-and-handler teams."

I did a quick count and noticed that we were short one police officer.

He assigned a policeman to each team, except for Bailey and me. When he finished giving out instructions, he asked if we had questions. No one did, so they all lined up to let the dogs sniff the shirt he was holding, then the teams moved out and started on their way.

Gilbert walked over to Bailey, Marcie, and me. He nodded at Marcie and asked if she could keep an eye on Chelsea.

Marcie agreed and walked away.

"Are you my police team member?" I asked.

"Only if I can't convince you to stay here."

"Bailey and I trained for this. He may not have been doing Search and Rescue as long as Hilda and some of the others, but he's got the best nose. You know that. You know how good he is. I can't believe you don't think we can handle this search. I—"

"Hold on. I didn't say you couldn't handle it. I know you're trained and capable. I also know how good Bailey's tracking instinct is. But I also know you." He paused.

"What's that supposed to mean?"

"Pris, we're about to go tramping through the woods. There could be foxes, coyotes, and even bobcats."

I paused. "Bobcats?"

He nodded. "Plus, there are bound to be snakes and other vermin. I just thought that perhaps you'd prefer to stay here. I could take Bailey out and do the search. He knows me and I'm sure he'll work with me if you wanted to stay here."

It took every bit of courage I had not to pass Bailey's leash to Gilbert and run inside where it was warm and safe. But I knew the risks when I signed up. "I'm fine."

"You sure?" he asked.

I nodded.

"Good. Then, we're taking the area due east." He took out the shirt and placed it near Bailey's nose.

Bailey got a good whiff and then he put his nose to the ground.

"Let's go." Gilbert walked off in the direction that he wanted us to search.

Bailey took a few steps in that direction, but then he stopped.

"What's wrong?" Gilbert turned to me. "Didn't he get the scent?"

I looked at my dog, who was sniffing the air. I could tell by the way his nose twitched and the way he sniffed that he had the scent, but something was wrong. I stopped and got down on my knees. "What's wrong, boy?"

Bailey gazed into my eyes, and then he turned his head toward the southwest. He bayed and then tugged on the leash. He glanced back at me.

"He doesn't want to go that way."

"But it's the direction that the blood trail led from the car," Gilbert said.

"Bailey wants to go this way."

Gilbert looked from me to Bailey. "Are you sure he's picking up David Townsend's scent and not someone or something else?"

I wasn't confident of much in that moment. Bailey hadn't liked David Townsend much. Could he have decided that he'd rather track down a corn dog or a funnel cake instead of looking for the man who had almost kicked him?

Bailey turned and looked into my eyes. In that moment, I saw confidence. He was wearing his vest. He was working. Bailey the Bloodhound was on the trail.

"I don't care where the blood trail is leading. That's not the way to David Townsend. I trust Bailey."

Gilbert frowned. He gazed in the direction toward the east.

My heart sank. He didn't trust us. "Maybe you should head east, and Bailey and I will go south. I have my radio and I—"

"Pris, I trust you and I trust Bailey. If that's the direction you think we need to go, then we better get a move on."

My heart leaped, but there was a large lump in my throat that wouldn't go away. *Well, what if I was wrong? What if Bailey was wrong? What if—*

"Pris. Let's go!" Gilbert said.

I loosened the slack on Bailey's leash. "Okay, Bailey. Find!"

Chapter 31

Bailey kept his head down, lifting only to sniff the air briefly. Then it was back to work. He jogged at a good pace. Normally, he didn't go quite as rapidly, and I had to run to keep up. I tripped over a log and Gilbert helped me to my feet.

"Can I help?" he asked.

The question came out of concern for my safety and not because he didn't trust my ability. So, I handed him Bailey's leash and he and Bailey moved much more rapidly.

I might have to consider jogging with Tabby if I was going to stay in shape to keep up with Bailey. *Yeah, not likely.* I still stumbled over logs and broken tree branches as we trekked across fields. The autumn leaves falling from the trees and covering the ground might have made a picturesque scene if we were traveling at a reasonable pace, but I had to take two steps for each one of Gilbert's.

Sweat dripped from my forehead and periodically I caught a whiff of a musty scent I suspected was coming from me rather than the great outdoors. Nothing romantic about a stinky, sweaty person huffing along while trying not to wheeze or fall flat on your face.

Gilbert glanced back. "Are you okay?"

"'I'm wasted on cross-country. We dwarves are natural sprinters. Very dangerous over short distances.'"

Gilbert stopped. "What?"

"It's a line from *The Two Towers* movie."

"*The Lord of the Rings?*" he asked.

"It was a joke . . . Never mind." Gilbert and I had been dating only a few months and he hadn't discovered that I was a *Lord of the Rings* geek yet. I'd learned that revealing too many eccentricities at one time wasn't good for a relationship. Nope. I'd wait to let him know the extent of my geekiness until we'd been dating for at least six months. No need scaring off a potential suitor too quickly. Some peculiarities should be doled out in small doses over time. I rubbed my side and worked to take in as much oxygen as I could as quietly as I could.

Gilbert looked at Bailey and then looked around. "We can stop. You need to catch your breath. Or, if you want to wait here, Bailey and I could—"

"Nope. No way!"

"Pris, I know he's your dog. I also know you are trained and capable of following the trail. Bailey's your dog and—"

I was shaking my head like a metronome. "Nope. No way."

"You're still mad about earlier? You think I don't trust you, but I do. I was only thinking—"

"That's not it, either." I leaned against a nearby tree and massaged a cramp in my calf.

"Okay, then, what?" Gilbert gave me a hard look.

"There's no way I'm staying out here in the wilderness alone. That's how those women in horror movies get killed. They split up." I gave him a serious look. "You have a gun. And while bloodhounds aren't known for protection, I know Bailey would take on a bobcat, a yeti, or an armed killer. He'd tackle whatever threat came my way. So, there's no way that I'm parting from either one of you."

"I could give you my gun." He grinned.

"So I could shoot myself in the foot? No, thank you. I'll pass." I stretched my calf out and bounced around like a boxer before a fight. "I can do this. I just needed to catch my breath. And, Gilbert, even though I know you would never actually give me your gun, I do appreciate you lying to make me feel better."

He scratched his chin. "That obvious?"

"Yep, but I appreciate it. Now, let's keep moving." I clapped my hands together.

"You sure?" he asked.

Are you serious? Of course not. I'm lying through my teeth.

"Yeah. I'm sure. Let's go."

You're not the only one who can lie when needed.

Just as we started to move, Gilbert's radio squawked. A half second later, my radio did the same.

There were lots of voices that were choppy and full of static.

"Repeat," Gilbert said.

"Found . . . Body . . . Man."

Chapter 32

"Is he alive?" Gilbert waited several beats and repeated his question. *"Is he alive?"*

We waited for several seconds but got no response.

"Come on. Let's go." Gilbert had to give Bailey a couple of tugs before he was willing to let go of whatever scent he was on and obey. Bloodhounds could be stubborn, but then so are policemen. Eventually, we convinced Bailey to come with us. He wasn't happy about it, but he trotted along.

When we got closer to the house, we saw flashing lights and a crowd gathered toward the east, the original direction Gilbert had wanted Bailey to go. He returned Bailey's leash and then took off at a run toward the activity. Bailey and I followed at a slower pace. Eventually, we got to the edge of the crowd.

I glanced around until I found Hilda and Teddy. I made my way toward them.

"Did Teddy find him?" I asked.

Hilda nodded and then bent down and scratched her Lab's ear. "He did. He's such a good boy."

"Was he . . . you know."

"He's alive. At least, he was when we found him. Officer Rodriguez called for an ambulance. The EMTs have been checking him out," Hilda said.

"Poor Chelsea. She and David Townsend really seemed serious," I said.

Something over my shoulder caught Hilda's attention.

I turned to look and saw Chelsea Baxter running full steam toward us. Marcie was following her.

"Uh-oh," I said.

When Chelsea reached the crowd, she shoved and pushed until she made her way to the inner circle. A policeman tried to grab her, but he must not have expected Chelsea to put up much resistance, because she was able to easily shove him aside.

Red-faced, the officer rushed to get back in the fray. This time, he was ready and made sure he had a firm grip on Chelsea.

"David," Chelsea screamed.

"You can't help feeling sorry for her." Marcie stood next to me.

Gilbert rushed ahead to help his officer and talk to Chelsea. I'm not sure what he said, but whatever he said was the final straw. Chelsea's knees gave way, and she collapsed on the ground in a heap.

Gilbert scooped her up and carried her over to a gurney.

He deposited her and then whispered to one of the EMTs who had come over to help. He looked up and our eyes met.

I wasn't expecting to talk to him. He definitely had his hands full. I turned to Marcie. "Let's go back in the house."

We headed toward the house. I heard my name and stopped.

Chief Morgan rushed to me. "Hey, this is a big mess and I could be tied up for a while. If I get someone to bring Chelsea back to the house, do you think your aunt Agatha would . . ."

"Of course, but you don't think Chelsea'll have to go to the hospital?"

"There's nothing wrong with her except nerves. She got herself worked up and then the shock . . . well, she just needs to be warm. Maybe a tranquilizer." Chief Morgan ran his hand through his hair.

"It had to be horrible stumbling across the body of the man you love like that." I shivered.

Chief Morgan turned. "What are you talking about?"

"Isn't he dead?" Marcie asked.

"No. And that's not David Townsend," Chief Morgan added.

"Not David?" Marcie asked.

Chief Morgan shook his head.

"Then who is it?" I asked.

"Hudson. Edward Townsend's valet," Chief Morgan said.

Chapter 33

*C*helsea was revived enough to refuse to go to the hospital. She was weak, but she mustered up enough energy to walk back to the house with assistance. She went to her bedroom and slammed the door. When Aunt Agatha and Mrs. Claymore knocked to check on her, she had refused to unlock the door. However, she must not have realized whom she was dealing with. Aunt Agatha wasn't going to take *no* without a fight.

Aunt Agatha reminded Chelsea that she was a guest in this house and that Mrs. Claymore, the housekeeper, had keys to every room. She also reminded her that they had been told to check on her, and that was exactly what she intended to do. So, Chelsea could stop acting like a spoiled prima donna. She knew the Baxter family, and she knew their parents had raised both Whitney and Chelsea to know how to behave in someone else's home. She could pretend like she had good manners and unlock the door, or they would unlock it and fulfill their assignment.

Chelsea unlocked the door.

Aunt Agatha entered, not in her wheelchair, and left a tray with hot tea on the nightstand. She informed Chelsea that Peter Alexander had been sent to get Dr. Williams.

Then she turned and limped out with barely a backward glance.

Marcie and I sat in the kitchen, drinking hot tea and updating Aunt Agatha.

"Hudson. Why would anyone hurt him?" I asked.

"Maybe they mistook him for David Townsend?" Marcie said.

Aunt Agatha limped around the kitchen in her compression boot.

"There is a resemblance, but why would they want to kill David Townsend?"

Marcie gave me a look that said, *Duh.*

"Okay, stupid question." I frowned and tried to make sense out of everything going through my head. "Why was Hudson driving David Townsend's car? And why would he have David Townsend's cell phone?"

"No idea. Maybe David Townsend asked him to bring his car around?" Marcie suggested.

"Ha! Not likely." Olivia Green was in the back corner of the kitchen. She'd been so quiet that I had forgotten she was there until she spoke.

All conversation stopped and all eyes focused on her. She must have felt the awkward silence because she blushed.

"I know it's not easy to make a Black woman blush," Aunt Agatha said. "But you're blushing."

"I'm sorry," Olivia Green said.

I was glad to see that I wasn't the only person who over-apologized. "Sounds like you know something," I said.

"Spill it." Marcie propped her head in her hand and gazed up at Olivia Green.

Mrs. Green fidgeted. "I didn't mean to interrupt your conversation. I shouldn't have been listening, but—"

"Now, you just cut that out right now." Aunt Agatha hobbled over to the table and sat down, propping her leg onto a chair. "This conversation wasn't secret. If it was, we would've gone someplace private. You're welcome to join in on this or any other conversations we have in here. Now, sit down and tell us what you know."

Olivia Green hesitated for several beats. Then she wiped her hands on a towel and sat at the kitchen table. "I really shouldn't have said anything. I hardly know Mr. David, but . . . well, when he got here from Australia, one of the first things he said he needed was a car." She kept her gaze focused on the table.

"Well, I suppose he didn't want to get trapped out here in the country without transportation. It's very isolated," I said.

"Edward had a chauffeur who took him around, didn't he?" Aunt Agatha asked.

Olivia Green nodded. "Yes, and Mr. Edward told him he could have Hudson drive him anywhere he wanted to go, but Mr. David laughed and said, 'No offense, old boy, but I don't need that mortician driving me around in your hearse.'"

"That was rude," Marcie said.

"Definitely bad manners," Aunt Agatha agreed.

"That's what I thought, too. But then Mr. Edward picks up the telephone and calls his friend at the bank and tells him he wants to set up a line of credit. His grandson needed a car, and he was to go pick out what he wanted and have the bank pay for it."

Aunt Agatha whistled. "How long had David been here?"

"Only a couple of days, but Mr. Edward wanted someone to shower his money on. He wanted David to be his grandson," Olivia Green said.

"Wow. It must be nice," Marcie said.

"No limits?" I asked.

She shook her head. "No limits."

"I'm guessing he bought an expensive convertible," I said.

"Natalie Evans drove him to River Bend that very afternoon and he came back driving a cherry red Mercedes-Benz convertible," Olivia said.

"I take it he didn't allow anyone else to drive it," I said.

"Not likely, and he certainly wouldn't have let Hudson drive it," she said. "He didn't like Hudson or Andrew Hicks."

"Why do you say their names together like that?" I asked.

"Well, Hudson and Andrew Hicks were close," Olivia said.

"You mean, they were lovers?" Marcie asked.

"No. I don't think so. I just meant they were close—drinking and gambling buddies. Andrew Hicks was a drunk and a womanizer. He used to come home in the early morning drunk as a skunk and stinking up the place with cheap perfume. Mary Elizabeth would stay here at the house until he came home and sometimes, he wouldn't come home at all. I don't know about Hudson. Personally, I think he has a crush on that female pariah, Natalie Evans."

"I wonder how Hudson's blood got in David Townsend's car." That's when it hit me. "How do we know it was Hudson's blood in the first place? David is still missing."

"Lord, don't tell me we have more injured people stumbling around this place." Aunt Agatha fanned herself. "I'll be glad when we go home."

"I thought you wanted to come to this mansion. Don't tell me you're ready to go home already?" Marcie teased.

"Too many people and too much going on in these big houses for me. I'll take my old house in town, thank you very much." Aunt Agatha sipped her tea.

"Well, we should be going home tonight. I mean, Gilbert only asked us to watch Hannah for the sleepover. Tomorrow's Monday and the girls will be back in school." I wondered if Gilbert would be able to leave with two murders, two injured men, and a missing person. Yikes, Aunt Agatha was right. There was a lot going on here.

Peter Alexander returned with Dr. Williams. Aunt Agatha rose to show him to Chelsea's room.

"I can show him the way. You rest your leg." Marcie stood up.

"She's being difficult and might need a little coercing to get her to behave. I better go." Aunt Agatha limped her way out of the kitchen and Dr. Williams followed.

Peter Alexander hesitated a moment and then turned to go, but I stopped him. "Peter, would you mind answering a few questions?"

He sat down. "More questions for the next Bailey the Bloodhound, Pet Detective, book?"

"No, actually I've been thinking about David Townsend. Now that Edward Townsend's death has been labeled a homicide, they'll run all kinds of tests. I was wondering if you think they could still check David Townsend's DNA against Edward's to determine if he's the true heir. Do you know?"

He thought for a minute. "I'm sure it's possible. Like you said, they can use DNA on mummies that have been buried for thousands of years. But they would need David Townsend's DNA for testing. And isn't he missing?"

"He is, but couldn't they use the blood from his car?" I asked.

"If they know it's his blood." Peter Alexander promised to contact his friends overseas. After Edward Townsend's death, he hadn't pursued the identity confirmation further. However, he was going to reach out.

Olivia Green, Marcie, Aunt Agatha, and I sat at the table after Peter left. It was warm, peaceful, and comforting. Aunt Agatha had supervised the making of apple turnovers and the kitchen smelled of cinnamon and spice.

"What are you thinking about so intensely?" Aunt Agatha finally asked me.

"Nothing," I said too quickly.

"'The lady doth protest too much,'" Marcie said, quoting *Hamlet*.

"She sure does. Now, what's got you worrying your bottom lip?" Aunt Agatha asked.

"Nothing." I felt the heat rush to my face. I knew I wasn't very convincing, so I decided to come clean and confess. "It's just all this talk about DNA testing made me wonder about . . . well, my identity."

"What do you mean? You know who your parents were." Aunt Agatha frowned.

"I know, but I don't know much . . . anything about my dad's family. I've always wondered who they were. And . . ."

"And why they never came to see you?" Marcie reached out a hand and squeezed mine.

I nodded. "I know my dad was white and my mom was Black. I always wondered if that had something to do with why they never tried to find me."

Aunt Agatha took a deep breath. "Child, I don't know. Your momma and daddy met in Africa. It was so far away, and the village was remote. They didn't have regular mail. It took months to get one word from her. The only information we had was what we learned from the missionaries that brought you home to us from the convent."

"Convent?" Olivia asked.

"My parents were volunteers in the Peace Corps. My mom went to school to be a teacher and then joined the

Peace Corps and went off to Africa. That's where she met my dad. He was a doctor."

Aunt Agatha nodded and continued. "They got married over there. It took so long for the letters to arrive, that by the time we finally got them, months had already passed. We would get a stack of letters at once and would check the dates and read them in order." She looked back in time and smiled. "Though the last group of letters were the ones where your mom was worried. Disease had broken out in the village. They thought it was cholera or smallpox, but . . . who knows. Anyway, they were worried about you." She patted my hand and formed a smile with her lips that never reached her eyes. "Your dad wrote that he wanted both you and your mom to return to the States. He was the only doctor for miles. He wouldn't leave. And your mom wouldn't leave him." She was quiet for a few moments and tears ran down her cheeks. "We tried reaching the American embassy, but it was so far from the village that they didn't know anything, either. All they could tell us was that no one matching their descriptions had survived. We thought we'd lost all three of you." She choked up.

I wrapped my arms around her, and we cried. After several moments, she patted my arm and pulled herself together.

Marcie handed us all paper towels.

"It was three months later that we got a letter from a nun at a convent. Your parents wanted you to be safe, so they made arrangements for a missionary to bring you home to Crosbyville. When your mama died, it 'bout killed your grandmother. Then she learned you were alive, and she was on a mission." She chuckled. "She called that embassy every day asking about you and trying to get word to the convent. They worked on getting all your paperwork so that you could travel. Finally, we got word that you were on your way home. That was the spark that rejuvenated your grandmother." She stared at me. "You look just like your mother. I see her whenever you smile."

"That's so sad." Olivia wiped her eyes, which were red from crying.

"And no one from my dad's family ever reached out?" I asked.

"Not that I know of. We have his name from the birth documents that they sent you home with. We know your dad's name was Robert Cummings, and he was from New England. Beyond that, we didn't know where to start looking. We kind of thought that maybe someone from his family might try to find you. Maybe he'd told his family more details than what we had. But, Pris, I don't even know if they know that you were born. Or that—"

"Or that I lived."

Chapter 34

We sat in silence for several long seconds, but then Marcie shattered the quiet. "Maybe it's time for you to look for them."

"What do you mean?" I asked.

"You can do one of those DNA tests they advertise on television. Ancestry or 23andMe. You just spit in a test tube and send it off and they can help find your relatives," Marcie said.

"I've thought about it, but . . ."

"But, what?" Marcie asked.

"What if they haven't reached out for a reason? What if they knew about me, but didn't care? What if they didn't want to be found?"

Bailey ambled over from the corner near the stove where he was curled up, and put his head in my lap.

"Then, you will know the truth and you will have clo-sure," Aunt Agatha said.

"Maybe you could hire that private detective," Olivia said.

We turned to stare at her.

"What?"

"I'm sorry." She blushed. "There I go butting into other people's conversations again. I'm going to learn to keep my big mouth shut."

"No." I reached out and hugged her. "You're right. I don't know why I didn't think of that myself. I could hire Peter Alexander to look for them. That way, if . . ."

"If they don't want to connect, then he can tell you." Marcie finished my thought.

I nodded.

"That's a darned good idea." Aunt Agatha patted Olivia Green's hand. "As my mom would have said, 'That's using your head for more than just a hat rack.'"

I promised to consult Peter Alexander tomorrow about possibly hiring him to find my father's family. Marcie wanted me to do it now, but I pushed back. She knew me well enough to know that I was waffling from fear of hearing that they weren't interested in getting to know me. But she backed down when I explained that I wanted to discuss things with Gilbert first.

Afterward, we spent time surfing the web, comparing DNA companies' promises. *Find relatives. Learn how your DNA can influence your health. Build your family tree.* Prices varied along with the claims that each company promised to deliver. In the end, I was more confused than before I started and put down my phone.

"Where're the girls?" I asked.

"Tabby and Carla took them to enjoy the last day of the festival." Marcie glanced at her watch.

"Didn't want them around with all of this craziness." Aunt Agatha waved a hand.

"We should probably text them and let them know that it's safe to come back." Marcie pulled out her phone and got busy.

"What time do you plan to go home?" Aunt Agatha asked.

"Will we get to go home?" Marcie asked.

"School starts tomorrow. The girls need to go," I said.

"I need to go, too. I have to work," Marcie said.

"It'll be good for them to get away from all of this, even if it's only for a few hours. Hannah and Clarice can go home, but what about Mary Elizabeth?" Aunt Agatha asked.

"How is Andrew Hicks doing?" I asked.

"Recovering. He's still sore. The doctor gave him tranquilizers, but I'm not sure that was a good idea." Aunt Agatha pursed her lips.

"Why not? He's got to be in a lot of pain. He was beat up pretty badly," I said.

"Because he's a weak man." Aunt Agatha must have noticed how confused we were because she continued. "I don't mean physically weak, although he is. I mean he's weak mentally and emotionally. He needs a crutch to keep him on the straight and narrow. Without the crutch to lean on, he falls off the wagon. He falls for cheap women. He falls for liquor. And he falls for gambling. He's too vulnerable to handle tranquilizers. You mark my words. Those pills will be just one more crutch."

We sat in silence for a beat. Then there was a slow clap.

We turned and, leaning against the doorway was Andrew Hicks.

His face was purple from bruises. His eyes were red. Any exposed skin that wasn't bruised was pale.

"What are you doing up? You're supposed to be resting," Aunt Agatha said.

"You're right." Andrew Hicks coughed. His body shook and he looked as though he would collapse.

Afraid that he would fall, Marcie and I ran to support him. We eased him over to a chair.

"You look like death warmed over." Aunt Agatha poured a cup of tea and handed it to Andrew Hicks.

He chuckled. "Rode hard and put away wet?"

"If that means you're looking raggedy, then, yes." Aunt Agatha turned to Marcie. "Can you find Mrs. Claymore and ask her for a blanket?"

Marcie left in search of the housekeeper.

"Now, what brings you in here? You're supposed to be asleep. That's why the doctor gave you those pills, isn't it?"

"You mean these?" Andrew Hicks put his hand into his pocket and pulled out a handful of pills and dropped them onto the table.

We stared at the pile of pills.

"You're right." He looked at Aunt Agatha. "I am weak.

That's why I didn't take those pills. I knew if I did, I wouldn't be able to stop."

"But, you must be in excruciating pain," I said.

"Nah. Not really. This is just physical pain. I can handle physical pain. It's the"—he turned to Aunt Agatha—"what did you call it? Mental and emotional pain? That's what I can't deal with."

Aunt Agatha was tough on the outside, but inside she was a softie. I could see that Andrew Hicks had gotten past her exterior and had touched her soft insides.

"You need your strength. Olivia, make him some eggs and toast."

"I'm not hungry," Andrew Hicks said.

"Did I ask you?" Aunt Agatha said.

"No, ma'am." Andrew gave a sheepish grin.

"Humph." Aunt Agatha poured more tea and fussed over Andrew Hicks for several moments. "And don't think I don't see what you're doing, either."

"What am I doing?" he asked innocently.

"Charming me the way you charm your way with all those loose women in town." Aunt Agatha got a slice of apple pie and warmed it in the microwave for a few seconds. Then she placed it in front of Andrew Hicks. "Eat that."

Andrew winked at me. He picked up his fork and ate his pie. "Hmm. This is good. Although, it would be better if I had a cup of coffee instead of this tea."

"Caffeine isn't good for someone in your condition." Aunt Agatha fussed while she got up and made a cup of coffee for Andrew in the single-cup coffeemaker.

Andrew Hicks ate in silence.

Marcie returned and wrapped a blanket around his shoulders. If he considered objecting, one glance at Aunt Agatha squelched it.

When Andrew was done eating apple pie, toast, and scrambled eggs with coffee, he leaned back in his chair. "That was good stuff." He patted his stomach.

"Now, maybe you can answer some questions," Aunt Agatha said.

Hicks raised an eyebrow but remained silent.

"Who beat the tar out of you?" Aunt Agatha asked.

"I owed some men money, and I couldn't pay it back."

"Gambling?" Aunt Agatha asked.

He nodded. "I thought I had come into a pile of dough, but . . ."

That's when the light bulb went on for me. "But my dog, Bailey, found it?"

He glanced down at Bailey and then reached out a hand and patted him on the head. "You just had to go digging under that boathouse?"

Bailey placed his head in Andrew Hicks's lap.

"You're a good boy, aren't you? You saved me."

Bailey gave a quick "Woof."

"Saved you?" I asked.

"I've done a lot of things. Your aunt was right. I gamble. I drink. I chase women. But, I've never stolen anything in my life. Not until I saw all that money. Edward Townsend had so much, and I needed it so badly, that I convinced myself he wouldn't miss it. I convinced myself that he owed it to Mary Elizabeth. She was an heir and she was entitled to some of the money. He was going to leave her something in his will. This was just an advance."

"But even if Edward Townsend intended to leave money to Mary Elizabeth, what does that have to do with you?" Aunt Agatha asked.

"I convinced myself that Mary Elizabeth would have shared with me." He shrugged. "I even convinced myself that I could win it playing poker. Then, I wouldn't need Mary Elizabeth's money. I could win it myself and put the money back. Anything over the fifty thousand dollars would be mine. I just needed the fifty grand as seed money." He shook his head. "I know it wasn't right, but I was weak." He looked at Aunt Agatha.

"Where did you get the money?" I asked.

"I found it."

"Where?" I asked.

"It was in a pillowcase. Shoved under some boxes in the old dairy. Somebody else clearly stole the money from Edward Townsend, and I stole the money from thieves." He chuckled.

We questioned Hicks a bit longer, but he claimed he had no idea who put the money in the pillowcase or how the pillowcase got into the dairy. His eyelids drooped and he looked tired.

"That's enough. You need your rest," Aunt Agatha said.

Andrew Hicks didn't argue. He merely thanked Aunt Agatha for the food and stood up.

He looked weak, physically weak, so Marcie and I helped him back to bed.

"Do you believe him?" Marcie asked the group when we returned.

"Mostly." I nodded. "I believe he found the money and thought he could take it, so he buried it under the boathouse. But . . ."

"But?" Aunt Agatha asked.

"But I think he knows who put it there. Or he at least suspects who put it there. And I think that knowledge is dangerous."

"You think whoever stole the money beat him up?" Marcie asked.

"No. I think he was telling the truth when he said the people he owed money to beat him up. But I think that he knows or suspects who stole it, and if the person who stole the money believes that Andrew took it, then I think he could still be in danger."

Chapter 35

*C*arla, Tabby, and the girls rushed into the kitchen full of energy and excitement.

"OMG! We just heard that Taylor Swift is doing a virtual concert tonight!" Mary Elizabeth screamed.

"Please tell me I can go?" Hannah held her hands together as she pleaded.

"What's a virtual concert?" Aunt Agatha asked.

"We have to go. I need to ask Chelsea right now. I'll just die if I can't go." Clarice headed for the door, but we stopped her.

"Hold on. Chelsea's not feeling well. She's resting," Aunt Agatha said. "And somebody needs to tell me what exactly is a virtual concert?"

"She's doing a live concert in Paris and it's going to be

live streamed in theaters around the world," Mary Elizabeth explained.

"It'll be almost like we were right there with her in person!" Hannah screamed.

"And one of those theaters is in Crosbyville?" I asked.

"No. Crosbyville's too small," Clarice said.

"It's going to be at the ACC at the University of Our Mother," Hannah said.

The University of Our Mother by the Lake was not only a large, prestigious Catholic university in the nearby town of River Bend, Indiana. It also happened to be my alma mater. The Athletic and Convocation Center, or ACC, was where the Fighting Leprechauns played basketball. It was also easily adaptable for concerts. I remember going to see concerts by *NSYNC, Destiny's Child, and Outkast in the same venue.

"That's great, but won't you need tickets?" I asked.

The girls pointed to Carla.

"Actually, my CPA firm got twenty tickets. My boss paid a small fortune and bought six of them awhile back. However, his entire family came down with the stomach flu and he can't go. So, he said the tickets are mine if I want them." Carla held up her cell phone. "I just need to let him know, and they'll be waiting at the box office for us."

The girls all screamed.

"Actually, I think it would be great for the girls to get away for a bit. Things are rather hectic—"

The screams that followed were so loud that no one could hear, so I stopped talking.

"What are you going to wear?"

"Tabby, will you do our makeup?" Clarice asked.

"Makeup?" I looked at Tabby.

"Glitter. I'm afraid it's the trend." Tabby shrugged.

"Please?" Hannah begged.

Gilbert is going to kill me.

"Leave it to me. I'll take care of the makeup, and they will still look like little girls. Scout's honor." Tabby held up three fingers.

I glanced at Aunt Agatha. She nodded.

"Okay," I said.

"Hey, I have one extra ticket if one of you wants to join the fun." Carla held up her phone to Marcie and me.

I glanced at Marcie. She wouldn't admit to anyone else that she was a Taylor Swift fan, but I knew my best friend.

"Well, as long as you have an extra ticket." She stood up. "I'm going to need to go home and find something to wear."

I tossed her my car keys. Tabby left to grab her makeup kit, and Marcie followed her out the door.

The girls screamed and ran back to the bedroom to get dressed.

After they left, the quiet in the kitchen was deafening.

"I should go up and make sure Chelsea's okay with Clarice going to the concert." I stood.

"Don't bother. I'll take her a tray of soup and tell her." Aunt Agatha stood and went over to the stove.

"I'm going to the library. I've wanted to spend time in that room ever since I got here." I stood. "Come on, Bailey."

The room was as lovely and relaxing as I remembered. I

stood inside the doorway and inhaled. The aroma of lemon-scented furniture polish, leather, and pine wafted up to my nose and filled my insides. I felt my heart rate slow down and a warm glow filled my insides. I looked at the hundreds of books that lined the walls and my lips curled up into a smile. This was my happy place. For a moment, standing there looking at the wonderful world of people and exciting new places that each book represented, I wanted to spread my arms wide, spin around in a circle, and sing like Julie Andrews at the start of *The Sound of Music*.

Instead of singing, I rushed to the bookshelves and ran my hands up and down the spines. I read the titles. The Works of Charles Dickens, *David Copperfield*. My heart skipped a beat and I gasped. The next book was *Oliver Twist*. *OMG! He has them all*. I quickly scanned the titles. I counted thirty-four total. I opened one of the covers and noted the date. These weren't the original printings but were published by Charles Scribner's Sons in 1907. The spines were cracked. The corners were worn, and the pages were yellowed from age and usage, the way well-read books should look. These weren't just books purchased by the yard to fill the shelves of a stately home. These books had been read and enjoyed throughout the years. I sniffed the pages. There was a slight musky smell that I loved. I pulled the books close to my chest and gave them a hug.

"Do you need a moment alone with those?"

I nearly dropped the books I was hugging as I swung around.

Gilbert stood in the doorway, grinning at me.

"I love this room. I could live here in this one room forever. All I'll need is someone to bring food in for me and Bailey."

He glanced around the room at all the books. "It's a nice room. I like the wood."

"How is Hudson?" I asked.

Gilbert stretched. "He'll live. He got cracked on the head pretty hard. He's probably got a concussion, but he refused to go to the hospital, so . . ." He shrugged.

"Can't you make him go?" I asked.

"Nope. Every person has the right to refuse medical treatment." He yawned.

His eyelids looked droopy and the lines across his forehead were more pronounced.

I replaced the books I'd been holding and walked over to him. I wrapped my arms around him and gave him a big warm hug.

He hugged me back.

I gazed up at him. "You look exhausted. When did you sleep last?"

He pondered the question for a few seconds then shook his head. "I have no idea. What day is it?"

I gave him a lecture about taking care of himself. It was the same lecture I'd given him many times before. He stifled a yawn and nodded in the appropriate places. The next yawn would not be contained.

"You're right. I haven't gotten enough sleep. I'm not taking care of myself." He grinned. "But you can hug me all you want."

"Are you sure you have the energy?" I kidded.

"I think I just got my second wind. Come closer and I'll show you how much energy I have." He pulled me closer and kissed me until I felt as though I were floating.

His radio squawked and this time, I was the one who swore.

He pushed the button. "This better be good."

The radio squawked something I couldn't understand, but Gilbert seemed to hear just fine, and he sighed before speaking into the radio. "I'll be right there." He turned to me. "Hold that thought. This won't take long." He kissed me.

I walked around the room a few minutes, but as his absence continued, I decided to make the best of the time I had alone in the library.

I checked out the furniture to determine which would be the comfiest reading spot. The sofa was closest to the fireplace, but there was an overstuffed chair in a corner with a floor lamp and side table nearby. The chair was perfect for tucking my legs up. So, I removed my shoes and did just that. "I don't think Edward Townsend will mind. Do you?" I asked Bailey.

However, my dog wasn't paying me any attention. Instead of curling up by my feet or even trying to climb into the chair with me, he had wiggled his way in between the chair and the wall. Once he'd gotten his one hundred pounds behind the chair, he started to scratch at the back of the chair.

"Bailey, stop. This isn't our furniture."

He didn't stop but continued to scratch.

I knew dogs scratching and digging at their bedding was supposedly an evolutionary behavior. My dog trainer said it stemmed from their desire to create a comfortable place to sleep. However, there were lots of comfortable places for him to curl up and take a nap without destroying furniture.

I got up and came around behind the chair. I grabbed hold of his collar and tugged, but Bailey was being stubborn.

"Okay, if Bailey won't stop scratching the chair, then I guess I better move the chair." I pushed the chair out toward the middle of the room and away from the wall and Bailey.

Moving the chair was harder than I thought. It was a solid, well-built chair. After I got it moved farther away, I saw it had been covering a large book.

I picked up the book. "Someone must have been reading this and forgot to put it back on the shelf." I glanced at the title.

The Holy Bible.

I looked carefully. It was a large, leather-bound book with gold letters. I opened the cover. The first few pages included a record of births, deaths, and the Townsend family genealogy that dated back to Edward Townsend's grandfather, a man named Archibald Townsend.

I wondered if Peter Alexander had looked through the Townsend Family Bible. He mentioned that you could get quite a lot of information from them, and he was right.

I sat down and looked at the names of Edward Townsend's ancestors. "Now, what was it Peter said? Mary Elizabeth's great-grandmother and Edward Townsend's mother were sisters."

Edward Townsend's mother, Grace, had one sister, Elspeth. Elspeth had a daughter, Mary. Mary had a daughter named Amy Elizabeth. "Oh, I'll bet Elspeth was an old-fashioned version of Elizabeth."

Bailey had given up scratching and was sniffing the rug and wasn't listening to me. When I was sure he wasn't intent on damaging the expensive rug, I returned to my research.

"There's no entry for Mary Elizabeth, but I'll bet she was named after her grandmother and her great-grandmother."

Bailey continued sniffing.

I looked at Edward Townsend's entries. Edward and Frederick were Grace and William's sons. Edward married Mary Alice and they had one son, James. James had one son, David. Frederick also had one son, Harold. Harold had one son, Jonathan. "That would make David and Jonathan cousins," I said to Bailey. He didn't bother looking up from his sniffing.

David Townsend's parents were James and Clara. There were dates for their marriage, the dates of James's birth and also of his death. "How sad. I can't imagine how much it must have hurt Edward Townsend to record the date that his only son died."

At the bottom of the page, there were numbers written as if recording a birth date.

50-40-32-23

"That can't be a birth date. The numbers are too big. Besides, it's too many numbers for a birth or death date. Too few numbers for a telephone or social security number." I studied the numbers.

Bailey's nose was fixed on a portion of the wall behind where the chair had been. He was standing on his hind legs and scratching at the woodwork.

"Oh no, you don't. Down." I put down the Bible and got up to pull my dog out of the room if necessary. As I put the book in my chair, a photo fluttered to the floor.

I picked it up and glanced at it without reading it, but then stuck it in my book and hurried to prevent my dog from destroying this lovely mahogany-paneled wood.

"Bailey, off. If you scratch that wall, I'll—"

I never finished declaring what I would do. In that instant, I heard a click and then a loud squeak. The wooden panel swung back, and the wall opened. I stood in complete astonishment and stared at the hidden door that had just opened before my eyes.

I stared at Bailey. "Holy secret rooms, Batman."

Chapter 36

I stood outside the secret room and texted Gilbert. Then I paced as Bailey explored inside. The room wasn't large. In fact, it was the size of a coat closet, but once inside, Bailey was distracted by something stuck under the floorboards. Closer examination showed that the wood boards could easily be shoved aside, uncovering a hole in the ground. The hole led down a flight of old stairs into an underground tunnel. There was something exciting about finding the secret room behind the bookshelf. My inner book nerd was thrilled.

However, I drew the line at exploring secret tunnels. Images of spiders, bats, and rats filled my brain, and no amount of coaxing would get me down those stairs.

After getting my text, Gilbert was able to leave the investigation and came back with a flashlight. He didn't have any qualms about going down the stone stairs, but I knew he wasn't a huge fan of snakes. I prayed he wouldn't find any, but at least if he did, he was armed. Besides, even though I tried to dissuade him, Bailey followed Gilbert down the stairs. Between the two males in my life, I felt confident they could handle all the creepy things lurking in that tunnel.

The only things either of them brought back up a few minutes later were spiderwebs.

"What's down there?" I asked as I brushed the dust and cobwebs from Gilbert's hair and back.

"Nothing. It's just a cold, dark room."

"It looks like pictures I've seen of priest holes."

"What's a priest hole?" Gilbert asked.

"It might not be a priest hole. It could just be a secret room, but I wonder why Edward Townsend needed a priest hole. Or a secret room, for that matter."

"What's a priest hole?" Gilbert asked again.

"Just what it sounds like." I did a quick Google search. "They apparently started in Great Britain during the reign of Queen Elizabeth I. Some Catholic priests plotted to have her ousted from power."

"When was that?"

"Late fifteen hundreds, early sixteen hundreds."

"You're joking."

I shook my head. "Nope. Needless to say, the Crown wasn't thrilled with these priests. The queen didn't like attempts to remove her from power so she retaliated. It was a dangerous time for Catholics, but especially for Catholic priests. I'm afraid she was rather brutal. Priests were tortured and imprisoned, some were even killed. Just because the head of the monarchy and the church was Protestant, didn't mean that all British citizens immediately converted from Catholicism. The struggle went on for years. Some rulers were less violent than others and priests were relatively safe. Other times, not so much. During the period when they were being persecuted, wealthy Catholics built secret rooms where priests or influential Catholics could hide. Hence the name 'priest holes.'"

"But that was hundreds of years ago and in Britain. What's a priest hole doing in Crosbyville, Indiana? As far as I remember from history class, Catholics never had to hide in the United States," Gilbert said.

"True." I shrugged. "I suppose it could have been used for hiding other things."

"Like what?" he asked.

"Maybe escaped slaves on the Underground Railroad? Liquor during Prohibition?"

"Is the house old enough to have been around during slavery?" Gilbert asked.

"I don't think so. I think it's more likely to have been built during Prohibition. Of course, it could just have been something that he did because he wanted to hide important papers, money, gold, or whatever."

"Gold? Like in gold bullion?" He chuckled. "I think you've been reading too many pirate novels."

"Seriously, after the Great Depression, lots of people didn't trust banks. It's possible that someone like Edward

Townsend might have kept large sums of money in his house."

"That's not a bad idea."

"While you and Bailey were checking out the tunnel, I explored the smaller room and noticed something." I walked back into the secret room.

Gilbert followed me.

I pointed to a camera on the wall. The camera on the inside of the room lined up perfectly with a wall sconce on the outside. From the outside, all you saw was the light fixture. Directly opposite the light on the inside of the room was the camera. There was a hole cut through the wall. Unless you were looking for the lens, you wouldn't have noticed it if you were standing in the office.

"Clever, but not that surprising." He shrugged. "Lots of people have concealed cameras in their homes. Maybe he was trying to catch the staff pocketing the silver."

"True, but this is hidden in his office, nowhere near the valuable silverware."

Gilbert stepped back inside the room and closed the door so he could look at the trajectory of the camera. "Interesting. It's pointed at his desk and that painting."

"Maybe there's something more valuable in the study than in the kitchen." He stuck his head out of the door and looked around the room again. "Some of those books could be rare, signed first editions. Or, that painting might be a Picasso or Rembrandt worth millions."

"You have a point about the books. I'll bet some of them

are valuable, but I can't see a book thief breaking in and stealing them, can you?"

"Hard to smuggle out unless you came with a suitcase."

"As for the painting." I squinted at the painting that was in the direct path of the camera. "I'm not an art expert, but it doesn't look valuable to me. Maybe Marcie could tell us, but I'm sure of one thing. It is *not* a Picasso. Still . . . why hide the camera? Nothing would deter a thief more than an obvious camera."

He opened the door and walked over to the painting. He examined it for a few moments and then pulled the frame forward. The painting was on a hinge and opened like a medicine cabinet. Behind the frame was a wall safe. "Bingo!"

Chapter 37

*O*pening the safe of a dead man isn't easy. At least, it's not easy for the police. Gilbert made a phone call to the district attorney and learned that he would need a court order to get into Edward Townsend's safe.

"What about David Townsend?" I asked.

"He hasn't officially been named as Edward Townsend's legal heir, but since Edward Townsend had a trust, and he named your aunt Agatha as executor, she should be able to open the safe," Gilbert explained.

"That's all good and fine, but I don't know the combination," Aunt Agatha said from the doorway.

That's when my mind went back to the numbers I'd found earlier in the Townsend family Bible. I hurried back to the chair and picked up the book. I flipped to the front.

"Don't tell me you have a sudden overwhelming desire to read the Bible?" Gilbert joked.

I pointed to the numbers at the bottom of the page. "You don't suppose this could be the combination, do you?"

Gilbert frowned. "Maybe, but why write it in the Bible?"

"Lawd, with all the PIN numbers, passwords, and security codes folks have to remember nowadays, you have to write 'em down somewhere." Aunt Agatha chuckled. "The family Bible is probably the safest place."

"What do you mean?" Gilbert asked.

"What criminal planning to steal from you is going to take the time to stop, open the Bible, and read?" I asked.

"Good point," Gilbert said. He carried the heavy book to the safe. He reached out a hand but stopped before spinning the dial. "I should wait until the court order comes giving me permission to open the safe."

"Pshaw." Aunt Agatha limped over to the safe. "I don't need to wait. Edward Townsend named me his executor. I'm opening the safe." She glanced into the book and then turned to me. "Pris, you read those numbers off."

I glanced over Gilbert's shoulder and did as I was instructed. "Fifty. Forty. Thirty-two. Twenty-three."

Aunt Agatha spun the dial toward the right. Then left. Right. And left. Aunt Agatha tried to open the safe, but it wouldn't unlock. She repeated the steps again and again. Still, the safe wouldn't open. She turned to me. "Do you want to try? Maybe I did something wrong."

"No. I watched. You didn't do anything wrong." I bit my

lower lip and tried to hide my disappointment. "I guess I was wrong. This must not be the combination to the safe."

Gilbert stared at the safe. "No, I think you're right. I think this is the combination."

"Then why won't it open? What am I doing wrong?" Aunt Agatha asked.

"I had a case a few months ago . . . guy had a safe just like this. We got a court order and waited for a locksmith to open it. It was tricky." He studied the safe closely. "Turns out, there's a trick to opening this type of safe."

"What kind of trick?" I asked.

Gilbert turned to Aunt Agatha. "Are you willing to consent to my opening this safe?"

"Have at it." Aunt Agatha waved her hand.

"Pris, would you record this?" Gilbert asked.

I pulled out my phone and swiped until I got the camera. I pointed it at him and recorded. He repeated his request for consent to open the safe to Aunt Agatha. When she agreed and stated her name, Gilbert turned the dial to the left four times.

"Counterclockwise?" I asked.

"Yeah, most locks start the opposite way. Clockwise. Plus, you have to pass the first number four times. What's the next number?"

I told him and he spun the dial clockwise three times and then stopped on the second number, Forty. We repeated the process for the last two numbers. Gilbert alternated between spinning clockwise and counterclockwise and reduced the number of spins as he progressed. So, by the time we got to the last number, twenty-three, he passed it twice and then stopped. When he finished, he slowly turned the dial to the left until it wouldn't turn any more. Then he turned the handle under the dial.

There was a satisfying double click, and Gilbert swung the door open.

"Wow. That's amazing," Aunt Agatha said.

"Nothing like my gym locker from high school," I said.

"The locksmith called it a high-security mechanical lock."

I held my breath while Gilbert opened the door wide.

Aunt Agatha and I craned our necks to look inside. I held the camera and recorded the contents. Several envelopes and a few pieces of paper were lying loose on top of the envelopes. There was a black jewelry box, a flash drive, and a key.

Gilbert donned a pair of rubber gloves from his pocket and took the items from the safe.

"What's with the gloves?" I asked.

"Edward Townsend was murdered. He had a camera pointed at the safe. The two could be connected. I have no idea. Better safe than sorry," he said.

I looked over his shoulder as he unfolded the papers and glanced through the contents of an envelope.

"Last will and testament." He picked up another envelope. "Marriage certificate for Edward Townsend and Mary Alice Livingston." He pulled out another document. "Birth certificate for James Townsend. Death certificates for Mary Alice and James Townsend." Gilbert placed each document on the desk.

"What's in the box?" Aunt Agatha asked.

Gilbert examined the box. It had a small lock. Too small for the key that was included in the safe. Fortunately, it wasn't locked, and he was able to push a button and open the lid. Inside were several pieces of jewelry. They first examined a woman's ring with one large diamond and a gold wedding band.

"Woman's diamond ring." Gilbert put the ring down and picked up the band. He held it up to the light. "Gold band. Engraved initials, *M.L.* and *E.T.*, along with a date."

He put the ring back and picked up each of the other items. "Diamond earrings. Woman's ring. Ruby with diamonds. Matching ruby bracelet. Ruby earrings. Gold enameled locket with a picture and a lock of hair inside." He named each item before returning it to the box. Then he picked up the key. "One key. One flash drive."

Gilbert glanced around for a computer. "Did you by any chance bring your laptop?"

"It's upstairs." I stopped recording and quickly sent the video to Gilbert. When I heard his phone chime, confirming he'd received it, I headed toward the door. "It'll just take a minute to grab my laptop."

I made it as far as the door when it was suddenly flung open.

Marcie rushed in. "Chelsea's gone."

"Gone? What do you mean gone?" Gilbert switched to Chief Morgan and asked.

"She's not here. She's gone. Her car's gone. She got a call

on her cell and then flew out of here like a bat out of hell. I couldn't stop her."

Peter Alexander followed Marcie inside. "Chelsea's not the only one."

"Who?" Chief Morgan asked.

"Natalie Evans is gone, too."

Chapter 38

*C*hief Morgan swore. Blood rushed up his neck and he looked as though he was ready to explode. He got on his radio and rushed out of the room.

I started to follow but was halted when he stopped and turned.

"No. I need you to put everything back in the safe and close the door."

Aunt Agatha was still in the library. She was sitting in the big comfy chair that I'd occupied earlier. Instead of reading Dickens or the Bible, she was looking at the envelope that was labeled *Last Will and Testament*.

"Gilbert wants me to return everything to the safe." Aunt Agatha handed me the will.

Before adding it to the other items in the safe, I took my phone and used the Notes app on my phone to scan the will.

"What are you doing?" Aunt Agatha asked.

"Scanning it. That way, you can take a look at it later."

"I've already looked at it."

"Okay, then I can take a look at it." I swiped my phone and sent her a copy of the scanned document.

"How did you do that?" she said as she looked at the scanned document.

That was a rhetorical question, so I didn't bother to answer. Instead, I returned the will to the safe, closed the door, and then read Edward Townsend's last will from my phone.

"Nothing shocking. Ten thousand dollars to each of his staff. The housekeeper, Mrs. Claymore. His cook, Mrs. Olivia Green. His chauffeur, and Hudson the valet." I paused. "Hmm."

"What's that supposed to mean?" Aunt Agatha asked. "Ten thousand dollars is a lot of money."

"It is for common folks like you and me, but for someone as rich as Edward Townsend, it doesn't seem like much."

"He didn't have to leave them anything. I mean, he was paying them."

"Oh, I know, and I'm sure it's the thought that counts. It'll come in handy. But . . ."

"But?"

"But, when you've worked for someone rich, I think people may have . . . well, expectations of more."

Aunt Agatha opened her mouth to argue, and I held up a hand to stop her.

"I'm not saying it's right. I mean, it's his money and he can dispose of it however he wants. You're right. He paid them all a salary and, technically, he didn't owe them any-thing. It's just that, in a lot of the manor house mysteries that I read, the relatives and servants all seem to have ex-pectations, and they're willing to kill to get their hands on the money." My brain went back to the four *L*'s. Lust, love, loot, and loathing. I shared it with Aunt Agatha.

Now it was her turn to ponder the implications of Ed-ward Townsend's bequests. "Well, ain't that the truth. The *love* of money could easily cause someone to *loathe* a wealthy relative and *lust* after their *loot*."

"Exactly."

"That's just wrong." She shivered. "The Bible says, 'The love of money is the root of all evil'—1 Timothy 6:10."

I kept reading. "The bulk of his estate is to go to his closest living heir. If no heirs are found, then the estate is to be kept in trust and divided among the following charities." I paused and read down the list. "EQUUS Foun-dation, Thoroughbred Aftercare Alliance, World Horse Welfare, Thoroughbred Charities of America . . . and a host of others. From the sound of these, I think they're all horse related."

"I'm not surprised. Eddie loved horses. He always used to say that the key to his heart and to his wealth was in his horse barn." Aunt Agatha dabbed at her eyes with a hand-kerchief. "But, you're right about the money. Ten thousand dollars isn't much for people who cooked, cleaned, and cared for him when he's leaving money to animals."

"Especially given the size of his estate. According to

Carla, Edward Townsend's estate is worth well over a billion dollars. More like two billion."

"Good Lawd." Aunt Agatha's mouth dropped open. "I had no idea he had that much money. Did you say *billion* with a *B*?"

I nodded. "Yes, and as a trustee, you stand to profit, too."

"Well, I don't want his money. I never did want his money." Aunt Agatha shook her head and twisted her handkerchief. "If I'd wanted his money, I could have married him. Good Lord, that man would ask me just about once a month."

"I didn't know you and Edward Townsend were that close."

"We were good friends back in the day, and that's the end of that." She sniffed and wiped her eyes.

When she was calm, I continued. "Do you want to know how much you'll receive?"

"No, I don't. I don't have to take the money, do I?" She paused. "Although, I suppose, I could donate it to charity or something." She took a deep breath. "I can't imagine he would give the trustees more than the people who worked for him, so maybe a couple thousand dollars could do some good." She took a deep breath. "All right. How much?"

"The trustees get half of one percent of the value of the trust." I watched my aunt's face carefully. I saw the relief cross her brow.

"Well, thank God. I thought you were going to say he left some outrageous amount of money."

It took a great deal of effort, but I controlled my lips. "That half of one percent would equal somewhere around ten million dollars divided three ways, so you would only get a measly three million."

Aunt Agatha must have swallowed because she started to choke and went into a coughing fit.

I hurried over and patted her on the back.

Tears ran down her face and I felt horrible for causing her distress. I ran to the kitchen and came back with a glass of water.

Aunt Agatha was still coughing, but she didn't look as though she would pass out. She sipped the water and gradually, the coughing slowed and eventually stopped. Her hand shook as she drank the water. When she was finished, she stared. "Please tell me you're joking."

"I'm afraid not." I shook my head. "Carla said the estate has to be valued and it could be years before everything is paid out. There's got to be an audit and even though Edward Townsend wanted to avoid probate, the estate will likely have to go through the courts and probate."

"Three million dollars? Pris, what am I supposed to do with all of that money?"

"Enjoy life. You could retire. You've worked hard your entire life. You and Grammy Bell raised me, a child you never planned for. You put me through college and supported me and my crazy dream to write children's books. This is your chance to finally get to focus on yourself. You could hire someone to take over the diner. Travel. Take a cruise around the world." I squeezed her hand. But she was shaking her head before the words were out of my mouth.

"That dang fool. I should've known he'd try to pull something like this." Noting the surprise on my face, Aunt Agatha softened her gaze. "Honey, I know you mean well, but I don't want to retire. I love what I do. I love my diner. I love cooking, and I have plenty of people that I can cook for every day. I enjoyed raising you. You're my family." She caressed my face.

"But, you could do anything you wanted. You'd be free."

"I'm free now." She grunted. "Well, as free as a human has any right to be. No, I don't want the burden of dealing with all of that money, and trust me, that much money would be a burden and not a blessing. It don't seem to have done Eddie much good. Despite all of his money, he didn't have his family around him and had to hire someone to track down what family he had left in the world. It don't look like he had too many friends, either, aside from that Jay Barlow. And now it looks like somebody up and killed him— killed both of them." She shook her head. "Nah, I don't want that kind of trouble. I'll help manage the trust to the best of my ability, but I don't plan to get trapped by all that money."

"I love you." I pulled Aunt Agatha into a hug.

Bailey had been sitting nearby, but when we embraced, he decided to join us. He nudged his muzzle under my arm until he was able to wiggle in between us.

His maneuvering caused me to drop the flash drive that

I had been holding. I picked it up. "I forgot to put this in the safe with the rest of the items." I glanced around. On the floor below the picture, I found the key. "Darn it. This must have fallen, too."

"Gilbert was going to look at that anyway. Maybe you should go bring down your laptop, so when he gets back, he can just pop it in and take a look."

I tilted my head to the side and gave her a hard look.

"What? I'm only thinking about Gilbert."

I suspected that Aunt Agatha's suggestion was due more to nosiness than a desire to save time for Gilbert, but I had to admit that I was nosy, too.

I hopped up and ran upstairs. I grabbed my laptop and quickly returned to the library.

Aunt Agatha tapped her hand on the Bible, which was still in her lap, while we waited for Gilbert to return.

I tried to avoid the appendage hanging off the side of my laptop and focus on other things, but my gaze kept returning to the flash drive. After what felt like an hour, but was actually only a couple of minutes, I gave in. "My laptop may not even be able to read the files. Maybe I should just try and open them to make sure?"

"I thought you'd never ask. Hurry up." Aunt Agatha scooted out of the chair and stood so she could look over my shoulder.

I opened the flash drive.

"What kind of files are those?" Aunt Agatha pointed.

"Movies."

"Movies? Like the kind you see in the theater?"

"I don't think so. The files aren't big enough." I scrolled down the list of file names that appeared to be dates. "The file sizes are small, so if I had to guess, I'd say they were the videos he'd recorded from his camera."

"Oh, good. Let's look at it."

My hand gripped my mouse and the pointer hovered over the file. Bailey had been lying quietly beside the desk, but suddenly, he sat up. Barked. And then trotted out of the room.

A commotion from the hallway stopped my finger from opening the file.

Gilbert was yelling, and my normally docile bloodhound was growling.

I got up and rushed through the door.

Chapter 39

*I*n the hallway, a crowd was gathered. Two EMTs, Hudson, Gilbert, Mrs. Claymore, Olivia Green, Andrew Hicks, and Bailey. Bailey growled and lunged while Gilbert grabbed hold of his collar.

"Bailey. Stop," I yelled.

I hustled over to Gilbert and took control of Bailey's collar. Bailey stopped lunging and buried his growl deep inside his belly. Only when I was standing close to him could I hear it.

"Are you sure you have him?" Gilbert asked, maintaining his grip.

I nodded and he let go.

Bailey was wound up like a top. However, he didn't lunge and the growl was low and contained.

"Now, what's going on?" Chief Morgan scowled at the staff.

Mrs. Claymore and Olivia Green took one look at his face and hurried back toward the kitchen.

One of the EMTs turned to Chief Morgan. "He refused treatment. We just wanted to make sure he got here safe."

Chief Morgan nodded.

The second EMT released his grip on Hudson. "You have a concussion and should go to the hospital and be seen by a doctor. But we can't force you."

"That's right. You can't. Now, leave me alone," Hudson said.

The EMTs exchanged a look with Chief Morgan. He shrugged and they relaxed.

Hudson and Andrew Hicks glared at each other.

Chief Morgan turned to Hicks. "Why are you up?"

It took Hicks so long to answer, I thought he wasn't going to. After what felt like an eternity, he tore his gaze away from Hudson. "I heard his voice. Whoever clubbed him, obviously didn't hit him hard enough. I thought I'd finish the job."

"If you think you're man enough to do the job, then go for it." Hudson took a step forward, but Chief Morgan stepped in between the two men.

Peter Alexander must have been watching and listening from the parlor. He stepped forward. "Can I help?" He locked eyes with Chief Morgan, who made a slight inclination with his head.

Peter moved to Andrew Hicks and took a firm grasp of his arm. "Let me help you back to bed."

Andrew paused for a few moments but then took a step forward. However, the effort must have been too much. He stopped and doubled over in pain.

The EMTs rushed over to help. "Take him to the library. It's the closest place where you can work on him." Chief Morgan nodded toward the library door.

When they were gone, Gilbert turned his attention to the valet. "Now, maybe you can tell me just what you think you're doing?"

Hudson opened his mouth, but suddenly his knees folded.

Gilbert reached him before he collapsed completely. He helped the valet into the library, leaving me and Bailey alone in the hallway.

I glanced down at Bailey. "Listen, I'm not sure what has your hackles up, but cut it out. Now isn't the time."

Bailey sat and looked up at me.

"Don't give me that innocent look."

He snorted and gave his head a shake.

"Pris, who are you talking to?" Gilbert came back into the hall.

"Bailey." No use pretending I didn't talk to my dog. Gilbert knew better. "How are they? Hudson and Andrew Hicks?"

"The EMTs are checking them both out." He rubbed his hand through his hair. "I guess it's good to have someone other than a veterinarian take a look at Hicks."

"What's wrong?" I asked.

"I've got two dead bodies and three missing people."

"You don't think . . ." I couldn't even get my mouth to form the words to suggest that Chelsea, Natalie, and David were dead. I shuddered.

"I think somebody clobbered Hudson. He claims he didn't see who did it, but . . ." He shook his head.

"Plus, there's the blood you found in David's car," I said.

"Right. We found blood, but not a body. He must have been well enough to have gotten away or . . ."

"Or?" I asked.

"Let's just say, I need to find him." He glanced down at Bailey. "When we were out before, he got a scent, right?"

"Yeah, I could tell by his body language. He was on a trail."

"Good. Then, I want to try again."

"Okay, I can—"

"Pris, I need you to stay here. There's a killer out there somewhere and I would feel a lot better if you were safe here. Actually, I'd feel a lot better if you went to see Taylor Swift with Hannah and the rest of the girls, but I guess that's asking too much."

I reached over and hugged him. "Yes, that's asking too much."

"Let me take Bailey out, alone. You stay here where it's safe. I'll keep an officer on duty outside. Plus, Peter Alexander's here."

"Do you trust him?" I asked.

He thought for a few moments, then nodded. "I do."

"Okay."

He pulled away and stared into my eyes. "Okay? Just like that? No arguments?"

"Just like that. No arguments." I'd had enough of tramping through the woods.

He kissed me. He reached over and took Bailey's leash.

"Who are you looking for?" I asked. "Natalie? Chelsea? Or David?"

"From everything I can determine, Chelsea and Natalie both left of their own free will. Both took their own vehicles. They're adults. I have no evidence that a crime was committed against either of them. Although, I want to talk to both of them as material witnesses. I've got a BOLO for Natalie and Chelsea. Call me if either one of them shows up."

I nodded.

He picked up a bag that was lying on the table. One of David Townsend's shirts was in the bag. He put the shirt under Bailey's nose and let him take a good whiff.

Bailey sniffed the shirt and then gave his head a shake. He put his nose to the ground and moved toward the front door.

"Let's go, boy." Chief Morgan opened the door and the two of them went out on the hunt.

Chapter 40

I couldn't help saying a brief prayer as Bailey and Gilbert left. As far as towns go, Crosbyville was relatively safe. Not much happened here, when compared to larger metropolitan areas and the nearby towns of River Bend and Chicago. At least, that's what I'd learned since I started dating the chief of police. He loved his job and was full of information about crime statistics, along with advice for physical safety. However, no matter how safe the area was, I was always aware whenever his radio squawked and he left, there was the possibility that he could be injured . . . or worse. While most people ran away from danger and avoided difficult situations, Gilbert and the men and women who swore to serve and protect were the ones who ran toward danger.

So, I prayed. I took a deep breath. At least Bailey was

with him this time. That thought brought a smile to my face. Bailey was a good dog.

"What are you smiling about?" Aunt Agatha asked.

I'd been absorbed in my own thoughts and hadn't even noticed that my aunt had come into the hall. She was back in her wheelchair. "I was just . . . wait. What's wrong with smiling?"

"Nothing. I just want something to smile about, too. We're here in this house where two people have been murdered. We got two people who've had the snot beat out of them, and three folks missing. And your boyfriend, one of the only folks around here who can legally pack heat, just left with your dog, who'd rip the throat out of anyone who tried to hurt you."

I could feel my lips slide downward from a smile into a frown. "Bloodhounds aren't really the best breed for ripping out throats, but—"

Aunt Agatha waved away my protest. She surprised me by reaching down into her compression boot and sliding out a wooden rolling pin. She glanced around her shoulder like a shoplifter looking for store security. Seeing the coast was clear, she handed me the rolling pin. "Here."

"Where did you get this?" I stared at the rolling pin.

"From the kitchen. Where do you think?" She stared at me as if my mental capacity was in question.

"I figured that, but why did you take it?"

"I'm not stealing it. I have far better rolling pins than that one at the diner. This is just a cheap wooden one." She frowned. "It's good for most things and will get the job done. Personally, I prefer my marble rolling pin. You can't flour it to prevent the dough from sticking, but I can put it in the freezer and chill it and that does the same thing. Plus—"

"Aunt Agatha!" I needed to get her refocused before she got too far down into the rolling pin comparison. "Why did you take this? What am I supposed to do with it?"

"Protection." Her tone implied she was still questioning my mental acuity. "We're here alone. You're a pretty good batter. At least you used to be."

I wasn't just a good batter. I was an amazing batter. At least, I used to be when I was in high school. I still held the record for RBIs and home runs, which I broke during the Indiana State Softball Championships. I finished my senior year with a .515 batting average, a .646 on-base percentage, and a 1.212 slugging percentage, along with thirty-four home runs and eighty-five RBIs. I was more than a good batter. I was a darned good batter. I had also been a good pitcher, but gave that up to a better pitcher, Marcie. Aunt Agatha knew all of that already. She and my grammy Bell had attended all of my games. My puzzled expression asked the question that my lips hadn't.

"There's a murderer on the loose and I probably couldn't outrun a hundred-year-old man with only one good leg." She patted the compression boot. "But that doesn't mean I intend to go down without a fight."

"Okay, so I have the rolling pin." My lips twitched. "What else are you hiding in that boot?"

"I couldn't fit anything else in the boot." Aunt Agatha

reached beside her back in the wheelchair and held up a bottle of wine. "So, I grabbed this."

"Are you planning to get the killer drunk?" I joked.

"Don't be ridiculous. Of course not." She slipped the bottle back behind her back. "I wouldn't knowingly drink with a killer." She pursed her lips.

"Okay . . . so what are you going to do?"

"I may not have set the state record for RBIs and home runs, but I can swing that bottle and buy us some time until that boyfriend of yours returns."

I chuckled. "Let's hope that Bailey and Gilbert find the killer. Or better yet, let's hope the killer is one of the three people who are missing."

"How does that help? Missing doesn't mean they can't find their way back. I don't know that I can sleep in this house another night." She shivered. "Did Gilbert mention anything about when we could go home?"

"I didn't get a chance to talk to him about it before he was gone again." I shook my head. "I thought you wanted to stay here?"

"I did, but that was before we knew that Eddie was murdered and before Jay Barlow was killed. Now I'll be happy to go home."

"The girls have to go to school tomorrow, so I'm sure that we should be free to go home," I said, although even to my own ears, I didn't sound convincing. "I'll ask Gilbert when he's back."

Aunt Agatha patted my hand. "Don't worry. *When* we

get through this, and we will get through this"—she held up the bottle—"we're going to open this bottle and celebrate."

I laughed. "Maybe you should have grabbed a corkscrew."

Aunt Agatha reached into a pocket and held up a corkscrew.

Chapter 41

The front door flew open. It would have hit the wall with a bang, but the spring door stopper halted the swing and pushed it back. Before the door closed, Natalie Evans blew inside like a tornado.

"Where is he? Where is that lamebrained chief of police?" Natalie stormed through the door. She halted when she saw me.

Two state police officers followed Natalie inside.

"Well?" Natalie scowled.

The shock of seeing Natalie Evans and the two cops tied my tongue. I forced my mouth open. "Natalie? What are you doing here?"

She stopped, folded her arms across her chest, and tapped her foot impatiently. "That's exactly what I'm trying to find out. Now, where is that idiot?"

"Gilbert?"

"Duh!"

"Chief Morgan isn't here. Now, maybe you can calm down and stop acting like a spoiled two-year-old in the middle of a temper tantrum for two seconds," Aunt Agatha said.

Natalie glared. "Spoiled? You haven't begun to see the temper tantrum that I'm going to throw when I get my hands on that thick-skulled Neanderthal." Natalie marched about four feet, turned, and repeated, pacing in small circles.

The two officers looked from me to Aunt Agatha.

"Gentlemen, would you like to sit down?" Aunt Agatha asked.

The officers exchanged glances. One of them cleared his throat. "We'll just wait here for Chief Morgan. Do you know how long before he returns?"

I glanced at the time. I had no idea how long Gilbert would be, then I remembered I could call him. I pulled out my cell phone and was just about to call when the front door opened.

Bailey was the first to enter. His nose twitched and I could tell by the proud set of his ears and the way he pranced, he was a happy bloodhound.

"Bailey." I squatted down and gave my dog a good scratch.

Seconds later Chief Morgan walked in along with David Townsend and Chelsea Baxter.

There was a brief pause. Everyone looked at one another.

Then the chaos started.

"How dare you have me dragged here like some common criminal," Natalie said.

"What's she doing here?" Chelsea glared from Natalie to Chief Morgan.

"You can't do this," David Townsend said at the same time.

Chief Morgan put two fingers in his mouth and whistled like a sailor. "Quiet."

Everyone stopped.

Chief Morgan turned to the state police officers. "Where'd you find her?"

"River Bend Airport." He reached into a pocket and pulled out an airline ticket and a passport.

"Bhutan?"

"I hear it's lovely at this time of year." Natalie frowned.

"Luggage?" Chief Morgan asked.

"She'd already checked her bags so we didn't want to hold up the entire plane to have them unload it, but we can notify the airport in Chicago and they'll—"

Chief Morgan waved away their protest. "That'll be fine."

The officers nodded. "Do you need us to hang around?"

Chief Morgan shook his head. "No. I've got it under control. I've got officers patrolling the grounds. We've got it."

"Yes, sir." They shook hands and then walked out of the door that Chief Morgan held open for them.

"Now, everybody into the library so I can get to the bottom of this mess," Chief Morgan ordered.

Natalie frowned and looked as though she meant to resist.

"Or, I can haul all of you down to the jail and get your statements there. Your choice." Gilbert scowled.

I was surprised to see that Natalie Evans was the first to comply. She unfolded her arms and marched into the library.

Chelsea hooked her arm in David's and the two of them followed.

Aunt Agatha gave Bailey's ears a scratch, then she said, "You found him, didn't you, boy? You deserve a special treat. Come with me and I'll get you taken care of in the kitchen."

Bailey barked at the T-word. He and Aunt Agatha headed toward the kitchen.

"I think I deserve a special treat, too." Gilbert grinned. He took two steps closer and pulled me into an embrace.

I reached up to kiss him.

Before our lips touched, Aunt Agatha cleared her throat. "Don't forget to ask him."

She rolled out of the room, taking all of the romance of the moment with her.

"What are you supposed to ask me?" Gilbert gave me a wary look.

"About going home. The girls have school tomorrow and we were only supposed to be here for one night for Mary Elizabeth's birthday sleepover."

He rubbed his neck. "Of course. You're all free to go whenever you want."

"All of us?" I gave a pointed look at the closed door of the library.

"Well, most of you are free to go." He took a deep breath. "Mary Elizabeth, Hannah, and Clarice. Marcie, Tabby, Carla, Aunt Agatha, and you."

"Oh, thank you," I joked. "Have I been officially cleared as a suspect?"

"You were never a suspect. You didn't even know Jay Barlow and barely knew Edward Townsend."

"What about Chelsea and Andrew?" I glanced around to make sure no one was listening. "Clarice and Mary Elizabeth can't leave if their legal guardians are still here."

"Even if I could be sure that Andrew Hicks hadn't killed Edward Townsend to increase Mary Elizabeth's inheritance, he's not in physical shape to care for her." He paused.

"And Chelsea?" I asked. "Surely, you don't believe she killed Edward Townsend and Jay Barlow?"

Gilbert was silent.

"Come on. You can't be serious. Chelsea Baxter?"

"Didn't you used to call her the Wicked Witch of the West? Or was it the Wicked Witch of the East?"

I waved away his arguments. "East. West. It doesn't matter. Chelsea Baxter may be wicked but she would absolutely *NOT* have clubbed an old man on the head."

"Not her style?" he joked.

"And risk breaking a nail? No way!"

"Well, she and David Townsend have gotten close very quickly. She admitted that she needs money and David Townsend stands to inherit a lot of it. Plus, I'm not crazy about that little stunt she just pulled."

"Stunt?" I asked.

"Sneaking out of the house to meet Townsend in the boathouse. They were preparing to escape. Chelsea may not have been the one who actually wielded the weapon that killed Jay Barlow, but she may very well have been an accessory after the fact."

I stared.

"Clarice can go, but Chelsea Baxter stays."

"Clarice can't stay by herself."

"I'll call DCS."

"You can't do that! Clarice has been through too much already. First her parents are killed, and then her aunt Whitney is murdered, and now Chelsea is possibly arrested . . . That poor kid has been through the wringer, and you know very well that you are not going to call the Department of Child Services." I put my hand on my hip and channeled my best impersonation of Aunt Agatha.

Gilbert shrugged. "You're the one who told me she can't stay alone."

"Ugh!" I glared. "The girls can stay at my place." He started to speak, and I interrupted. "*All* of the girls can spend the night at my house. I'll see that they get to school in the morning and hopefully, you will have figured this whole thing out by the time school's out."

"What?"

"You heard me. I have a deadline and I haven't gotten any writing done since I've been here. So, you better get busy."

Gilbert walked toward the library. At the doorway, he stopped and turned.

"Go on. You've got work to do."

Gilbert muttered something that sounded like *stubborn women.*

"What was that?"

"Nothing." He opened the door and entered the library.

"Men." I turned to leave when I remembered I'd left my laptop in the library. I needed it to work on my manuscript. "Darn it." I leaned against the doors to the library and listened. *Can I slip in, grab my laptop, and slip out?* I took a deep breath and reached for the knob.

The door swung open. The two EMTs walked out of the room.

Shocked, I backpedaled to avoid a collision, and I tripped. My arms flailed as I worked to avoid falling on my backside.

Thankfully, one of the EMTs had good reflexes and reached out and grabbed me around the waist, preventing my fall.

"You okay?" he asked.

"Fine. Sorry." I felt the heat rush to my face.

"Don't apologize. We were just—"

A radio buzzed and the EMTs were immediately on alert. They both rushed down the hall and out the front door without a backward glance.

I glanced back at the library. The doors were open. I headed toward them but stopped as my cell phone vibrated.

One glance at the contact's picture brought a smile to my face before a moment of panic squeezed my heart. "Cameron, is everything okay?"

"Well, hello to you, too," she said in her clipped tone. "Can't I call my favorite client without anything being wrong?" Cameron chuckled.

"I'm sorry. Where are my manners? Hello, Cameron. How are you?"

Cameron Prescott was the founder of Prescott Literary Agency and my agent. She was a New Yorker with a tough-as-nails reputation, which was a bit scary for a Midwestern schoolteacher turned children's book author. I heard that once during difficult negotiations on behalf of one of her clients, she had brought one of the publisher's lawyers to tears. However, my experience was completely different. With me, Cameron was cheerful, encouraging, and enthusiastic. At least, she was whenever we spoke. She'd spent twenty years as an editor herself at one of the big five publishers before she left and started her own literary agency. Prescott Literary Agency had a long list of award-winning, bestselling children's books. Signing with her had been a dream come true, and I hoped that I wouldn't let her down.

We both laughed at her use of the term *favorite client*. I had it on good authority that she called every client her *favorite*. Still, it sent a warm fuzzy feeling through my bloodstream whenever I heard it.

"Good. Following up. How're you with that deadline for book three?"

Ugh. Do I tell her that I haven't written one word? That I have spent the past couple of days babysitting three tweens at a mansion where two people have been murdered? That I realize that I have less than one month to pull this thing together and hit the ultra-aggressive one-month deadline that I'd insisted, against her recommendation, on setting?

Or do I lie and tell her that all is well? That I'm almost finished and on target to finish on schedule? That's when the idea struck me. Maybe I straddle the fence and tell the truth without telling the whole truth. In other words, hedge.

"You won't believe what happened. I met a real private investigator and he let me interview him. He's here in Crosbyville working on a missing person . . . well, it wasn't really a missing person case like you would think. It wasn't a case of someone who lived here and disappeared. It was more like . . . finding a lost heir. Anyway, there was this wealthy businessman, Edward Townsend, who—"

"I read about that."

"Umm. You did?"

"Billionaire. Estranged from his family. Looking for his long-lost heir."

"That's right." I stared at the phone. "How did you hear about it?"

"Big news. Stuck in my mind. Turns out I knew his heir."

"What? You know David Townsend?"

"Knew."

Knew. Past tense. As a former editor, Cameron was even more of a stickler for words than I was. But it still took a few moments for the full impact of that one word to hit me. "What do you mean, *knew*?"

"I met him once before he died. Loved the British accent, but—"

"Wait. Died? David Townsend isn't dead."

"Pretty sure he's dead. Could be wrong. Haven't spoken in years."

My brain tried to adjust to the new information, but I couldn't make sense out of anything. However, I did latch on to one thing. "British accent? Do you mean Australian?" Some Americans might not be able to tell the difference between an Aussie accent and a British accent, but Cameron would.

"No. I mean *British*. Very public school." She mimicked her best royal accent.

"Okay, you lost me. What's a 'public school' accent?" I asked.

"Used to be the 'upper-class' accent or pronunciation coined by phonetician Daniel Jones. He changed it later. 'Received Pronunciation, or RP.' Anyway, back to your deadline—"

I pulled the phone away from my ear. "Hey, I'll be right there," I said to no one. Then I put the phone back. "I'm sorry, but I have to go. I'll call you later. Okay?" I didn't wait for her response before ending the call. Whew! I needed to get busy writing. Cameron Prescott was a wonderful person and deserved better than a slacker client who wasn't keeping up with her deadlines. After all, agents made money only when they sold material. I suspected that Cameron's other clients were bringing in a lot more money than me. Still, I needed new tires. I needed to make this deadline.

I mentally resolved to do better. I wasn't involved in this murder investigation. I wasn't even involved in the hunt for a missing heir. None of this impacted me one way or the other. The murders were Gilbert's problem. He was smart. He could figure out who murdered Edward Townsend and

Jay Barlow. He didn't need my help. Nor did he want my help.

I took a deep breath. I should just get my laptop and write my book and forget about all this madness. That would be the smart thing to do. But, I wasn't feeling smart. I was feeling curious.

I picked up my phone and googled *received pronunciation*. It gave a more in-depth and boring explanation than the one I got from Cameron, which was basically the same thing she'd told me. Next, I googled *David Townsend*. There were thousands of them. Black. White. Old. Young. Short. Tall. All sizes. None of them resembled the one sitting in the library and purporting to be the grandson of a billionaire.

I heaved a sigh and walked into the library.

Chapter 42

I needn't have worried about anyone inside the library noticing me. A meteor could have fallen inside that room, and no one would have noticed until the space rock crash-landed.

On first glance, herding cats would have been the description that came to mind. Chief Morgan and Peter Alexander had their hands full.

Chelsea and Natalie Evans were hurling insults back and forth from one end of the room to the other.

A red-faced David Townsend was pointing and yelling at Hudson, who scowled back.

Chief Morgan gave his New York whistle again. The commotion dropped down a notch but didn't stop completely. So, he followed it up. "Quiet!"

This did the trick, although the silence drew attention to my presence.

"Can I help you?" Gilbert asked.

"No. I just forgot my laptop." I rushed over to the desk. I picked up my laptop and turned to rush out of the room. I was almost at the doors and just a few steps from the safety of the hallway before I realized something was wrong. I stopped.

"Forget something?" Chief Morgan asked.

I looked at my laptop. It wasn't there. I rushed back to the desk and looked. Nope. I scoured the floor. Maybe I dropped it.

"Lose something?" Peter Alexander was the closest to the desk.

"Yeah . . . I—" I turned to Chief Morgan.

He joined us at the desk. "What is it?"

"The flash drive. It was in my laptop for when you got back. Was it returned to the safe?" I asked.

"The flash drive from the jewelry box?"

I nodded.

Chief Morgan went to the wall, moved the painting, and opened the safe. The envelope was still there, along with the box, but the flash drive and key were gone.

"All right, who did it?" Chief Morgan exploded.

Everyone gathered closer, mumbling at once and feigning innocence. Most of them may very well have been innocent, but at least one of the people in that room was a thief, and probably a killer.

"Did what?"

"What are you talking about?"

"I want my lawyer."

"I'm going to sue the city of Crosbyville, the police department, and you personally for every cent you have." Natalie smirked. "And don't even think about searching me for whatever it is your girlfriend has lost without a warrant."

Gilbert's ears were on fire, and he looked like a volcano ready to blow his top.

"What on earth is all this shouting?" Aunt Agatha rolled into the room from the hallway, along with Bailey.

For a moment, I gazed at my bloodhound and my heart constricted. Bailey had a nasty habit of pilfering objects. Could he have taken the flash drive and the key? *Think. When was the last time you saw the objects?* My mind flashed back. Was it just a few hours ago? Gilbert, Aunt Agatha, and I were in the library. Then Gilbert took Bailey to look for David Townsend. Aunt Agatha and I were alone in the library when I'd gone upstairs to get my laptop.

"Pris, what happened to that drive? It was evidence," Chief Morgan said.

"I forgot to put it back in the safe, and . . . we . . . I was curious," I said.

"You had it right the first time. *We* were curious. I suggested she get her laptop," Aunt Agatha admitted.

He closed his eyes. "Then what happened?"

My mouth was suddenly dry as the Sahara. I licked my lips. "Well, then I put the flash drive in my laptop."

"And?"

"It was full of movies. Videos from the . . ." I used my eyes to draw a line toward the wall that hid the priest hole and the secret security camera.

Chief Morgan turned to Peter Alexander. "Make sure no one leaves this room." Then he grabbed me by the arm and marched me into the hallway. When we were clear of the library he closed the doors. "Pris, I can't believe you did that. You knew this was evidence."

"I'm sorry. I didn't mean to—"

"To what? Lose evidence?"

"But, it still has to be in that room. One of those people has to have it. The only people who left the house are the two EMTs, and they almost certainly wouldn't have taken it. All you have to do is search—"

"Pris, you don't understand." He took a deep breath. "It's not about the flash drive anymore. You've destroyed the chain of custody. Even if I found the flash drive and there was a video of one of the suspects murdering Edward Townsend, I couldn't use it in court."

"Why not?" I asked.

"Because a good defense lawyer would challenge the evidence. They could say that the flash drive had been tampered with. Someone might have replaced the real flash drive with a duplicate version that incriminates their client."

"But no one would have time to do that. How could they? How could they create a duplicate?" My voice sounded whiny, but I couldn't help it.

"I don't know. Maybe they edited the video to make someone look guilty who wasn't. Or maybe they simply deleted the one video on that flash drive that was more damning than all the others. Or the one video that would explain why their client looked guilty, but really wasn't." He ran his hand through his hair.

My lower lip quivered. I wanted to talk—to apologize. But it took all of my energy to hold back the tears that stung the backs of my eyes. If I opened my mouth, I would start blubbering, so I kept my mouth closed. I put my head down, and felt the first tear escape and run down my nose. I saw it hit the ground, but I refused to wipe away the traces. The second tear followed and then another and another.

Gilbert pulled me to his chest and wrapped his arms around me to comfort me, but I didn't deserve comfort. So, that only made me cry harder.

"It's okay. Please, don't cry." Gilbert placed his chin on my head.

"No . . . it's . . . not." I sniffed. "It's not okay. I shouldn't have been nosy. I shouldn't have moved the flash drive. I should have put it in the safe with the other stuff."

He pulled away and lifted my chin. "It's not your fault."

"Stop trying to make me feel better. It's just making me feel worse."

"That doesn't make any sense, but I'm not saying this just to make you feel better. I'm being honest. It wasn't your fault. It was my fault. I'm the one who should have put the flash drive in the safe. Not you. That was my job, and I screwed up."

"No. You trusted that the flash drive would be there. You—"

He was shaking his head. "No. It was my responsibility,

not yours. I'm sorry. I shouldn't have tried to shirk my responsibility and place the blame for my mistake on you. Can you forgive me?"

His apology only made the tears flow more. I sobbed.

Gilbert held me and shushed me as if he were comforting Hannah. Eventually, the tears slowed down to a trickle, and he gently lifted my head. He kissed my face and then his lips moved down to my mouth. The kiss started slow and gentle, but quickly a warmth started in my core. In the same way that a log added to a fire will grow in heat and intensity, so did that kiss.

"Excuse me, Chief, but we have a situation that I think needs your attention."

Neither of us heard Peter Alexander enter the hallway until he spoke.

Gilbert swore under his breath and then pulled away. "What kind of situation?"

Having just gone on an emotional roller coaster from a blubbering basket case to red-hot passion in less than sixty seconds, I needed an extra minute to pull myself together.

Before Peter Alexander could explain, there was a loud crash from the library as a piece of furniture hit the floor. Someone screamed, and Bailey gave his deep, "I'm going to rip your face off" bark.

Gilbert rushed through the doors into the library, followed by Peter Alexander. I hesitated a few seconds before I heard another bark. "Bailey."

Chapter 43

In the library, Chelsea Baxter and Natalie Evans were locked together and rolling around on the floor while David Townsend attempted to pull them apart. Hudson and Andrew Hicks were yelling at each other. Aunt Agatha had a firm grip on Bailey's collar while he lunged and growled.

Chief Morgan and Peter launched into the fray and within seconds, they each had one of the women in hand. Gilbert, who had grabbed Chelsea, shoved her toward David Townsend. "Keep a firm hold on her."

David complied.

Chief Morgan turned his attention to Andrew and Hudson. "Sit down. Shut up. Or I'll lock both of you up."

"On what charge?" Hudson asked.

"Disorderly conduct." Chief Morgan scowled. His threat worked, and everyone slowly quieted.

Lastly, he turned to Bailey. "Bailey, down!"

Bailey hesitated a half second, but slowly slid down into a sphinx position.

"Now, what on earth happened?" Gilbert asked.

Everyone started to answer at once.

"Silence!" Gilbert yelled, and turned to Aunt Agatha. "Can you tell me what happened?"

"Good Lawd, I don't know that I can." Aunt Agatha shook her head. "Well, after you and Pris left, David Townsend accused Hudson of trying to kill him to get Edward Townsend's money. Andrew claimed Mary Elizabeth was an heir and was entitled to the money. That's when Natalie jumped in and defended him." She pointed at David Townsend. "Then Chelsea jumped in and said some not-very-kind things about Natalie. And, well, I don't know. Before I knew what was what, Chelsea and Natalie were fighting like two alley cats." She fanned herself. "Bailey started growling and it took everything I had to keep him in check."

I hurried over to my aunt. "Are you okay? Maybe you should go in the kitchen and get a cup of tea to help steady your nerves."

"A glass of whiskey would do a better job," Andrew Hicks said.

"You know, I think I will. I'm not a young woman and all this commotion is upsetting." She rolled over to the side of the room. At the door she stopped. "Bailey, come."

Bailey stretched and got up and followed Aunt Agatha out of the room.

Gilbert glanced at each person. "Now, there's a key and a flash drive missing. I'd like permission to search—"

"Nope. No way. Absolutely not." Was the general consensus.

"Your girlfriend lost the evidence and I'm not submitting to a search without a search warrant," Natalie Evans said.

"That can be arranged. No one's leaving this house—this room—until I find that flash drive," Gilbert said.

"Then, you better call for a female officer, and I would recommend you get the district attorney on the phone because I promise you that I will be suing as soon as the search is over." Natalie flopped down on the sofa next to Andrew Hicks.

"Look, mate, I don't know anything about a flash drive. What exactly was on this flash drive?" David Townsend asked.

"And what kind of key are you looking for? What does it open?" Chelsea asked. "Maybe the housekeeper has an extra key."

The door opened and Aunt Agatha and Olivia Green entered. Olivia Green pushed a tea cart with coffee and tea near the desk. When she was done, she glanced at Aunt Agatha, who nodded.

"Are you sure you don't need help?" Olivia asked.

"No, I'm sure I can manage. Thank you." Aunt Agatha smiled.

Olivia Green glanced over her shoulder once. Then she walked out of the library and closed the door behind her.

I moved over to assist Aunt Agatha. She poured and I served. I was never a graceful waitress, but I managed to get the beverages distributed with minimal spillage.

When everyone was served, Hudson reached in his jacket and pulled out a flask. He held it up. "I don't know about anyone else, but I could use a bit of Irish luck." He splashed a bit of the amber liquid into his cup and took a sip.

"Give me that." Natalie Evans walked over and grabbed the flask. She sniffed it, shrugged, and then splashed a bit in her cup. She took a sip and then held up the flask.

Andrew Hicks and David Townsend both nodded. Natalie put a splash from the flask in Andrew Hicks's cup. Then she frowned at Chelsea Baxter as she moved past her to add a splash to David Townsend's cup. Chelsea took a tight possessive hold on David Townsend's arm while Natalie merely rolled her eyes.

When she finished, Natalie emptied what was left in the flask into her own cup. "Oops. I guess that's the last of it." She grinned and took a sip. "I think I'll skip the coffee."

Hudson returned the empty flask to his pocket.

Everyone sipped their drinks and the tension in the room decreased.

"Now, who wants to tell me what happened?" Gilbert asked.

Peter Alexander gave a more detailed explanation, but it was essentially the same as the story Aunt Agatha had shared.

David Townsend coughed.

"Fine. Let's hear your side." Gilbert turned to face David. "What happened to you? Why'd you run?"

He cleared his throat gruffly. "I wasn't running."

Gilbert squinted and folded his arms across his chest. "Okay, let's hear it."

"I got a note to meet Chelsea at the old dairy, so I—"

"I never sent any note," Chelsea said.

David shrugged. "I got in my car and headed to the dairy, but there was a large tree limb blocking the road. I got out to move it out of the way when the lights went out." He coughed.

"Someone hit you?" Gilbert asked.

David Townsend nodded. He coughed and took a sip of coffee.

"Did you see who it was?" Gilbert asked.

David Townsend coughed as he shook his head, but something in his eyes made me doubt that he was telling the truth.

Gilbert must have seen the same thing. "Look, if you know something . . . anything that will help get to the bottom of this, now is the time to come forward."

"I have no idea what you're talking about, mate." David Townsend coughed more.

"If you're worried about your safety, I can assure you the police will protect you, but we need your help," Gilbert said.

Natalie snorted.

"Do you have something to add, Ms. Evans?" Gilbert flashed her a hard look.

"Me? I don't have anything to add to this farce, except to say that the *police* haven't done a very good job of providing protection so far."

Gilbert scowled.

David Townsend continued to cough with more intensity and frequency.

"Go down the wrong pipe?" Andrew Hicks asked.

David Townsend's face turned redder and redder. He clutched at his throat and his eyes got bigger.

Initially, we ignored the coughing, chalking it up to a throat tickle. That was until Townsend's actions became more frantic, and his face went from tanned leather to red to purple.

Gilbert was the first to react. He rushed over to David Townsend. Just as he reached him, David Townsend collapsed.

Gilbert caught him and helped lower him to the floor. He loosened his collar. "Call 911."

I pulled out my phone.

Chelsea Baxter stared down at David Townsend as he lay on the floor.

My hands shook as I dialed, but I managed it.

"Nine-one-one. What's your emergency?" the dispatcher asked.

"We have a man who's . . . He's coughing. It looks like he . . . I don't know . . . It looks like he's choking to death." I stopped abruptly. Why had I added that last part? "He's on the floor and he's—"

"What's the location of the emergency?" the dispatcher asked.

My mind went blank. If I ever knew the address for Townsend Farms it had fallen through the creases of my brain like coins in a seat cushion and was lost forever. I glanced up. "Does anyone know the address?"

Natalie Evans rattled off the address, which I relayed.

"What's your telephone number?"

"Seriously? Can't you see that on your screen?" I asked. My voice had gone up an octave or two as I tried not to watch Gilbert and Peter performing CPR on David Townsend. But just like when driving by a car crash on the interstate, I couldn't stop myself from rubbernecking. I had to look.

"We need to confirm the phone number in case we get disconnected," the dispatcher said patiently.

I forced my brain to focus and recited my telephone number.

"Tell me what happened," the dispatcher said.

"I don't know. He seemed fine. One minute he was drinking coffee and the next minute he was choking," I rattled on. "We thought maybe it went down the wrong pipe, but it was just coffee, so it shouldn't have blocked his airway. I mean—"

The dispatcher asked for the patient's name and age. I answered the name without help. When it came to age, I repeated the question and looked to Chelsea Baxter for help, but she was frozen like a deer caught in the headlights of a car.

"About thirty-five," Peter Alexander said from the floor where he and Gilbert were alternating between chest compressions and breathing into David Townsend's lungs.

"Is he awake and conscious?" the dispatcher asked and typed.

"I don't know," I said.

"Is he breathing?" More typing.

I repeated the question but got no answer. "My boyfriend . . . um, I mean the chief of police is performing CPR. Look, I don't know the answers to these questions. Can't you just get someone out here to help?"

"An ambulance is on the way, but I need these answers to make sure we can provide the best care," the dispatcher said calmly. "If someone is providing CPR, then chances are good that your friend will be okay until the ambulance arrives. Please try to remain calm."

Calm? Are you joking?

"She said an ambulance is on its way," I said.

Gilbert stopped the CPR long enough to place his hand on David Townsend's neck and take his pulse. The look on his face told me the answer before the words left his mouth. He sat back on his heels. "He's dead."

Natalie Evans screamed.

Chelsea Baxter collapsed in a heap on the floor.

Chapter 44

The EMTs who arrived this time around weren't the same ones who had been here earlier. This time there was a man and a woman. Since there was nothing to be done for David Townsend, they focused on Chelsea. Her diagnosis was shock, which I believed. She was pale and shivered as though she were freezing. Given all the shocks she'd had in the past few hours, she'd certainly earned it.

This time, she didn't decline a free trip to Crosbyville Memorial Hospital. In fact, she didn't speak at all. They strapped her to a gurney and wheeled her out to the ambulance.

To my surprise, Aunt Agatha got out of her wheelchair. "I can't let that poor child go to the hospital alone." She limped to the passenger side of the ambulance.

One of the EMTs looked as though he meant to tell her she couldn't go, but a stern look from Aunt Agatha froze the words in his throat. He gave a glance to Gilbert, who gave a slight nod indicating that she should be allowed to accompany their patient.

The EMT helped Aunt Agatha into the ambulance and closed the door. Then he went to the back and climbed in with Chelsea.

The Townsend estate swarmed with police and forensics. There were so many people moving around, I couldn't keep track. The county coroner attended to David Townsend while everyone else took pictures. Measurements. Fingerprints. The professionals did their jobs while keeping the civilians at bay.

If I thought Gilbert was in a bad mood earlier, it was nothing compared to his mood after David Townsend's death. He barked orders that nothing was to be touched. He ordered us into the kitchen. Then he instructed two uniformed officers not to let us out of their sight. His mood was so bad that not even Natalie Evans challenged him. She tucked her attitude away and followed the rest of us into the kitchen. Like sheep headed for shearing, we marched into the kitchen one after the other and sat in a tense silence.

The atmosphere in the kitchen was one of shock with a sprinkling of fear. *Who killed David Townsend? Was there a serial killer on the loose? Who would be next? Will any of us make it out of here alive?* Melodramatic, but those were the thoughts that ran through my mind before I squashed them down. Given the side-eye everyone was giving one another, I wasn't the only one asking those questions.

One by one, officers came to the kitchen and requested one of us accompany them. Peter Alexander went first. After thirty minutes, the officer returned and requested Andrew Hicks. Hudson went next, leaving Natalie Evans and me alone with the two uniformed officers. Hudson's interview took nearly an hour and stretched my nerves to near the breaking point. Natalie alternated between pacing the floor and impatiently drumming her fingers on the table while tapping her foot. Finally, Natalie Evans had her turn and left.

I sat in the kitchen. The police officers left, first one and then the other, leaving me alone with only Bailey for company. He must have realized that I was on edge because he placed his head in my lap and gazed up at me with his large, expressive eyes.

Staring into Bailey's eyes and rubbing his ears had a calming effect on me. Given the way his tail wagged against the kitchen floor and his eyes rolled back in his head, he was enjoying it, too. Finally, one of the policemen came back and asked me to follow him to the drawing room where Carla and David Townsend had talked of embezzlement.

Gilbert sat behind the desk that Carla had occupied earlier. He looked up when I entered. "Do you have any insight? Anything to add to this mess?"

In the hours that I'd had to wait for my turn, I'd gone

over and over what I would say. What could I say? I didn't have the slightest idea what had happened to David Townsend. "Do you know who he is?"

Gilbert looked up at me and stared. "What?"

"I'm fairly certain he wasn't David Townsend. Not the real David Townsend, anyway. I just wondered if you knew who he was."

Chapter 45

In my head, my statement had gone differently. I had no intention of quite so abruptly dropping the information that Cameron had shared. However, nerves and stress got the better of me, and I blurted out what Cameron had told me.

The vein on the side of Gilbert's head vibrated like a plucked guitar string. He clinched his jaw and frowned. When I finished talking, he swallowed hard before saying, "You knew he wasn't David Townsend and you didn't think to tell me? Pris, I—"

I held up a hand. "Hold on. I only found out a few minutes before he died."

"Still, you should have—"

"What? Interrupted you while Chelsea and Natalie were fighting to say that my agent told me that David

Townsend, the *real* David Townsend, spoke with a British accent, not an Australian accent, and that she believed he was dead?"

"Yes." Gilbert paused. "No, but . . ." He took a deep breath. "Tell me what she said. *Everything.*"

I repeated everything Cameron had said, including everything about the "public school" accent. It wasn't much. "That's it. That's all." I waited and watched Gilbert's reaction. "Honestly, I wasn't sure she was right. I mean, David Townsend is a common enough name. When I googled him, there were thousands of responses. Besides, I thought . . ."

"What?"

"I thought someone with Edward Townsend's money would have investigated all potential heirs thoroughly. He was a billionaire. He could certainly afford to pay someone to investigate." I hung my head. "I'm sorry."

Gilbert took a deep breath. He walked around the desk and pulled me into his arms. "I'm sorry, too. Here's another example of me blaming you for something I should have figured out myself."

"It may not be true. Is there a way to find out?" I looked up at him.

"The coroner will take fingerprints. It's standard procedure, but that doesn't mean we'll find anything."

"Why not?"

"David Townsend wasn't born in the United States. If he hasn't committed a crime, then chances are slim that he'll show up."

That's when I remembered the conversation I'd had

with Peter Alexander. I told Gilbert that Peter had wanted
to have Edward Townsend do a DNA test. He also mentioned a friend at Interpol who might be able to check if
David Townsend—or whoever he was—was in the database.
"Of course, he was only thinking about it from the stand-
point of determining if David Townsend . . . or . . . geez,
what do I call him?"

"For now, let's continue calling him David Townsend.
Who knows, it might really be his name." Gilbert ran his
hand through his hair.

"You think he's really—"

"I don't think anything right now. All I'm saying is that
David Townsend might really be his name. That doesn't
mean he's Edward Townsend's heir. Until we know who he is
for sure, we'll continue referring to him as David Townsend."

Something in Gilbert's voice made me look more closely
at him. "What are you not saying?"

"If he is David Townsend, great. If he's not . . . then
considering how much information he knew about the
Townsend estate, he had to have help to pull this off. Someone else knows who he is and if they know we're onto them,
then they may start to feel desperate."

"You think they're dangerous?"

"Well, someone killed him."

Chapter 46

Killed? What do you mean? It was an accident, right?" My knees suddenly felt weak.

Gilbert shook his head. "I'm pretty sure he was poisoned, but for the life of me I can't figure out how it was done."

"Poisoned? But, that's impossible. How? The only thing he had was coffee and we all drank the same thing. Aunt Agatha made the coffee. Surely you don't believe she—"

"Of course not. I don't believe Agatha poisoned him." His lips twitched. "In my experience murderers follow their personality types. Based on your aunt's personality, if she wanted to kill someone, she'd probably beat them to death, but she wouldn't poison them."

"Well, I'm glad that you know that. At least, I think so.

Then who?" I paused. "I served the coffee." I folded my arms and stared. "You're not going to suggest that I—"

"Don't be ridiculous."

I sighed. "Okay, then who . . ." That's when it hit me. "Natalie?"

"She poured the whiskey," Gilbert said.

I let my mind go back to the scene in the library. Hudson took the flask from his pocket and poured whiskey in his own cup. Then Natalie took the flask and poured whiskey in Andrew Hicks's cup. Then she poured the contents of the flask in David Townsend's cup. Last, she emptied the rest of the flask into her own. I shook my head. "It's impossible. She poured the whiskey from the same flask in everyone's cup, including her own."

"That's the problem." Gilbert paced. "I don't know how she managed it, but it's the only thing that makes sense. Maybe she used some kind of sleight of hand, so it looked like she was pouring from the flask when she was really pouring in poison from someplace else."

I thought for a moment and then shook my head. "If she did, then I have no idea how she managed it. I certainly didn't see her."

"Yeah, me, either, but I've got the lab running a toxicology screening on the flask, the cups, and pretty much everything that could possibly have contained poison. If she poisoned him, I'll find it."

"What about the flash drive and the key?" I asked.

"We've searched all of the suspects. Unless the killer swallowed them, I have no idea where they are."

"Gilbert, why do you think David Townsend was murdered?"

"Beats me." He shrugged. "I'd say it was probably something to do with the money. There were billions at stake. Murder has been done for a lot less."

"If the killer wanted the money, then as the next in line, Mary Elizabeth could be in danger."

Gilbert frowned. "I can assign protection. I'll have an officer on guard."

"That'll scare her. I'll take her to my house like we planned. Bailey will watch out for strangers." I glanced over at my dog, who was lying on his back with all four legs in the air, rolling around with a goofy grin on his face.

Gilbert laughed. "That's your protection?"

"Hey, he can be mean if he has to." I looked at Bailey. "Can't you, boy?"

Bailey drooled with his tongue hanging out of the side of his mouth. He wiggled his back on the floor, scratching himself.

Gilbert chuckled. "Okay, how about I put a plainclothes officer on watch outside just in case Bailey needs backup."

"Okay."

We talked a bit longer, but an active crime scene is a busy place. It wasn't long before Gilbert was needed.

I wandered out of the drawing room and went upstairs to pack. I was more than ready to go home. Had it been only two days? It felt like an eternity. So much had happened. I went through the milestones in my mind. "First, Edward Townsend arranged for his friend Jay Barlow to come to Crosbyville but died before he arrived. Next, Jay Barlow was attacked and later murdered. Then we learned—"

Bailey barked.

"What?"

Bailey nudged my hand with his nose and then stared up at me.

"What?"

Bailey started to dig in the mattress as though he were trying to unearth buried treasure.

"Hey, cut that out. This isn't ours. You'll ruin the bedspread trying to dig—" I stopped and stared at my bloodhound. "Dig? Is that what you're trying to tell me? That I forgot that you dug up that satchel with the money?"

Bailey sat down and licked his paws. Mission accomplished.

"That's right. You found the money. Good boy. *Then* Jay Barlow was attacked and murdered. Then we learned that Edward Townsend's death wasn't natural. He was murdered, too. Aunt Agatha was named a trustee of Edward Townsend's estate, which was probably going to make her a millionaire if she kept the money. Yikes. I still can't wrap my mind around that. Andrew Hicks was beaten to within an inch of his life. Carla discovered someone was embezzling money from the Townsend estate. David Townsend—or whoever he was—was attacked. Someone attacked his attacker and then David disappeared. You found the secret room." I turned to look at Bailey, who was curled up on the bed, watching me pack.

"I found the flash drive and the key."

Bailey barked.

"Okay, you found the flash drive and the key." I scratched his ear absently. "Then Chelsea disappeared. The valet, Hudson, was assaulted. Natalie Evans disappeared. You and Gilbert found David Townsend and Chelsea. The police found Natalie Evans at the airport in River Bend with a one-way ticket to Bhutan." I shook my head and made a mental note to look up Bhutan. I took a deep breath and continued. "The police brought Natalie back to Crosbyville. Someone took the flash drive and the key from the library." Losing that evidence hurt. I don't care what Gilbert said, I felt responsible. I sighed. "Finally, David Townsend died." I grabbed my laptop and typed everything in order. Then I shook my head like an Etch A Sketch to erase the image of him lying on the floor, dying. "If Gilbert's right, David Townsend was murdered. Although, I still can't see how anyone could have murdered him. That's a lot," I said to Bailey.

Bailey rolled onto his back to allow me easier access to rub his belly. I complied.

"I'm supposed to be writing my book." Something in that long list of events struck a chord. Glancing through the list, one item stood out. "Now, I wonder why Natalie Evans tried to leave the country."

Chapter 47

Most of the police traffic was gone by the time Marcie, Carla, Tabby, and the girls got home from the concert. They came home covered in glitter and singing at the top of their lungs into hairbrushes held like microphones. Clarice had the nicest singing voice of the three girls, but Hannah was the best dancer. Still, lack of talent didn't stop any of them.

Upon learning that we were moving the sleepover to my house, the girls whooped and ran upstairs to pack. While they were gone, I filled Marcie, Carla, and Tabby in on what they'd missed.

"Holy serial killer, Batman. Three murders make a serial killer, right?" Tabby said.

Carla poked Tabby in the ribs.

"I mean, I'm sure your hunky chief of police can handle it and that nobody else will die," Tabby said.

Carla poked her again.

"Ouch. I just mean—"

"Stop talking. You're just digging yourself a bigger and bigger hole." Carla scowled.

Tabby zipped her mouth closed.

"Does Gilbert have a suspect?" Carla asked.

I shrugged. "Beats me. You know he doesn't tell me things like that."

"I think getting out of this house is a good idea." Marcie shivered. "You want me to sleep over, too?"

I did, but I didn't want to be too needy. "I'd love it. If you don't mind."

"I don't mind. Just drop me at home first. I need to grab work clothes for tomorrow and my car. Tomorrow morning, the girls can ride with me to school."

"Thank you." I couldn't contain my joy and hugged Marcie.

"What are best friends for?" Marcie asked.

They went upstairs to pack while Bailey and I took one last stroll downstairs. The doors to the library were closed, but earlier there had been a policeman on guard and the yellow crime scene tape cordoning off the room from snoopers. The officer was gone, but the tape remained. *Darn it.* I had hoped to have one last look at that Bible.

I stared longingly at the door for several moments and then turned to leave. That's when I heard a voice and stopped.

I turned back and noticed that the tape was still in place, but one of the two doors wasn't closed completely.

They must still be working. I paused a few moments. I turned again to leave, but then the voice got louder.

"What do you mean, 'what did I do with it'? I didn't take it. What did *you* do with it?"

The voice was reaching a whispered screech and, after two days, I recognized Natalie Evans's nasal tone without even seeing her.

"Well, if I didn't take it and you didn't take it, then, who did?"

I strained to hear the answer to that question, but was thwarted in my efforts when Bailey, who had previously been sitting quietly by my side, decided to enter the conversation by barking.

"Shhh." I glared at him, but I might as well have saved my energy because that only got him excited. He stood up and barked louder.

The door opened and Natalie Evans stared at me. "Snooping?"

"No . . . we were just . . . looking for a book. I wanted to . . . I was looking at it earlier and with all the excitement, I didn't get to finish, and I left it in the library," I rambled on.

It was clear that Natalie didn't believe me.

"If you're done, I'd like to . . ." I waved my hand toward the room.

Natalie paused a few moments, then stepped aside so that Bailey and I could duck under the crime scene tape and enter.

I glanced around the room, looking for the person Natalie had been speaking to, but the room was empty. She had a cell phone in her hand and must have been on the phone, which explained why I had heard only Natalie's voice.

Natalie folded her arms and tapped her foot while she waited for me to get whatever I claimed I'd need. That's when I saw the Bible sitting where I'd left it. I walked over to the chair, aware that Natalie Evans was watching me the entire time.

I picked up the Bible and turned to leave.

"Planning a little light reading?" Natalie said.

"It's still the number-one bestseller."

"Seriously?"

"Yeah. The Bible and Shakespeare still top the—"

"Who cares." Natalie waved her hand. "I don't care how many copies of the Bible sell every year."

Several thoughts went through my mind. *Maybe you should read it sometime. Especially the part about "loving thy neighbor as thyself." Or "doing unto others as you would have them do unto you."* Instead, I said, "Well, there are lots of good stories in here."

Natalie narrowed her gaze and cocked her head to the side. "If you're such a devoted Christian, don't you have a Bible at home?" She pointed at the large book that I was clutching to my chest. "That one must weigh a ton."

I crossed my fingers. "Well, I moved recently and some of my books are still boxed up." I took a few steps toward the door.

"You could get a free one in any hotel room in the world,

thanks to the Gideons." She tilted her head to the side. "Why haul that door stopper home?"

"I can't just take a Bible from a hotel room. That would be wrong."

Natalie rolled her eyes and mumbled something that sounded like a reference to Mary Poppins.

"What was that?" I asked.

Natalie glared but didn't repeat her comment.

Emboldened, I continued. "Taking a Bible from a hotel would be stealing, and I'm pretty sure that even if the hotel didn't prosecute you and send you to jail, stealing a Bible would get you a one-way ticket to hell. 'Do not pass Go. Do not collect two hundred dollars.'" I focused on meeting Natalie's gaze and prayed that I looked innocent. If I didn't look innocent, then I hoped I looked empty-headed.

It must have worked, because after a few moments she yawned and looked away.

Two steps from the library door and freedom, Natalie stopped me again.

"I don't know what you think you heard, but I did not steal that flash drive or key, and if you tell your boyfriend I did, I will sue you for every dime you and that fleabag dog of yours ever made with your idiotic books."

Okay, that was the last straw. Natalie Evans could insult me, but insulting my dog meant war. I stopped and spun around. "First, I know you think the sun, moon, and every planet in the solar system revolve around you, but trust me when I tell you that they do not. You are not the center of the universe, and I couldn't care less who you talk to, what you say, or what you do. Secondly, Gilbert Morgan is the chief of police. He doesn't need my input, and as an officer of the court, if he requested information about your conversation or any conversations related to this case, then as a law-abiding citizen, I would answer."

Natalie opened her mouth to interrupt, but I was on a roll and in no mood to be interrupted and I bulldozed right over her like a construction worker with a backhoe.

"Third, and most important, my dog does not now, nor has he ever had fleas, but if you continue to insult me and my dog by spouting off lies, then I will take this massive book and shove it up your—"

"Pris!"

I didn't realize Gilbert was standing in the doorway listening until he spoke. The flame that fired up my temper and brought me within inches of a catfight with Natalie Evans flickered out like a match on a windy day. I spun around and dropped the Bible I'd been holding.

Before I could pick up the hefty book, Gilbert beat me to it and picked it up.

"Nice backpack." Natalie smirked.

Gilbert was carrying a pink Barbie backpack that obviously belonged to Hannah. He glared at Natalie.

The photo that I'd picked up before Bailey found the secret room and stuck in the book fluttered to the ground.

Gilbert picked up the photo.

"Well, well. I guess we know what it takes to turn the

mouse into a lion." Natalie cackled. "Insult the dog and the claws come out. *RAWRR*."

My face was hot, and I was dizzy from the blood rushing to my head. I alternated like a ticking clock between wanting to slap Natalie Evans into the middle of next week and wanting to slink out of the room like a snake. I didn't get a chance to do either.

"What's going on?" Gilbert asked.

"Nancy Drew was listening at the keyhole and overheard a personal conversation," Natalie said.

I hate being called Nancy Drew.

"I was not listening at the keyhole. I was standing outside the door, about to enter, when I heard someone talking—"

"Tomayto, tomahto." Natalie flipped her hand and waltzed toward the door. "I'm going to my room."

When Natalie left, the air pressure in the room dropped, and I was able to breathe.

Gilbert lifted my chin and looked into my eyes. "You okay?"

I took several slow, deep breaths and nodded. "That woman is so obnoxious. I can't believe I let her get under my skin. That's what irritates me more than anything else. It isn't so much what she said, although if she insults Bailey one more time, then I will reach down her throat and rip her tonsils out." I took a deep breath and paused a beat. "I'm angry with myself for letting her get to me more than anything."

"She really must have irritated you if you threatened her with this." Gilbert held up the Bible. His lips twitched. He tried to control them but failed and burst out laughing.

"OMG! I'm going to hell. I threatened to shove a Bible up her . . . well, you know."

When Gilbert finally stopped laughing, he asked, "Do you want to talk about it?"

I told him about the conversation I'd overheard. He asked a few questions, but I couldn't answer them. Eventually, he held up the Bible. "Do you really want to take this home for some light reading?"

"No. I just remembered the photo that Bailey found earlier and it triggered something."

"What?" He gazed at the photo. "Do you know who they are?"

I stared at the photo. Based on the clothes and hairstyles it must have been taken about ten years ago. "It looks like it was taken in one of those photo booths at the mall. But something's off . . ."

"I remember cramming into those booths when I was in school and making goofy faces. But I was never this well dressed."

"That's it. They're wearing school blazers. It's what kids in the UK wear. And that's David Townsend. Or, the man who claimed to be David Townsend." I stared at the photo.

"Not just claimed to be. Your agent was wrong," Gilbert said.

"What do you mean?"

"We did a DNA test. The guy who died shared around twelve percent of the same DNA as Edward Townsend."

"Twelve percent isn't very much," I said.

"No, but it's enough to prove that he was technically an heir. We know Edward Townsend only had one son and one grandson."

Something flitted across my brain. I stared at the photo again. "Two of these boys look almost exactly alike. They could be twins."

Gilbert looked again. "True, but Edward Townsend's son didn't have twins. He only had one son. And to be honest, even the third kid looks like the other two."

"Edward Townsend had one son, James. James had one son, David," I said.

"Right. What's your point?" Gilbert asked.

"Edward Townsend had a brother . . . Let me see that Bible."

Gilbert placed the heavy Bible onto the desk and we flipped to the beginning with the genealogy.

"Here it is. Frederick and Edward Townsend were brothers. Each of them had one son. Edward's son was James. Frederick's son was Harold." I traced the names in the book.

"James's son was David," Gilbert said.

"Harold's son was Jonathan." I expected Gilbert to be excited by my revelation, but he just looked confused.

"So?"

"Marcie said that Jonathan and David looked so much alike that people used to mistake them for twins." I held up the photo. "I'll bet you anything that two of these boys are David and Jonathan."

"So?"

"That would mean that our David Townsend was possibly Jonathan Townsend. He wasn't Edward Townsend's grandson, but he would still be an heir. Edward Townsend would have been his uncle. That would explain why his DNA was similar, but only by twelve percent. Edward Townsend was his uncle."

"Great-uncle," Gilbert said.

"Jonathan would have been a closer heir than Mary Elizabeth. At least, I think that's how it would have worked. Although, I guess that would depend on how the trust or the will was set up. Mary Elizabeth was only a cousin. I think a second cousin."

Gilbert glared at the photo. Eventually, he sighed. "Maybe. I'll have to check with an attorney, preferably one who isn't a sulky minx with an attitude." He flipped the photo over. Nothing was written on the back. "It would have been great if someone had labeled it, *David, Jonathan, and friend* along with the year."

I glanced at the photo. "Maybe we could figure out who the third boy is and find out from him?"

"Another cousin?" Gilbert asked.

I shrugged. "Beats me. Although he looks familiar."

We discussed the photo until Marcie came downstairs.

"Am I interrupting anything?" Marcie waggled her eyebrows. "Please tell me I'm interrupting something."

"Don't be silly, but . . ." I glanced at Gilbert.

He gave a slight nod and I held out the photo. "Do you recognize anyone?"

Marcie's expression spoke volumes. "That's David." She

pointed at one of the boys. "And that must be Jonathan. He looks so much like David. Geez! It's been fifteen years."

"What about the other boy?" Gilbert asked.

Marcie stared, but eventually shook her head. "Sorry."

Gilbert tucked the photo into his pocket.

Marcie turned to me. "We're all packed and ready to go."

"Do you still want this?" Gilbert pointed to the Bible.

"No, thanks. I have one." I smiled.

We said our good-byes and then he went to say good-bye to Hannah.

Aunt Agatha sent me a text message stating that she was staying at the hospital overnight with Chelsea.

I couldn't help but feel guilty for all the uncharitable thoughts I'd had about Chelsea. It was hard to feel bitter toward someone when they were in the hospital. Chelsea had been through a lot in the past few months. Regardless of how I felt about her, I wouldn't wish all this hardship and grief on anyone . . . well, maybe Natalie Evans.

Perhaps I should have taken that Bible home after all. Apparently, I still needed a lot of spiritual growth.

Chapter 48

I dropped Marcie at home to pack and then drove Bailey and the girls to my house. Clarice and Hannah had stayed overnight at my house before, but this was Mary Elizabeth's first visit. My entire home could have fit inside Edward Townsend's mansion several times. It didn't take long for the three girls to get acclimated. Before I finished unpacking, they were running through the house at top speed, followed by Bailey.

We'd had pizza the night before, so I went for the second-best sleepover meal—tacos. A quick check of my fridge and pantry showed I had almost everything necessary for tacos, Mexican rice, and refried beans. The only thing missing was ground beef and taco shells. I sent a quick text to Marcie, and she agreed to pick up the needed items.

The girls helped with the prep. Many hands made for light work and by the time Marcie arrived, everything else was ready. I arranged the ingredients like a taco bar, allowing each girl to add their favorites. When we finished, they helped load the dishwasher and then headed upstairs to watch movies.

Alone in the kitchen, Marcie and I sat at the table and sipped coffee. Despite spending the entire weekend together, this was the first opportunity we'd had to sit and talk together. I filled her in on everything that I knew or thought I knew about David and Jonathan Townsend.

"Wait. That's a lot. We need to write this down. Hold on." Marcie hopped up and ran out to her car. After a few minutes, she came back with a large sketchbook. Marcie was a talented artist. She flipped over some amazing sketches that she'd done of the horses, Mary Elizabeth, Hannah, Clarice, and Bailey until she found a blank page.

"Wait." I reached out and flipped the page back. "Is that David Townsend?"

Marcie colored. "Yeah. I was sitting outside and saw him and Hudson talking. There was something about their faces that made me want to sketch them." She stared at the drawing and then shrugged. "I don't know. There was something about the lines that caught my attention. They have similar bone structures. Plus, they both have blue eyes that are so vivid and intense." She frowned. "It's hard to tell here because this is just a sketch, but if I had my colored pencils—"

"Their eyes. That's it."

"That's what?" Marcie asked.

I reminded Marcie about the photo I'd found and how I thought it was David and Jonathan Townsend when they were teens. "They looked so much alike I could see why people thought they were twins."

Marcie stared at her drawing and frowned. "You know . . . I think you're right. It's not David. It's not here."

"What's not here?" I asked.

"I can't believe I forgot about that." She smacked her head and pointed at the picture. "When David and I were dating, he told me a story about a joke he and Jonathan had played." She paused. "It wasn't funny, not to me anyway. In fact, I thought it was downright cruel."

"What was it?" I asked.

"He said he and Jonathan switched identities all the time. Once, when David was dating this girl . . . I don't remember her name now . . . but anyway, Jonathan pretended to be David and she couldn't tell the difference and even made out with him." Marcie colored.

"That is cruel. That poor girl."

"I know. Anyway, I told David that if he ever tried anything like that with me, I would punch his lights out." Marcie took a deep breath. "That's when he shared the secret to how I could always tell them apart."

Now she had my attention.

"David said that he, Jonathan, and his half brother, Sonny, all looked alike. All three of them had blue eyes and

the same nose, but each of them had one unique charac-
teristic."

I held my breath and waited.

"David had a birthmark. It was a small brown circle near
his right ear. If he wore his hair long on the sides, then no
one would see it."

"I don't remember seeing a birthmark on the person who
presented himself as David Townsend. Did you?"

Marcie thought for several moments but then shook her
head. "I wasn't really close enough to him, but I don't remember a birthmark."

"Do you remember anything else?"

"I can't believe I forgot this." Marcie's eyes widened and
she frowned. "Jonathan was allergic to blueberries."

"That would explain why Aunt Agatha remembers David Townsend loving her blueberry pies. Since Jonathan was
the person who was impersonating him, he said he was allergic to blueberries."

"I'm sorry, Pris. I should have remembered this."

"Don't be ridiculous. That was fifteen years ago. I can
barely remember conversations I've had fifteen minutes
ago."

"But maybe David, or rather Jonathan, would be alive if—"

"Don't even think that. It's not your fault that Jonathan
Townsend decided to pretend to be David and got himself
killed. I mean, why didn't he just come clean and admit
who he was? He was still an heir."

"No. He couldn't." Marcie shook her head. "Remember,

Frederick and Edward Townsend had a big fight. Edward Townsend cut off his brother. As Frederick's grandson, he was disinherited. Is that a word?" She glanced in my direction.

"I don't know, but if it's not, it should be." I stood up and paced across the kitchen. "So, Jonathan was allergic to blueberries. That explains why Jay Barlow had brought that container of blueberries. I'll bet he remembered Jonathan's allergy and was going to test him."

"Do you think Jonathan killed him?" Marcie asked.

"I don't know. He might have."

"Wouldn't he have risked anaphylactic shock? You said there were blueberries all over the shed when you found him."

I thought for several minutes. "Maybe he had an EpiPen?"

Marcie shrugged. "Maybe."

"Okay, so David Townsend had a birthmark and Jonathan Townsend was allergic to blueberries. I don't know if the medical examiner can test for a reaction, but Gilbert could certainly check Jonathan's room and his belongings to see if he had an EpiPen. Most people with severe allergies will have something to indicate what to do if they're exposed."

Marcie paused. "Would he need to do anything? Gilbert knows that the guy wasn't David Townsend. Isn't that enough? Does he have to prove that he's Jonathan Townsend?"

"I don't know. I'm sure he'd want to figure out who the dead guy was so he can notify family, if nothing else."

"Right. Good point." Marcie paused, looked at her drawing again. "You said there was something in the picture. Something about their eyes."

I picked up the sketchbook. "Your drawing told me who the third man was in the photo that Gilbert has." I pointed to the sketch of Hudson. "Hudson . . . Sonny. David Townsend's half brother."

Chapter 49

I called Gilbert and told him everything that Marcie had told me about David and Jonathan Townsend. He was at the police station and said he'd ask the coroner to check for a birthmark or blueberry allergy and hung up.

"Could Hudson really be David Townsend's half brother?" I asked.

"I don't know."

"Try to think about everything David told you about his family."

"That was a long time ago." Marcie sighed.

"What happened between his mother and father? How did he end up with a half brother?"

"His mother, Clara, was beautiful. She was also a flirt. She cheated on James and he divorced her. That's when James moved with David to Australia. Clara remarried. She got pregnant and died in childbirth. I think, or soon afterward."

Marcie glanced down and got quiet.

"What?"

"I don't think Clara wanted to get remarried, but she got pregnant and I think Edward Townsend mandated a wedding," Marcie said.

"How? He was thousands of miles away and didn't have anything to do with her after she and James were divorced."

"Edward Townsend was rich. He used his money to get what he wanted. He didn't want a loose daughter-in-law—or an ex-daughter-in-law. So, he put conditions on the alimony and child support," Marcie said.

"How? If she was entitled to child support, then Edward or James would have to pay."

"I think Clara wasn't mentally stable. David said she would have . . . 'spells.' I think she suffered from some form of mental illness. Sometimes she would be okay. Then other times, she wasn't. She did some bizarre things," Marcie said.

"Like what? Do you remember anything David said?"

Marcie thought for a few moments. "Like running naked through Harrods department store. And threatening to jump from the top of Tower Bridge. She did some really dangerous things. Those were the things that allowed James to have custody."

"That's sad. She probably needed medication. Instead, her husband divorced her and took her son away to Australia," I said.

"Yeah. The thought of losing one son made her desperate and she agreed to anything Edward Townsend's lawyers said to keep her other child and the money." She shook her head. "Honestly, I don't know if keeping David would have been a good idea, but . . . anyway she remarried and had the baby, but then she died not long afterward."

"What happened to her baby?" I asked.

"His father raised him. I think he drank." Marcie frowned. "As soon as Clara died, Edward Townsend stopped the money."

"Okay. Well, I guess that makes sense. I mean, the second husband and his son weren't related to Edward Townsend. It's a bummer, but . . ."

"I think the second husband, David's stepfather, was bitter about the money. He hated Edward Townsend. He'd get drunk and say all kinds of things about him. David felt guilty. He hated that he had so much and his stepbrother didn't have much of anything. So, he convinced his grandfather to pay to send Sonny to the same fancy boarding school that he and Jonathan went to. That way, Sonny got a good education and he got to spend time away from his father."

"I guess that's a good thing, right?"

Marcie shrugged. "David said Sonny never really fit in at the school. He was surrounded by kids with wealth and privilege, but he didn't belong."

"Kids can be cruel, too. If they knew that he wasn't rich, they probably teased him," I said.

Marcie nodded. "That's exactly what happened. David took up for Sonny, but he thought that made it worse. Sonny resented that he needed a protector. Then he'd go home for holidays and spend time with his dad and come back even more bitter." She was silent for several moments. "I know it made David sad, but . . . what could he do?"

I thought for several moments. "I don't suppose James would have adopted—"

"The child of the man his wife cheated on him with? No."

"So, what happened?"

"I have no idea. David was in Crosbyville one day and the next day, he was on a plane to Australia. I never saw or heard from him again."

"Did you write?"

"Yes, but he never responded. Eventually, my pride wouldn't let me continue trying."

I reached out and squeezed her hand. "I'm so sorry. I had no idea. How come you didn't tell me?"

"More pride?" She took a sip of coffee and glanced at the sketch she'd made of the man we now believed was Jonathan Townsend. "That was one reason I wanted to talk to him. I wanted to find out what happened. Now I guess I'll never know."

Chapter 50

*T*hanks to Marcie, getting the three girls ready for school in the morning wasn't the chaos I'd experienced the first time Hannah and Clarice had stayed overnight. There were no tears. No hairspray or hair-teasing mishaps. And no wardrobe calamities. If I didn't know otherwise, I might have believed Marcie had spent time in the military. She was up and tossing out orders that kept not only the girls but Bailey and me on task.

At six, Marcie got up, showered, and dressed. I was ordered to get up and get breakfast ready. Bailey was put outside to take care of business. Then she got each of the girls busy brushing their teeth, getting clean, and dressing. By the time I'd finished preparing bacon-egg-and-toast sandwiches, all three girls were downstairs. Before we went to bed last night, we'd made lunch for all of them, so they

were able to grab their lunches and be on their way in record time.

After they left, Bailey and I stood in the kitchen in a
daze. I glanced at my bloodhound. "What just happened?"

Bailey shook himself.

"Yeah, I have no idea, either."

I made myself a cup of coffee and nibbled on the remaining bacon and eggs. Then I went upstairs and got cleaned
and dressed.

Today, I planned to write. I sat down at my laptop in
the formal dining room, which I had converted into a home
office. I opened the manuscript and reacquainted myself with
The Case of the Dancing Dachshund. "Let's see, dachshund
Maximillion Murray has disappeared. Carey believes he was
abducted. If Max fails to show up in three days for the reading of Uncle Herbert's will, then he stands to lose fifty
million dollars."

"Fifty million dollars is a lot of money." I paused. "Edward
Townsend's estate was a lot bigger, but . . . it's certainly
enough to drive a desperate person to a life of crime." I
glanced at Bailey. "What do you think?"

Bailey was engaged in cleaning himself.

"Ugh. Cut it out."

Bailey looked up at me and then curled up in the dog
bed I kept next to my desk.

I pondered the case for several minutes and then typed.

Anna posted pictures of Max around the neighbor-
hood asking anyone with information on the where-

abouts of the missing dachshund to get in touch. The headline, REWARD FOR INFORMATION, was meant to motivate volunteer search teams, and it worked.

For two days, Anna sifted through emails, texts, and calls while Bailey put his nose to work tracking down the most promising leads.

Unfortunately, none of the tips had helped them sniff out the location of the missing heir.

Time was running out. With only one day left until the reading of the will, they were desperate. Would this be the case that left the detective baying at the wrong prey?

I spent several hours writing and rewriting. I fleshed out the beginning and got a good start on the middle of the story. When my stomach growled for the second or third time, I stretched and went to the kitchen to get lunch. A tuna fish sandwich, chips, and an apple stopped the growling, but something still gnawed at my insides.

Bailey finished his midday meal and sat waiting for me to drop a morsel or two his way. I wasn't a fan of the crusts and removed them when I made the sandwich. Our routine meant he had to wait until I finished eating before he got a bite. He'd waited patiently with only the occasional whimper. So, I shared the crusts and a few thin slices of the apple.

He gulped down the snack and licked his lips.

"I still have a lot of writing to do to make that deadline. I should get back to work."

Bailey walked to the back door and glanced back at me. The second part of our lunchtime routine involved a walk. I glanced at the time. "We have time for a quick walk, but then I have to get back to work."

I hooked Bailey's leash to his harness, grabbed a few plastic bags for waste, and then headed outside.

Walking around our neighborhood wasn't as exciting for a bloodhound as roaming the park, but there were still plenty of scents to satisfy my hound. He sniffed everything in sight while I mentally reviewed my story as we walked downtown Crosbyville. Sifting through the story elements, I couldn't help but notice the similarities between the book and the current situation. Subconsciously I'd incorporated the search for Edward Townsend's missing heir into the plotline. There was a large inheritance and a missing heir.

My cell phone vibrated. One glance showed me it was Gilbert. I smiled and answered.

"Have you solved the case yet?" I asked.

"Good afternoon to you, too," he grumbled.

I chuckled. "I'm sorry. Good afternoon. What's gotten you in such a bad mood?"

"I've been interrogating Natalie Evans."

"Ahh. That's enough to put anyone in a bad mood. Let me guess. She's threatening to sue you, the Crosbyville Police Department, and the city of Crosbyville?"

"Yep, but she's now including the entire state of Indiana."

"Can she do that?" I laughed.

"Beats me, but I can tell you nothing would give me more pleasure than to lock her up."

"Did you find out anything that would make that a possibility?"

"She claims that she couldn't have poisoned David Townsend because she drank the whiskey, too."

"That's a good point. Unless the poison was in David Townsend's cup before the coffee and the whiskey were added, then there's no way she could have done it."

"I know, but I just got the toxicology report back, and it's thrown a wrench into the works."

"Why? What poison did they find?"

"None."

"But if he wasn't poisoned, then what killed him?" I asked.

"That's the two-billion-dollar question."

Chapter 51

*G*ilbert and I chatted for a few more minutes. Our conversation eventually slid into sweet nothings. I caught a glimpse of myself in the window of a florist shop. I had a silly grin, and my face was flushed. Before I could make too big a fool of myself, Gilbert got another call and had to hang up. Although, his promise to finish what he started when he came by later to pick up Hannah made me even hotter, and my grin was sillier than before. I disconnected and fanned myself to reduce my internal temperature.

I glanced around and saw that I was close to the Blue Plate Special Café. Aunt Agatha had sent me a message earlier saying that Chelsea was sedated and sleeping, and she'd felt comfortable leaving her for a few hours. I offered to pick her up, but Aunt Agatha had run into a friend who offered to give her a ride. However, she might need a ride back to the hospital later.

If Chelsea was better, there was a good chance that she would be released. Still, I wasn't sure if she would be well enough to care for Clarice. Andrew Hicks was also still incapacitated. Gilbert was the only healthy parental guardian of the three girls, and he was neck-deep in solving a triple homicide. I needed to face the fact that I'd likely have the three girls at least one more day. Which wasn't too taxing, considering they were back in school. Still, I needed to think about three square meals for four people. Five, if I could convince Marcie to stay overnight again.

"I can make dinner tonight and worry about tomorrow . . . tomorrow," I said.

"Excuse me. Were you talking to me?" A man in a three-piece suit with a bow tie and an old-fashioned pocket watch stopped and tipped his hat.

"No. Sorry. I was talking to . . ." I turned to point toward Bailey and then thought better of it. "No, I was talking to myself. Sorry." I apologized to the stranger again. Darn it. Natalie Evans's words floated back in my head. "You shouldn't apologize so much. It makes you look weak." *I had to stop apologizing so much.* I smiled at myself and ignored the puzzled look on his face. Then I turned and walked into the diner.

Aunt Agatha loved to cook and opening the diner had given her a wonderful outlet to share her gift with the community. It was also a great moneymaker for her since everyone loved her food and patronized the business from the first day she opened the doors. Downtown Crosbyville was quaint, with brick-storefront shops, an ice cream parlor, and antique and yarn shops. The Blue Plate Special Café wasn't large. It was an old-fashioned diner with a long counter. Barstools with aluminum legs and seats covered in black-and-white-checked plastic provided counter seating. The barstools matched the painted wood floors, which also were covered in black-and-white checks. In addition to the long counter, there were ten booths lining the walls with Formica-topped tables. My favorite features were the small jukeboxes that sat on each table, allowing the diners to listen to songs from the '50s and '60s for the outrageous sum of one nickel.

Luellen, one of the waitresses, waved at me. "Hey, Pris. You and Bailey here for a late lunch or an early dinner?"

"Neither. I just want to pick up a chocolate cake for dessert if you have any left." I glanced at the glass dessert carousel on the back counter.

"You're in luck. I had to make a chocolate cake for my son's birthday and decided to make two. With Agatha laid up with her ankle in that boot, I figured she might need a bit of help with the baking. She don't like sharing her recipes, but I've seen her mixing that cake often enough that I was able to re-create the recipe." She leaned forward and whispered, "Don't tell Agatha."

"My lips are sealed."

Luellen went to the kitchen and boxed up the chocolate cake while Bailey and I waited at the counter.

Aunt Agatha's neighbor Debra Goldstein came into the

diner. She immediately squatted and greeted Bailey, whose tail was beating a steady rhythm against the bottom of the counter.

"How's my favorite peony-destroying bloodhound today?" She scratched Bailey's ears.

Mrs. Goldstein's peonies were her pride and joy. They'd won first prize in the annual flower show five years in a row. When I'd found Bailey covered in dirt with peonies strewn all over the yard, I was afraid that my aunt's neighbor would commit hound-a-cide and murder my dog. After her initial burst of anger, she took the loss of her prized plants in stride. I was fortunate that Mrs. Goldstein hadn't held a grudge, but she had installed a fence around her yard.

When she finished greeting Bailey, she stood up and greeted me. "Hello, Pris. How's Agatha doing? I heard she tore something in her leg."

I filled her in on Aunt Agatha's condition and reassured her that my aunt was mobile, still cooking, not in need of a get-well casserole, and would likely be available for their weekly mah-jongg game. Mrs. Goldstein was an avid mah-jongg player who was intent on teaching Aunt Agatha the game. Originally from Michigan, she'd spent many years in the South where casseroles were a panacea for illness and grief. However, while Mrs. Goldstein was a master where flowers were concerned, her cooking skills were sorely lacking.

"Good. We all love having Agatha join the game. She doesn't win often, but she brings great snacks." She laughed.

We talked a little longer, but then Luellen came out with my boxed cake.

"Can you let Agatha know that we're moving the game to the Crosbyville library this time?"

"Don't tell me you've been kicked out of the bookstore?" I chuckled. "Aunt Agatha told me that your mahjongg games get pretty rowdy."

"Well, they didn't exactly kick us out, although I think they aren't shedding a tear that we're gone." She sighed. "They changed the tables."

"What?"

"The tables. The bookstore used to have nice big tables that were perfect for playing mah-jongg and board games."

"I used to like to take my laptop and write. I'm sure the management wasn't thrilled, but I have to admit that I loved sitting there, surrounded by books," I said.

She nodded. "We met and talked and played mah-jongg for hours. We always patronized the snack shop and spent tons of money on overpriced coffee and pastries that weren't nearly as good as anything Agatha made. We also bought books. We weren't just taking up space. We bought things and supported the business. Plus, it was a great gathering spot." She shook her head. "Now they replaced the big tables with skinny tables and the most uncomfortable chairs on the planet." She shrugged. "Most of the group would rather support indie bookstores rather than the big chain stores, anyway. It's been hard finding the perfect replacement. We met at a restaurant, but that was expensive because everyone had to purchase a meal. Then we rotated between each person's home. It's Amelia Lawson Cooper's turn this week, but she has an electrician redoing her wiring. Those old houses are beautiful, but always in need of work. Anyway, Charlotte Littlefield offered a room at the library."

Before we finished talking, my phone vibrated. I glanced at the display and saw Aunt Agatha. "Speak of the devil." I answered and relayed the information about mah-jongg immediately. Aunt Agatha acknowledged that she had been reading up on how to master mah-jongg and was ready to kick some butt! My aunt has always been very competitive. She also promised to bring snacks.

I relayed the message, but then the back-and-forth got to be too much, so I passed the phone to Mrs. Goldstein.

I gathered from the side of the conversation I was able to hear, that Aunt Agatha was still talking smack. Mrs. Goldstein humored her and chuckled. The friendly banter made them both happy.

"Now, Agatha, you don't have to bring a full three-course meal. Simple snacks will be fine." To your average person, snacks would involve chips, dip, and cookies from the grocery store. For my aunt, snacks involved a salad, a meat with at least two sides, and dessert. Mrs. Goldstein returned my phone. Based on her smile, she knew it, too.

"Pris, I'm at the hospital with Chelsea. She wants to go home, but her clothes are still at Townsend Farms. She's not anxious to go back there, and I can't say I blame her. Would you be willing to—"

"You want me to pack her things and bring them to the hospital?" I asked.

"Would you? I know you and Chelsea aren't the best of friends, but—"

"Of course, I'll do it. Bailey and I are just leaving the diner. It'll take an hour, but I don't mind."

"Thank you."

Bailey and I said our good-byes to Mrs. Goldstein and left. We'd walked, so we made our way back to the house. I left the cake on the counter and put the roast that I'd taken out of the freezer in the morning in the Crock-Pot. On high, it would be done by the time Gilbert got home from work. Then Bailey and I got in the car and headed back to Townsend Farms.

The fall festival was over, so there wasn't much traffic going into and out of the property. I sent Gilbert a text letting him know my plans and also asking for permission to enter the estate. His response was curt.

K.

We stopped at the guardhouse. Despite Gilbert's blunt text, he must have called and given word that it was okay to admit me because the guard opened the gate and waved me through without any delays.

I took my time driving up to the mansion. It was daylight, and in the fall the trees created an idyllic country scene.

We pulled up to the house and like the first time, Mrs. Claymore was waiting.

"The police told me you'd be coming." She glanced at Bailey.

"I hope it's okay about Bailey. I didn't ask, but—"

"He's better behaved than some of the guests we've had recently." She grinned. "Olivia saved a ham bone for him. She'll be really disappointed if she doesn't get to see him. You be sure and stop by the kitchen before you leave."

I promised I would.

Bailey wagged his tail. The word *bone* had sent his saliva into overdrive and strings of drool dripped from his jowls.

I hurried upstairs to Chelsea's room. I hadn't expected her to have much, but I was surprised to find two large suitcases and a toiletry bag. *She must have planned for a longer stay.*

I took more care packing Chelsea's belongings than I'd taken with my own. Experience told me that no matter how careful I was, she'd find fault with something. Still, I folded, organized, and packed what I would consider to be two photograph-worthy suitcases. That luggage was perfection I'd never achieved with my own bags. It deserved to be immortalized for posterity. God knows I'd never be able to achieve anything so beautiful again. I took out my cell and snapped several photographs. *Maybe one day, I could re-create the feat for my own clothes.*

Before I dragged the suitcases into the hall, I crossed over to David Townsend's suite.

I opened the connecting door and entered. David Townsend's bedroom was massive. The floors were mahogany, and the walls were painted a deep burgundy. It had a large four-post bed with a canopy and was so tall, you needed a step to climb up on the mattress. The room had a large fireplace and a separate seating area. It would have been a nice room with a few feminine touches.

I grabbed a few of the items that clearly hadn't belonged to David Townsend and risked upsetting my neatly packed luggage by shoving them inside. When I stood up, I found Bailey's rear sticking out from underneath the bed.

"Get out of there."

Bailey ignored me.

I got down on the floor, prepared to pull the stubborn bloodhound by the collar. That's when I noticed that Bailey had something between his two front paws. It was a pill bottle. He was trying to pry the lid off with his mouth. I reached out and grabbed the bottle away from him. I slid out from the bed and frowned at Bailey. "Bad dog."

He didn't seem ashamed. In fact, if I had to categorize his expression, I'd call it pleased.

"You *never* open pill bottles. They're dangerous."

Bailey panted.

"Darned bloodhounds." I moved over to the luggage. Before I could toss the bottle into Chelsea's toiletry bag, I glanced at the label to make sure it was her meds and not David Townsend's.

One glance at the name and I froze. *Natalie Evans.* What were these doing there?

"Crap." The last person I wanted to run into was Natalie Evans.

"What are the chances that I can sneak into Natalie's room? Leave the pill bottle and sneak out without her seeing me?"

Bailey yawned.

"Agreed. Maybe I could just leave them with Mrs. Claymore and tell her I found them in Chelsea's room."

Bailey yawled. Normally, those are short. This one wasn't and sounded to me as though he was saying, *Coward*. Of course, that might have been my imagination on overdrive, but that's what it sounded like.

"Fine. I'll do it."

I dragged Chelsea's luggage into the hall. I knew which room had been Natalie Evans's, but I hesitated at entering. I knocked softly. When I got no answer, I twisted the doorknob. A creak behind me made me jump.

I looked around but didn't see anyone. I took a deep breath and put my hand out to open the doorknob again but balked. Instead of entering, I decided to take the luggage down to my car first. With any luck, I'd run into Mrs. Claymore. I knew she could hoist these bags without breaking a sweat and I could leave the bottle with her.

Unfortunately, Mrs. Claymore wasn't around. I lingered in the hall and even wandered through to the kitchen. Neither she nor Olivia Green was around. The big mansion was deathly quiet, which was scary.

"Let's get out of here," I said to Bailey.

The luggage was heavy, but I managed to get it outside and load it into my car. "You wait here. I'll be right back." I loaded Bailey into the car and rushed back inside.

I paused outside of Natalie's bedroom and took several deep breaths. I hadn't seen anyone enter the house, so I didn't bother knocking again. I opened the door and hurried inside.

I went to place the bottle on the dresser next to a round glass paperweight. The paperweight was identical to the one that was in the bedroom I'd used, except this one was blue and matched the decor. The bottle gave a strange, metallic rattle as I set it down. *What was that?* I picked up the bottle and looked through the orange plastic and around the label. That's when I saw that this wasn't filled with medicine. I pushed down and turned the lid to open the childproof cap.

Inside the bottle was a flash drive and a key. It was *the flash drive and key*. The ones that Edward Townsend had placed inside his safe.

Chapter 52

I wondered what happened to that."

Natalie Evans stood at the door.

My heart raced. My first instinct was to apologize for entering her bedroom and opening her pill bottle, but I swallowed it. Natalie wouldn't appreciate an apology. She would just say it made me look weak.

Besides, this wasn't hers. She'd taken evidence. Evidence that Gilbert needed for his chain of custody. She was a thief. She'd taken something that didn't belong to her. Thieves didn't deserve an apology. It was time to take the offensive. "This belonged to Edward Townsend. It's the flash drive and the key that were in his safe. You took them. What are you doing with these?" I asked.

"You're saying I took them? I'm not the one holding the

stolen goods. Maybe you should explain what you're doing with them and why you're planting evidence in my room."

Darn, she was good.

"I'm not planting evidence. I found this and was returning it to you. Your name's on the bottle." I held up the medicine bottle for her to see. She walked over to the dresser for a closer look.

"I've never seen that before."

"It's got your name on it."

She shrugged. "So what? That doesn't prove anything. All that proves is that you found one of my old pill bottles and used it to stick that evidence in so you could incriminate me. It'll never hold up in a court of law."

Sparring with Natalie Evans was a waste of time. She was smart. Regardless, I had the evidence. I had the flash drive and the key. "You can explain that to Gilbert. I'm taking this to the police station. You can argue with him and the district attorney."

I didn't think it was possible to scare the Queen of Mean Girls, but the blood drained from her face and Natalie Evans looked scared. When Natalie gasped, I realized she was looking past me, over my shoulder.

I turned toward the door.

A metal clip slid into place, making a clicking sound.

I glanced up into the cold blue eyes of Hudson, Edward Townsend's valet. He held a large menacing-looking gun in his hand. It was pointed at my heart.

Chapter 53

"I should have known you were lying when you said you hadn't taken it." Hudson pointed the gun toward Natalie Evans.

"I didn't take it. She did. She just brought that in here. She's trying to frame me. She wants her boyfriend to think I took it, but I didn't," Natalie said.

"I am not trying to frame you. I found this bottle and was just—"

"Shut up and give me that." Hudson held out his hand.

As much as I wanted to do exactly what he wanted, I couldn't. He'd shoot both of us, Natalie and me. Of course, if I didn't give him what he wanted, he could also shoot us and then take the flash drive anyway. My brain raced to find a solution that didn't lead to a bullet and death.

"Gilbert knows that I'm here. He also knows that I

found the flash drive and the key. He'll be here any minute," I said with as much conviction as I could muster.

"I don't believe you."

"It's true. Isn't it, Natalie?" I turned to Natalie for confirmation, but her gaze was locked on the gun, and she was frozen.

In the silence that followed, I heard Bailey outside, baying like a werewolf at a full moon.

Hudson threw his head back and laughed. It was a deep, low, menacing laugh that sent a shiver up my spine and made the hairs on my arms stand up. I glanced into those deep blue eyes. Eyes that were so similar to David's and Jonathan Townsend's eyes. Yet, they were different. It was like the veil was lifted, and what I saw made my pulse race.

Madness.

That revelation made my blood cold. I was trapped. Gilbert wasn't coming. I'd left my phone in the car, so even if the opportunity arose, I couldn't call for help. Even Mean Girl Natalie Evans was no help. She was paralyzed with fear. I couldn't even count on help from Bailey, since I'd locked him in my car.

I was in a room with a killer who had a gun pointed at me. I needed a miracle if I was going to get out of this alive.

Chapter 54

I needed to keep Hudson talking. Buy time for Mrs. Claymore or Olivia Green to come back. Time for someone to realize that we weren't at home. Gilbert knew I was here. Aunt Agatha knew I was here, too. Eventually, Chelsea would want her clothes. I just needed to keep Hudson talking long enough for the cavalry to arrive.

"You'll never get away with this." I inched closer to the dresser.

"That's where you're wrong. I already have gotten away with it. No one knows that I killed them. No one but you two, and I'm going to take care of that shortly." He lifted the gun and aimed.

"But they'll hear you. Mrs. Claymore, Olivia Green, and Andrew Hicks. If you shoot us, they'll hear it," I said hurriedly, remembering the paperweight on the dresser behind me.

"Good point." Hudson reached into a pocket and pulled out a device that he screwed onto the front of the gun. "I almost forgot the silencer. Thanks for the reminder." He laughed.

"Idiot." Natalie Evans snapped out of her frozen state long enough to scowl at me.

"But they know I'm here. My car's outside. My dog's outside. And, whether you believe me or not, Gilbert knows I'm here. He'll be here soon." My back was against the dresser. I couldn't see what I was doing. I moved my hand to rest somewhere near the paperweight.

Hudson grimaced, reminding me of the gargoyles that sat atop the old Crosbyville Savings and Loan building downtown. Those grotesque figurines were chiseled into the building's plaster facade. They sat atop the building, overlooking the street and every person who entered or left the building. As a child, I was terrified of those demonic creatures. One look at Hudson's face and I was a small girl shivering in fear, afraid to cross the threshold of the bank.

"Now, hand over that flash drive and key." Hudson extended his hand.

"Why did you do it? Why did you kill Edward Townsend?" I inched my hand closer to the paperweight.

Hudson's face twisted into a monstrous expression. The blood rushed up his neck and flooded his face. Spit pooled at the corners of his mouth. "Edward Townsend was a murderer. He got what he deserved."

I gasped.

My shock must have been reflected in my expression because he nodded. "Surprised? You didn't know that Edward Townsend was a murderer?"

"What do you mean?" I asked.

"Edward Townsend killed my mother."

Chapter 55

What?" My throat contracted, and I could barely choke out that one word from my throat. "I don't believe it."

"Believe it? Hah! That old man had everyone fooled. Everyone thought he was such a great man. A philanthropist. Always giving money away. Always helping others. Well, he didn't help my mother."

"What do you mean? I don't understand."

Hudson's eye twitched and he paced in front of the door. A few steps in one direction and then a few steps in the other. Never leaving a wide-enough gap for me to make a run for it.

"The great Edward Townsend. That's how you people here in the States . . . in Crosbyville saw him, but let me tell you. He had another side. When my mum was sick. My mum. His daughter-in-law was sick. He cut her off. He let her die. That's the real Edward Townsend."

My mind flashed back to what I remembered about David Townsend's family. "Are you talking about Clara?"

"Yes. Clara. My mother." Hudson walked faster. His breathing increased. His eye twitched faster. I never noticed his British accent before. He must have been hiding it. But as he spoke, his accent became more and more pronounced as his speech became short and clipped.

"I heard she was very beautiful."

He stopped pacing and smiled—really smiled. "She was the most beautiful woman in the world." He stood smiling for several moments as his mind went back in time. The scowl returned. The pacing resumed and his twitch returned. "She was beautiful. Then he killed her."

"I'm sorry. How did she die?"

"She died because Edward Townsend refused to give her the money she needed. She needed medicine. She was sick. She needed to go to the hospital. A good hospital. She couldn't afford it because he cut her off. He cut off her money because she got pregnant." The spit at the corners of his mouth increased and he dripped strings of drool like Bailey. "She died giving birth to me." He pounded his chest.

"I'm sorry. She was divorced from James by then and—"

"Don't talk to me about him. Do *not* mention that name to me." Hudson shouted. "He was no good. He didn't love her. He left her. All he cared about was his son, David. He left her. He left us to die in England while he went off to Australia."

"How old were you when your mom died?" I asked.

"Three days." He stopped pacing. "I was only three days old." Tears ran down his cheeks.

If we could keep him calm, maybe we had a chance.

"Three days? You can't possibly even remember your mom." Natalie Evans found her voice. Sadly, it was full of vinegar. "And Edward paid to send you to that fancy boarding school with David and Jonathan. He paid for your education."

Darned Natalie Evans. I glared at her and willed her to be quiet. Geez. If she didn't have anything nice to say, the least she could do was to keep quiet. Instead, she'd gotten Hudson revved up and pacing again.

"Education." Hudson spat on the carpet. "Yeah, he paid to send me to a fancy boarding school, but everyone knew I didn't belong. I wasn't rich. I was just David and Jonathan's poor relation. I was only there on sufferance. They put up with me because my older brother had a rich grandfather. They didn't dare upset the great Edward Townsend. Heaven forbid. The headmaster couldn't risk losing out on Edward Townsend donating a few million dollars to build a new rugby pitch or a library."

"Hypocrite. You took Edward Townsend's money, just like they all did. Just like *we* all did. Edward Townsend paid for your expensive private school education and anything else your deadbeat dad was able to weasel out of him. And your mother got what she deserved. She was just a tart who got herself knocked up and then came crawling to Edward Townsend to support her illegitimate son and deadbeat dad."

Natalie spewed hateful words that poisoned an already-confused mind.

"You shut up. You don't know anything. Don't you say anything about my mum. I know what happened. I know what he did. My dad told me. He told me everything. You just shut up."

"What did your dad tell you?" I asked softly.

"He told me what happened. He told me he pleaded with Edward Townsend, but the high-and-mighty man wouldn't even send a pound. That's how she died. She died because Edward Townsend caused it."

"I'm sorry." I couldn't see the paperweight, but my fingers touched the cold glass ball.

"Edward Townsend needed to pay. He needed to pay for killing my mum. So, I planned this. I planned it with Jonathan."

"How?" I asked.

"David died. He's been dead for years, but Jonathan looked so much like him that he knew he could pass for David. They'd done it for years at school. Switched places. Edward Townsend didn't know. He was too stupid to figure it out. He'd cut Jonathan's grandfather out. He was Edward Townsend's flesh and blood. But he wasn't going to get a cent. He deserved to inherit. So, he pretended to be David."

"And you?"

"I got a job as Edward Townsend's valet. We used the names of schoolmates as references. I'd been to fancy houses most of my life. I saw what valets did. I learned the job quickly." He scowled.

"You're obviously as crazy as your mother." Natalie sneered.

"I. Am. Not. Crazy!" Hudson hit the wall with the fist that wasn't holding the gun, punctuating each word. He stood, foaming at the mouth. Blood dripped from his knuckles. His gaze darted wildly around the room from Natalie to me. His entire body shook with rage. That's when he remembered the gun. He lifted it and straightened his arm.

He pointed the gun at Natalie and fired.

Chapter 56

*E*verything felt as though it was moving in slow motion. Natalie screamed. The gun fired with a pop. I grasped the paperweight in my hand, wound up my arm, and let the glass ball fly, hurling it at the valet's head.

He dropped to the ground.

Within seconds, Bailey flew through the door, followed by Gilbert. His gun was drawn and pointed.

Gilbert kicked the gun away from the outstretched hand of Hudson as he lay unconscious on the floor. "I heard a shot. Are you okay?"

"Yes. I'm fine." I turned to look at Natalie Evans.

Natalie was standing against the wall as blood poured from her shoulder. She stared at the blood. "He shot me."

I hurried over to her.

Gilbert knelt beside Hudson. He handcuffed him and then pulled out his phone and called 911.

"Pris. Are you okay?" I heard a clump as Aunt Agatha limped into the room carrying a bottle of wine like a bat.

"Aunt Agatha?" I asked, not turning away from Natalie.

"Praise God. I heard that shot and my heart stopped. I was so afraid—" She saw me trying to stop the blood pouring out of Natalie Evans's shoulder and went into action. "Sweet mother of God."

Aunt Agatha put down the bottle, took over my position, and ordered me to get towels.

I went to the bathroom and grabbed every towel I could find and hurried back into the room.

A white-faced Natalie Evans was now lying on the bed and Aunt Agatha was pressing the end of the bedspread into her shoulder to stop the bleeding.

Mrs. Claymore entered with more towels, and I grabbed Bailey's leash and stepped out of the room to make space for the EMTs.

My knees didn't buckle until I was in the hallway. The last thing I remember was glancing into Gilbert's face before the lights went out.

Chapter 57

When I woke up, I was being cradled in Gilbert's arms while Mrs. Claymore waved a bottle of smelling salts under my nose. The vinegary scent brought water to my eyes, and I tossed my head from side to side.

"Are you okay?" Gilbert whispered.

"I'm fine . . . Now." I laid my head on his shoulder. "What happened?"

"I was hoping you could tell me."

"I mean, how did you know to come? I left my cell in the car. How did you . . ."

"Mrs. Green wanted to make sure Bailey got his treat. She was waiting for you by the kitchen, but when you didn't come, she got worried. She heard Bailey howling and beating against the windows trying to get out and she really got worried. So, she found Mrs. Claymore and they went in search of you. They heard shouting from the room and called for help."

I glanced at Mrs. Claymore. "Thank you." I looked around for Mrs. Green, but didn't see her. "Where's Mrs. Green?"

"She's in the kitchen. Once she knew you were okay, she said her nerves needed releasing." Gilbert grinned.

I gave him a look.

"She's baking," Gilbert said.

I struggled to get up. "I need to thank her." I headed for the door but stopped. "How did Aunt Agatha get here?"

"After Mrs. Green called the police, she called Agatha, who took an Uber." Gilbert shook his head. "Your aunt is a determined woman."

The EMTs removed Hudson. He was alive but had a concussion. They took him to the hospital for observation. Considering he had killed at least three people, attempted to kill one, and had been planning to kill me, I wasn't too upset about the concussion I'd given him.

Gilbert coordinated things while I slipped down to the kitchen to thank Olivia Green.

I found her beating dough with her fists. When she saw me, she wiped her hands on her apron and pulled me into a hug.

"Oh, thank God. I'm so glad you're okay." She squeezed me tight.

"Thank you. Gilbert tells me that you saved my life," I croaked.

She released me. "Lord, no. It's Bailey you have to thank. He was going crazy trying to get to you. When I opened that car door, he flew out and ran straight up those stairs." She glanced down at Bailey, who was curled up in the corner, gnawing on a large ham bone.

Aunt Agatha limped into the kitchen and sat down at the table.

"Is she . . . ?" I asked.

"She'll be okay. They're taking her to the hospital. The bullet went right through and missed all the important stuff."

Olivia Green poured coffee into mugs, and we sat and drank.

Gilbert entered and came and squatted in front of me. "Are you feeling well enough to give a statement?"

I nodded.

He pulled out his tape recorder and waited.

I filled him in on everything that happened.

"How is Hudson related to David Townsend? I thought his brother was named Sonny?" Aunt Agatha asked. Then, it hit her. "Oh, Sonny . . . Hudson . . . Sonny. I get it."

"That man has problems." Mrs. Green sipped her coffee.

"His mother suffered from mental illness, and I suspect Hudson inherited it, too." I glanced down, and realized that I was still clutching the medicine bottle with the flash drive and key. I handed them to Gilbert.

He frowned at them. "I wonder why Hudson was willing to kill to get his hands on this."

Gilbert sent an officer to get his laptop from the car. When he returned, he put the flash drive into the USB port. A few clicks later, we were watching a movie. Most of the movies on the drive were simply snippets of people entering and leaving the study. Mrs. Claymore cleaning. One of the day maids dusting. One of the videos showed Natalie and Hudson kissing. Another showed Hudson opening the safe, removing the money, and placing it in a pillowcase.

When we finished watching all of the videos, Gilbert removed the flash drive and put it in a plastic bag. He wrote the date and time along with his initials on the front. Then he asked me to date and initial the bag as a witness.

"Any idea what that key opens?" Gilbert asked. I picked up the key and stared at it. "What's this?"

Gilbert took the key and held it up to his eyes. He squinted. "It looks like a horse."

"That man was crazy about horses," Aunt Agatha said. "He lived and breathed those animals. That's how he made his money, you know."

"I didn't know." I turned to look more closely at Aunt Agatha. "I thought he made his money in the stock market or buying and selling bonds or something."

"Well, he did later, but he started off with horses. He and his brother, Frederick, used to work on a horse farm. They did everything and saved and saved until they bought their first horse. Then they bought another and another. Well, Frederick had a gambling problem. He sold some of the stock and told Edward the horse died." She stopped and shook her head. "Edward was devastated. Later, Edward found out what happened. He and Frederick had a big fight and that was the end of the business."

"I still don't see how Edward made his money," I said.

"Edward rebuilt the stock, but he didn't have the heart

to go into horse breeding full-time. That's when he started buying and selling commodities and then stocks, bonds, real estate . . . you name it. You see?"

I shook my head.

"The horses were his heart, not his business. He never could be objective about the horses. He regretted letting that come between him and his brother. But he never could eliminate horses from his life completely." Aunt Agatha chuckled.

"What's so funny?" I asked.

"Oh, nothing. It just reminded me of something Eddie used to say." She grinned.

"What was that?" Gilbert asked.

"He used to say that the key to his heart and his wealth was in his horses." She sipped her coffee.

Gilbert and I exchanged glances. Then we both got up and hurried outside.

The Townsend estate was huge, with multiple barns and the equestrian center, but they were new. The old horse barn seemed the best place to start. At the barn, we looked around. There was a tack box with a lock that looked about the right size for the key. I pointed it out to Gilbert.

He slid the key into the lock and turned it. It opened. He lifted the lid.

Inside were letters, photographs, and a diary.

Chapter 58

*G*ilbert took the tack box and all of the evidence back to the police station.

Bailey, Aunt Agatha, and I drove home.

Chelsea had been released from the hospital and surprisingly, she wanted to see Clarice. So, Marcie dropped her off after school.

Mary Elizabeth's parents had finally wrapped up their overseas work and were on their way back to the US. Their flight was scheduled to land at O'Hare later this evening. Andrew and Mary Elizabeth took the South Shore commuter train from River Bend to Chicago to meet them.

Hannah and I finished the preparations for our roast and by the time Gilbert arrived, we had a full three-course meal ready and waiting, thanks to the chocolate cake I'd picked up earlier.

After dinner, Bailey and Hannah went to watch movies while Gilbert and I cleaned up.

Gilbert shared that as the only surviving heir, Mary Elizabeth would likely inherit the entire Townsend estate.

"Good thing Hudson is locked up or he might have . . ." I shuddered, unable to finish that thought. "Anyway, at least Peter should get the finder's fee."

"He'll be a rich man when the dust settles, but it's probably going to take years before everything is resolved." Gilbert grinned. "Peter Alexander won't be the only millionaire."

"Aunt Agatha?"

Gilbert nodded. "She can franchise the Blue Plate Special Café. With luck, she could be more famous than McDonald's."

"That's exactly what she doesn't want." I chuckled. "She wants to give all of the money away to charity, but I think Carla talked her out of it. She's going to connect Aunt Agatha up with a good financial planner."

"She doesn't want to retire? Take it easy? Buy a big house and hire a ton of people to cook for her like Edward Townsend did?" Gilbert asked.

"Absolutely not. In fact, one of the things she wants to do is convince Mary Elizabeth's parents to donate the Townsend Farm to the community. She wants to use the horses for equine-assisted therapy."

"What's that?" Gilbert asked.

"Similar to pet-assisted therapy, horses are also great for helping with mental and emotional issues." I shrugged. "She's still researching things right now. In the meantime, she and

Carla did get Mary Elizabeth's parents to agree to keep the staff on the payroll. Andrew is coming back to help with the horses, too."

"That's good," Gilbert said.

I loaded the dishwasher. "Okay, now are you going to tell me what was in Edward Townsend's diary?"

"He may have been older, but his mind was certainly sharp. Edward Townsend had been documenting discrepancies he found in his accounts for over six months. He knew someone was embezzling his money. He figured it was Natalie. I have no idea why he locked the diary in the barn instead of putting it in a safe deposit box, but everyone said he didn't trust lawyers or banks." Gilbert shrugged. "We may never know the answer."

"Yikes." I poured us both coffee and sat down at the table. "Why'd he keep her on?"

"With Hudson's help, Natalie found David . . . I mean Jonathan. Edward must have suspected that Natalie wasn't a person of integrity, but Jonathan was very convincing. He knew all of the right answers and he looked like David. I think Edward wanted to believe Natalie had really found his grandson." He shrugged. "He couldn't trust Natalie with his money, so he added Carla as a trustee. I guess he knew if money was being embezzled, she'd track it down and put a stop to it."

"She did, too. Is that why Natalie tried to make a run for it?" I asked.

"She hasn't given a statement yet, but that's what I think. Carla was getting too close to figuring out what she'd done.

Plus, I think she must have started to see that Hudson was unstable."

"One of those videos showed Natalie kissing Hudson. Were they a couple?" I asked.

"I suspect Natalie used him, just like she used David . . . I mean Jonathan Townsend." Gilbert sipped his coffee.

"They were using each other. Hudson and Jonathan must have used Natalie to convince Edward Townsend that Jonathan was David. Anyway, Hudson killed Edward Townsend because he blamed him for his mother's death. He killed Jay Barlow because he knew the secret for telling David and Jonathan apart."

Gilbert nodded. "That's why Barlow had the blueberries. He was going to expose Jonathan."

"So, why did Hudson kill Jonathan?"

"Hudson was afraid that Natalie and Jonathan were going to double-cross him. He'd taken that money from the safe, remember?"

"Then Andrew Hicks found the money and moved it."

"But Hudson didn't know it was Hicks who moved it. He thought it was Jonathan or Natalie. So, he set a trap. He sent a message for him, making Jonathan think it was from Chelsea. Then he put a large tree limb in the road. When Jonathan got out to move the limb, he clubbed him."

"How did Hudson get hurt?" I asked.

"We don't have proof yet, but I think it was Natalie. She noticed that Hudson was jealous and unstable. She must have been hiding out and saw him hit Jonathan and that's when she hit Hudson."

"Geez." I glanced at Bailey. "So, which one of them killed Jonathan?"

"Hudson." Gilbert turned to look at me.

"You know how he did it?"

"I think so. When you asked me to test if Jonathan was allergic to blueberries, that's when I realized how he'd been poisoned. The killer, Hudson, had put the blueberry juice or extract into the flask. He even took a sip. Natalie drank it, too. Only someone like Jonathan Townsend, who was allergic to blueberries, would be affected."

"And it killed him. Hudson killed him. Right there in front of us." I shuddered.

Gilbert reached out his hand and squeezed mine. "It's over now. Now you can forget about all of this and get back to working on the next Adventures of Bailey the Blood-hound, Pet Detective, book."

"I think I'll use some of this in my book. I just wish . . ."

"What?" Gilbert asked.

"Oh, nothing. It's too bad that Hudson was a valet. I've always wanted a reason to say, 'The butler did it.'"

Gilbert smiled. "Didn't anyone ever tell you what Hudson's last name is?"

I shook my head. "I assumed it was Hudson."

Gilbert shook his head. "Hudson's his first name. His last name is Butler."

The Adventures of Bailey the Bloodhound

....

The Case of the Dancing Dachshund

In the wood-paneled library Mr. Goodwin, Uncle Herbert's lawyer, sat behind a massive desk.

Carey Murray looked nervously around the room. The only other person present was Hudson, Uncle Herbert's long-serving butler.

Mr. Goodwin glanced at his watch. He cleared his throat, unfolded a document, and adjusted his glasses.

As he began to read, the door was suddenly flung open, and in trotted Bailey, followed by his human, Anna.

He sniffed the air and then made his way to the bookshelf. He pulled one of the books forward. A lock clicked. A panel swung open, revealing a secret room.

Inside the room, tied up with a muzzle covering his mouth, was a dachshund.

"Max." Carey rushed to her beloved hound and pulled off the muzzle. "Who did this to you?"

"It was Hudson. The butler did it!" Max said.

Hudson rushed toward the door but found Bailey blocking the exit. The police arrived and handcuffed Hudson before he could escape.

"I would have gotten away with it if it hadn't been for that blasted bloodhound."

"Who is that talented investigator?" Mr. Goodwin asked.

"That's Bailey the Bloodhound, Pet Detective!" Anna said.

THE END

Acknowledgments

I have been blessed to know people who possess a vast amount of information and unique skills, who are willing to share their knowledge and expertise with me. Thanks to Debra Goldstein, for legal help and for brainstorming, supporting, and listening. Thanks to E. L. Reddick, for the support and encouragement, and for listening and allowing me to bounce ideas off you. You're the best. And thanks to Kellye Garrett, for the sprints and encouragement that helped me get to THE END.

Thanks to my family: Jacquelyn, Christopher, Carson, Crosby, and Cameron Rucker. Thanks to Jillian, Marcella, Drew, Marcella Merkel, and William. Your love and support have helped more than you will ever know.

Thanks to my amazing agent, Jessica Faust at BookEnds Literary, and editors, Liz Sellers and Michelle Vega at Berkley.

Special thanks to Mary Elizabeth Hicks, for permitting me to use your name to create a character for this book. Your love of horses, animals, Taylor Swift, and reading were my inspiration.

Valerie Burns, writing as **Kallie E. Benjamin**, is the author of three mystery series. She is a mentor in the master of fine arts program for writing popular fiction at Seton Hill University in Greensburg, Pennsylvania, where she earned her own MFA degree. Valerie currently lives in North Georgia with her two poodles, Kensington and Chloe.

VISIT VALERIE BURNS ONLINE

VMBurns.com
f VMBurnsBooks
⊙ VMBurnsBooks

Ready to find
your next great read?

Let us help.

Visit prh.com/nextread